Midnight Blue

An Avery Shepard Detective Mystery

J.H. Graham

Malice Books

Published by Malice Books
P.O. Box 188045
Sacramento, CA 95814

ISBN: 0692661441
ISBN-13: 978-0692661444

Also by J.H. Graham

THE AVERY SHEPARD DETECTIVE SERIES

Red Jade

Midnight Blue

Midnight Blue

CHAPTER 1

No one ever called Eddie Durance "Two Gun" back in the bad old days. That was something the papers cooked up later. But nowadays you never read about him— if you read about him at all— without seeing that silly nickname in quote marks. "Bootlegger" will be there too, usually in the same sentence, along with "murder."

Murder was the last thing on my mind that afternoon in August, a year to the day since V-J Day, when I turned into the long driveway of the McElmon ranch in the Valley.

It had been a perfect summer so far. I was newly remarried with a young stepson, and in recent months had opened up my detective practice again after a stint in the Army Reserves. My wife Bobbie and I had a great time taking Donny ocean fishing and to the ball games, going on camping trips in the mountains and spending time at the ranch with the McElmons, who strictly speaking were not family, although the distinction had long since been lost on us.

As I pulled up in front of the big open-bay garage we were greeted by the McElmon small fry and their father, known to me as Buster, who carried his namesake Robert Junior— called Mac in the family— on his broad shoulders. Mac and Donny were both five and had become fast friends.

"Donny, Donny!" Mac shouted. "Guess what— you're

spendin' the night wif us, an' Jem's having a campout wif a tweasure hunt an' you an' me are invited. It's a 's'prise.'"

"Not much of one now," Buster laughed, lowering his small son to the ground. I lifted Donny out of the Buick and the two boys dashed into the garage in pursuit of the older kids.

Buster, Bobbie and I waited for their dust to die down before following them, skirting Buster's motorcycle, their ancient Ford station wagon, and a tangle of bicycles and scooters and wagons, and made our way to the woodshop in one corner, where eight-year-old James– the oldest McElmon boy, known to us as Jem– showed off the redwood garden chair he'd been working on.

"Me and Dad built it," he said. Tall for his age and lanky, he resembled his father in looks with black hair and turquoise-colored eyes. "Well, it was mostly Dad," he corrected himself. "But I helped."

"You sure did," Buster said, resting one of his big paws on the boy's shoulder. "You're getting to be pretty handy with tools. Better put 'em away and get washed up for supper now, huh?"

I'd met Buster when he was a kid, on his own in Los Angeles without any family, and had looked after him until he was of age, though I think it's fair to say he looked after me, too.

Edith Austin and Buster's wife Lyric– who he called Lys and the rest of us called Swish for some long-forgotten reason– stood arm in arm waving to us from the top of the stone steps that led to the back lawn and terrace from the drive.

Edith and I had started out as operatives working for Swish's father, Harry Price, who'd been one of the first private detectives in Los Angeles. He later took me on as a partner. Then when Harry died, Edith came in with me. We closed the office not too long after Pearl Harbor and went our separate ways– me back into the Army and Edith to a war job up north in Seattle. Now she was sailing to Honolulu,

2

Hawaii the day after tomorrow to live with her sailor son Arthur and his bride, a local girl. She had come back to Los Angeles to put her affairs here in order and say goodbye to old friends. After staying a week with Bobbie and me, she'd spent the last two nights at the ranch. Swish had organized this family party as a sendoff for her.

Swish, in a bright yellow sundress that showed off her willowy figure, put her arm around Bobbie and the two of them led the way across the lawn to the house.

"You look like you just stepped out of *Vogue*," Bobbie said. "No one would ever guess you just had a baby."

"A tummy hasn't got a chance around here, what with running around after the rascals and the upkeep on this place," Swish said laughingly over her shoulder. "Poor Edie. She thought she was coming out for a rest and we put her to work weeding the vegetable garden."

"Oh, I've loved every minute of it, my dear. I've so missed having a garden," Edith said, then glanced down at her middle. "Only I don't seem to have lost any of *my* tummy, worse luck."

Edith's figure was rather broader than it once was— though she could say the same thing about me— and her hair had gone white. But she still had a spritely step and twinkling gray eyes.

After we had tiptoed inside to have a peek at Diana, the latest McElmon— postwar model, asleep in her pink and white nursery, Buster made frozen daiquiris for the ladies and got beers out of the icebox for us. We relaxed outside on the back patio with its well-oiled glider and blue-cushioned chaise lounges.

It was that hour in Los Angeles at midsummer when the air was balmy but not too hot, with just a hint of the cool evening to come. Birds chirped back and forth to each other among the branches of the ancient oaks and olive trees. The kids had an early supper of weenies roasted on the outdoor fireplace and chased each other around, trampling the beds of petunias and lamb's ears until Swish clapped her hands and called out that it was time to put the chickens to bed.

"I'll do it!" Kit yelled, tearing across the lawn. Kit– Katherine– the McElmon's oldest kid and only daughter– was named after my sister who they never got to meet but, in a way, had brought all of us together. Like Jem, she had her father's black hair and turquoise-blue eyes and the slender grace of her mother.

The other kids– more or less indistinguishable in their summer uniforms of blue jeans, striped tee-shirts and canvas tennis shoes– howled in protest and took off after her, bound for the dirt lane that led to the barnyard and its dilapidated outbuildings.

"No, me!"

"But it's my turn!"

"Wait for me!"

"I wanna see the chickens in their beds, too!"

Buster grabbed a couple of fresh beers for us, and with his shotgun slung over the crook of his arm, we followed them at a more leisurely pace.

The fading sunlight cast golden shadows through the feathery branches of the pepper trees that lined the lane and made the scrubby, barren hills off in the distance look almost inviting. There was a rustling in the palm tree, and an owl flew out of it in search of dinner.

Buster paused by the gate and was quiet for so long that I glanced up at him. He'd gained back the weight he lost while in the Pacific, flying transporters in the combat zone for the Marines, and looked to be back up to his usual healthy one-eighty, five pounds above his top fighting weight in his boxing days. He was as handsome as ever, maybe more so– tall and deeply tanned, though there were lines around the turquoise eyes that hadn't been there before. Now I saw that there were tears running down his face. I put my hand on his shoulder and we stood like that for a moment. Then Buster sighed deeply.

"I've got everything I ever wanted," he said. "Lys, the

4

kids, this place. I don't have anything to kick about. I'm happy as fuck. I was just thinking about where I was this time last year, when we heard it was all over. And the ones who didn't live to see it."

"It's rough," I said and we both fell silent. From the barnyard came high-pitched shrieks and peals of laughter, followed by protesting clucks from the hens.

"They were just kids, most of them. They ought to have been going to college or starting families of their own," Buster said after a while in his soft, lilting voice. "Lys has got her art classes at the hospital, and even the babies do their bit, bringing flowers to the boys out there. I feel like I want to do something for them, too. I dunno— maybe have some of them come out here to stay for a while. They could do some work around this place, until they figure out what they want to do."

"Sounds good," I said. "It wouldn't take much to get that old bunkhouse in shape," I added, gesturing to a long, low outbuilding with peeling white paint that had been applied during the McKinley administration by the look of it. "We could probably salvage most of the lumber from that old milking shed we pulled down."

He grinned at me. "I was hoping you'd say that, but I didn't like to ask. You've put in enough sweat around here this summer already. Don't know how I would've done it without you."

"I didn't mind— you know that," I said. "Besides, it gave Bobbie and Swish a chance to get to know each other better. And Donny loves it out here, around your brood."

"He's a swell kid," Buster said. He turned his steady gaze on me. "It's good to see you so happy, Ave. You and Bobbie going to have one of your own soon?"

"I dunno," I hedged. We'd talked about it when we were first married, but living in my cramped bachelor apartment— and no prospects of getting anything better— it hadn't seemed like a good time. Then we'd had the ordeal of moving to a new place, and Bobbie's custody case with her ex for Donny. "Bobbie's got a lot going on right now. She's got to get Donny ready to start school in the fall, and we're still settling in at the house and all. Maybe it's too soon."

He laughed. "I bet Bobbie doesn't think so. Have you seen her face when she holds Diana? There's nothing to worry about. You'd make a great father," he added soberly. "After all, you raised me."

"I'm not sure who raised who," I said.

He laughed and threw one of his big arms around my shoulders in a half bear-hug.

Then the lane was filled with the sound of young voices shouting and tennis shoes pounding on dirt as Kit and Jem came roaring past in a dead heat. Mac and Donny trailed far behind, their shorter, chubbier legs working in double-time to try to keep up.

"Whoa, you four– slow down!" Buster said, laughing again.

We turned and headed back toward the house. It sat well back from the road, a rambling place laid out, as Buster put it, "spread eagled" on a hill, with a weathered split-shingle roof and an open, ivy-covered porch running the length of it that looked out over a sloping front lawn. It had started out as an old adobe farmhouse, abandoned until an Englishman who was some sort of somebody in motion pictures bought it in the thirties and spent a lot of money making it over, adding two low-slung, board-and-batten wings and all the modern conveniences. By the time Buster and Swish bought it a few months ago, though, the place had sat vacant for years and had a forlorn, unloved appearance. Now it had come to life again, filled with the sound of laughter and screen doors endlessly creaking open or banging shut. The lights of the kitchen cast a yellow glow through the bay window and I could see the girls inside bustling around.

"This is a great place to raise kiddies," Buster said, reading my thoughts as usual. "Though Kit insists she'll be a social outcast 'round these parts if we don't have a swimming pool. I guess I better see if I can get ours working."

I slapped him on the back. "That kid doesn't need a pool to be popular. Hell, in a couple years what you'll need is a moat– to keep boys like you from coming around courting her like you courted Swish."

Buster gave me a crooked grin and brought the shotgun up to his shoulder. "A boy like me comes around here," he said, "he's going to get an ass full of buckshot."

We had our supper on the floodlit terrace– steaks grilled on the outdoor barbeque with French-fried potatoes and a big green salad with tomatoes picked that morning from their own vegetable garden and mixed by Swish at the table, washed down with red California plonk– and talked about books, movies we'd seen lately, Rita Hayworth's hair, the atomic bomb; the United Nations, seamless stockings, car telephones, the price of used cars, and any other topic anyone deemed fit for conversation. Buster, who had worked for Douglas Aircraft before he went into the Marines, told us about the job offer from Lockheed he was mulling over, and Bobbie, who had worked at Lockheed during the war, teased him about going over to the enemy.

Edith said she hoped we would all come and visit her on the islands.

"With air travel getting faster all the time, who knows– maybe you won't always feel so far away," she said a bit wistfully. "You'll come and see me often, I hope."

"You can bet on it," Buster said. "Hawaii's beautiful, at least from what little bit I saw of it. I'd like to see it again with Lys, and the kids, too. But for now, this is close enough to paradise for me."

He put his arm around Swish and they smiled at each other. But there was an anxious look at the back of Swish's wide green eyes, I thought, and wondered why. Edith must have noticed it too and nudged me under the table. I shrugged.

When the coffee cups had been cleared away and

after-dinner liqueurs had been served, Edith folded her hands in her lap and fixed her keen gray eyes on Swish and Buster.

"All right, you two— out with it," she said. "What's wrong?"

"Nobody's sick, are they?" I put in. There'd been a polio scare going around. Bobbie was worried about it, too.

Buster exchanged a glance with Swish, then grinned. "How did you know something was wrong?"

"We're detectives, dear ones," Edith said.

Swish patted my hand. "The rascals are all fine. It's just that I had a strange phone call from a homicide detective earlier. He and his partner want to drop by tomorrow morning and ask me some questions."

I looked at her. "He didn't say what it was about?"

Swish shook her head. "Not really. That's what was so strange. I gathered it's something to do with Father."

The dancing flames in the outdoor fireplace caught the golden lights of her hair. Edith put her arm around her.

"Oh, well, then, it's probably about an old case Harry worked on," she said.

"We could stick around and be here when they show up, if you want," I said.

Swish shot me a relieved smile. "I wish you would."

We forgot about the police after that. It was almost time for the chickens to wake up again when the party finally broke up and Bobbie and I traipsed off by flashlight to the little ivy-choked guest cottage, tucked away in the trees a couple hundred yards from the main house.

"Those stories you were telling, Ave— are any of them true?" Bobbie asked as we were getting undressed for bed.

"Sure they are," I said. "Well, mostly true anyway."

"Sounds like you all sure had a lot of good times," she sighed.

"I like these times better," I said, holding her close. Her luxuriant red hair fell across my chest. After a while Bobbie breathed in my ear, "I'd better get something."

I relaxed my embrace but held on to her hand.

"Donny sure gets a kick out of being around the McElmon kids," I said.

"Uh-huh. He's so thrilled at being asked to Jem's campout with the 'big boys' tomorrow I could hardly get him to stop talking about it long enough to go to sleep."

"Diana's awfully cute."

"She's a doll." Bobbie bit her lip and gave me a sidelong glance. "Ave, are you feeling okay?"

I pulled her close again and kissed her. "What do you think about trying for our own postwar model?"

Bobbie wiggled up to a half-sitting position. "Say, how many of those liquors did you have, mister?"

I laughed and rolled over onto my side, facing her. "I'm not sloshed. Well I am, but not *that* sloshed. I mean, I know what I'm saying. It'd be good for Donny to have a brother or sister sooner rather than later, so they can grow up together. You know?"

Bobbie squeezed my hand, her brown eyes full of tears and understanding. Then she gave me her answer, with kisses everywhere and eyes that now burned hot and bright.

In the morning we gathered around the outdoor table again with bacon and eggs, crispy waffles and gallons of coffee. The kids had already had their breakfast and were off in the back forty reenacting the Battle of Guadalcanal from the sound of things. Buster, looking none the worse for wear from the late night, was dressed in his hot-weather work clothes– G.I. issue swim trunks, a tee-shirt and scuffed engineer's boots.

"I thought I'd tackle that old pool pump of ours this morning, see if I can't get it going," he said.

"If anyone can, you can, angel," Swish said.

"We'll get going as soon as we get rid of the police and leave you to it," I said.

"Don't rush off on my account," Buster said. "There's plenty of work to go around."

Edith grinned at him from under the brim of her

floppy straw hat. "I'm willing, but I've got some critical last minute shopping to take care of. Bobbie's going to help me choose a proper meet-the-daughter-in-law outfit. And I'm having my hair pruned and– oh, heavens, I've got a million other things to do."

"I'll pick some lemons and tomatoes for you to take back with you," Swish said. "And squash. No one leaves these premises with taking at least one squash."

Mrs. Bellinger, the housekeeper, with an apron tied around her expansive waist, brought out another stack of waffles. She'd worked for the McElmons off and on since Jem was born and doted on them all, especially Buster. A widow now, they'd persuaded her to move with them out to the ranch, where she had her own private quarters above the garage.

"I couldn't eat another thing, Mrs. B, honest," Buster protested.

"You need some more meat on those bones. You're too skinny yet," Mrs. B said firmly and smiled with approval as Buster, groaning, reached for another waffle.

We were slurping up our last cups of coffee when I heard the sound of a car in the driveway. Presently Mrs. B came out flanked by two men. One was tall and rangy, a hatless figure in aviator's sunglasses. The other was about three inches shorter and thirty pounds heavier than his companion, with a tan straw panama pulled low over one eye. They were detective sergeants Jeffrey Zankich and Jack Dawson of the Los Angeles police homicide bureau.

"Thanks for letting us drop in on you folks like this," Zankich, the tall one, said. He pocketed the cheaters and squinted, his dark, pomaded hair glistening in the sunlight.

Swish looked up at him with concern in her green eyes. "Nothing bad has happened I hope?"

"No– nothing to be worried about, ma'am," Zankich said. "We'd just like to ask some questions about an old case we're looking into."

I looked over at Edith and winked.

Buster made introductions at our end. We shook hands. Zankich's was smooth, with a firm grip. He was all of about thirty, with a tanned, handsome face, a slight build and a small, neat mustache. He wore a blue tropical worsted suit with a ruptured duck on the lapel, and an orange necktie punctuated by a green and purple trout.

We waited with polite curiosity, while the happy shrieks of the kids wafted over from the back forty.

"Er– would you like to come inside?" Swish asked, and led the way into the big, beam-ceiling combination living and dining room that had been the original farmhouse.

It was the kind of room where men, and children, and dogs could feel comfortable– tidy, but full of homey clutter. Old-fashioned braided wool rugs covered a worn oak floor. An L-shaped, chintz-covered sofa and oversized leather armchairs were grouped around a big, low, round coffee table– a Victorian relic that had belonged to Harry's not-so-dear departed mother, cut down to size and painted by Swish. There was an enormous weathered-brick fireplace at one end, flanked by bookcases that Buster and Jem built together in their garage workshop, the shelves sagging with their books and records. At the other end, nearer the kitchen, was a long antique oak dining table set with mismatched chairs and used more for art projects than eating, in good weather at least. Swish closed the swinging door to the kitchen and the French doors that went across the back wall, looking out over the terrace and the green lawn beyond it, and asked the men if they wanted any coffee.

"No thank you, ma'am," Zankich said. He waited for her to take her seat next to Buster on the sofa before settling himself into one of the arm chairs. "So, Mrs. McElmon, if I've got this right, your father was Harry Price– the detective? And he passed on in 1935?"

"Thirty-four," Swish said. "Mr. Shepard here, and Mrs. Austin used to work with him, if it's one of Father's old cases you want to know about."

Zankich looked across at me and Edith, then turned

back to Swish. "Well, it's a lucky break for us– finding you folks all together like this, I mean– but that isn't it, ma'am," he said. "Actually, it's about Axel Swann."

Four pairs of eyes looked at him in surprise.

"Goodness," Edith said lightly, "You don't mean you've found him at last?"

"Yes, ma'am," Zankich said. "We have."

Dawson's large, slightly protruding black eyes glanced vaguely out across the room. "What's left of him, that is," he said.

"Who," Bobbie asked, breaking the shocked silence that followed, "is Axel Swann?"

CHAPTER 2

On a balmy July evening in 1930, Axel A. Swann dressed in his midnight blue tuxedo, kissed his wife goodbye and drove into downtown Los Angeles to have dinner with his lawyer. Afterward Swann left the café and seemingly vanished into the night.

His fate had been debated by all and sundry– elevator operators, my barber, the kibitzers in Pershing Square, lunch counter cooks, shoe shiners, taxi drivers– a distraction from the hot, sticky dog days of summer.

Officials assumed from the start that bootleggers must have had something to do with it. National prohibition was still going strong then, and Swann had been a field agent with the local office of the federal dry enforcement bureau– or as the booze racketeers used to put it, a prohi.

By all accounts he was temperate in his personal habits and an honest, brave and diligent officer who was good at his job. While that might have made him the darling of the Anti-Saloon League, bootleggers took a dim view of it and were said to have vowed their revenge.

The leading theory was that he might have spotted drinking going on in one of the joints he passed on his way back to his car and, being a conscientious officer, stopped to make an arrest and got taken for a one-way ride.

The police gangster detail made sweeping raids of notorious dives and booked dozens of "suspected" bootleggers into Central Station for the rubber hose treatment. The District Attorney launched a war on eastern hoodlums, said to be pouring into Los Angeles in record numbers. In the end, though, none of it seemed to yield any information about Swann.

When no bullet-riddled corpse or blood-soaked auto turned up, they started to think he might have been kidnapped and was being held for ransom. Swann's wife, who contacted police when he didn't come home that night, told of mysterious phone calls and an even more mysterious black sedan seen cruising past the family home in the days leading up to Swann's disappearance. But the expected demand for cash never came so they gave up that idea for a while.

They considered that he might have met with an accident or had a sudden bout of amnesia, especially after Swann's car was found, clean and undamaged, parked in a garage less than two blocks from the café. Police searched all the hotels and rooming houses in the vicinity, but there was no sign of Swann.

A suicide alarm went up when a straw boater like one he'd been wearing that night was found near the bank of the lake at Lincoln Park. At least half the men in Los Angeles were sporting identical hats at the time, but the lake was duly dragged and to nobody's surprise yielded no body.

The kidnapping angle came up again after Swann's secretary came forward with a rather improbable story of having received a wire from Swann instructing her to bring all the documents from his safe to San Diego. She was to tell no one. All would be explained when they met. The girl had done as instructed, taking a steamer to San Diego, and waited for Swann at the appointed place. There, she'd been forced into a car– a black sedan, of course– by an unseen captor and was driven around blindfolded for a few hours before being released, unharmed, the papers intact. A rough-looking man who had been following her for some days before this incident may or may not have had something to do with it. The police dismissed the telegram as a hoax, possibly sent by bootleggers trying to get their hands on evidence in certain pending rum cases Swann had been working on. If so, they'd been disappointed as the papers turned out to be nothing but Swann's personal files.

Then there were the usual alleged sightings: an acquaintance claimed to have spotted Swann driving west on Sixth Street behind the wheel of a blue touring car; someone else saw him at the races in Agua Caliente. Reports that he was living at a ranch in Ensenada or taking a rest cure at a sanitarium in Ohio didn't pan out. Federal agents hastened down to Guadalupe to look at a recent corpse thought to match Swann's description. But it wasn't him.

In the end, with no evidence of foul play, the authorities came around to the idea that, while he might have been kidnapped or taken for a ride by bootleggers, it was more likely that he had gone off of his own free will and was alive and well somewhere. It was hinted that there might be a blonde in the picture.

Before long, new stories came along, pushing Swann out of the headlines. His name still came up now and then, when other people went missing under mysterious circumstances or a dusty skeleton turned up in some so-called "bootlegger's graveyard." These finds caused a flurry of excitement in the papers but never ended up revealing much of anything other than the grim fact that the deserts around Los Angeles were seemingly well supplied with old corpses. I couldn't remember having heard anything about him since before the war.

I looked up and found Zankich watching me. He looked older up close than he did at a distance. It was his eyes, mostly. They were a deep brown, almost black, and somber.

"So he's dead," I said.

"Yep. Long time," Zankich nodded.

"Where did they find him?" Edith asked.

"A construction crew was doing some excavating across the river over where the new freeway's going in, and they found some bones. We think he must've been buried in the cellar of one of the houses that used to be there."

"Holy hell!" Buster said.

"You're sure it really *is* Axel Swann this time?" I asked.

"It's him, alright," Dawson said with a grimace. "We took the skull to the lab and the teeth match up with his dental records."

"Good heavens, how awful," Swish said, shivering in spite of the heat. "So, do you think that poor man has been down there all these years, then?"

"From what we can tell, he was still dressed as he was the last time anybody saw him– in his dinner clothes," Zankich nodded. "There– uh– were some pieces of fabric found with him."

"Do you have any idea yet what happened to him?" I asked.

"There's a hole in the back of the skull that might have been caused by a bullet. Small caliber, most likely."

"Is it possible that it might have been self-inflicted?" Edith asked.

Zankich shook his head. "We don't think that's very likely, ma'am. He'd have had to bury himself for one thing. And there wasn't any gun down there with him. At least, none that we could find. We had to work pretty fast. The crew needed to get back to work."

The room fell silent again while we thought about that.

Presently, Zankich cleared his throat. "So, we're treating it as a suspicious death– for now. We're looking into it to try to see if it's worth reopening as a murder case. You can appreciate what we're up against, I bet. Sixteen years is a long time. A lot of the witnesses are dead or can't be located.

Swann's widow is still with us, but I don't know for how much longer. She's poorly. They've got her pumped full of morphine. I don't think she even understands what's happened."

His manner was easy, almost friendly. It seemed natural, not forced. Apparently he hadn't seen enough B-grade crime pictures to know that the private detective was supposed to be the natural enemy of the police detective.

"What is it you need our help with?" I asked.

"Well," Zankich began, clearing his throat, "we've been going through the old case files. There were about a million leads, but none of them seemed to lead anywhere. That's typical in a case like this, I guess. The federals had their hand in it, too, and the D.A, and the sheriff. I started comparing old witness statements. There's only about half a million of those. And not just from the original investigation."

"No?"

"Uh-uh. Seems the widow never believed he was dead, so she kept prodding them to reopen the case. Every once in a while, they'd look into it, like when some bones turned up– I guess you know about that? Nothing ever came of it. But after he was declared legally dead, the insurance company tried to get it reopened. Swann carried a lot of life insurance. I guess he would back then, in his line of work. The company kicked about paying up, since no one ever did find Swann's body. They sent one of their investigators out here to look into it. The D.A. put one of his investigators on it– a guy who had worked on the original case as one of us. That was all before my time. But it's there in the files. Some new information came out.

It seems there had been a meeting of the big bootleggers not long before Swann went missing. They were looking to organize, like in Chicago. Everybody's going along with it; only they can't risk Swann throwing a monkey wrench into the works, so the boys decided he had to go. They didn't want to get their own hands dirty, so they hired it done."

Bobbie looked up at him, wide-eyed. Edith's eyebrows shot up to her hairline, but she said nothing.

Dawson stared past Swish's left shoulder at the fireplace and picked up where Zankich left off.

"According to some of this other information that came out, Harry Price used to do favors for certain bootleggers sometimes, to pay off his gambling debts."

Buster frowned. "I don't understand. Are you saying you think it was Harry they hired to kill Swann?"

"We're just trying to run some old leads to ground," Zankich said gently. "It's early days yet. Nothing's been verified. Let's just say there's some interesting angles to this."

"Where did this particular angle come from?" I asked.

"It was in the witness statements from 1937. A police captain said he got it from a former police detective, who got it from an underworld informant. The informant himself had since died, so it never went any further."

"What makes you think it will now?" Buster asked.

Zankich's steady gaze met Buster's. "I don't know, sir, but when I went through the original case files, I found something. The police searched all the nearby hotels at the time and made lists of all the guests who were registered on the night Swann went missing. I paid most attention to the Hayward Hotel, because there was also some information floating around that Swann might have had a girl stashed there. I ran down the list, and I came across the name Harry Price."

"It's a fairly common enough name," Edith said.

"Yes, ma'am. But we want to find out if this one is your Harry Price. I've got photographs that were made of the original register books, the ones my predecessors copied the lists from. Maybe you'd recognized Price's signature?"

He drew an enlarged photograph out of his coat pocket and handed it to Edith.

She put on her glasses and held it up close to her face. "Yes, that's Harry's writing," she said in a dazed tone.

I took the photograph from her and peered at it.

There it was, about half way down the page:

DATE <u>Tuesday July 15</u>

NAME <u>*Harry Price*</u>   RESIDENCE <u>*Los Angeles*</u>
ROOM <u>416</u>

I handed it back to Zankich. "Okay, but what's the connection to that and Swann?"

"There was a bellhop at the Hayward who said he spotted Swann in the lobby that night. His was only one of about a hundred tips from witness claiming to have seen him, so I guess they didn't pay much attention to it at the time. But this bellhop knew what Swann looked like— apparently said he'd seen him there before."

"Any reason you know of why Price would be staying at the Hayward? Did he live there?" Dawson asked.

"No— we lived at the Biltmore then," Swish said.

"Were any of you with him, maybe?" Zankich asked. "I'd understand if you don't remember. It was a long time ago, after all."

"July?" I scratched my chin. "We'd have all been up at Camp Baldy."

It had been Harry's idea, in fact, going to the mountains, a late summer treat for the kids who had grown thin and wan, he thought, studying too hard for their college entrance exams in the fall and working extra hours for us in the office to earn the money for it. Harry had a new car— new to him, that is— a 1927 REO Flying Cloud that he won off a banker right before he jumped out of a window, and he wanted to show it off. So we went, taking housekeeping cabins on the creek. The kids gained weight and got brown as berries. They'd swim and hike all day, or else just laze around and read. Sometimes we rode horses up into the back country or went fishing. There was an outdoor dance pavilion and an orchestra for the young people in the evenings; Edith and her boy, who was nine or ten at the time, usually listened to the radio at the lodge while Harry and I played cards or pool. But Harry had gone to town one day while we were there to attend to some business. He was back by the next afternoon.

Dawson frowned at me. "He didn't say what business?"

"No, but if you knew Harry, you'd know that was usual for him," I said.

"Do you know if he did any work for bootleggers?"

"If they paid cash, I doubt he asked them what they did for a living," I said. "But he didn't take crook jobs, and he sure as hell didn't bump people off for money."

"But Price *did* know a lot of bootleggers, didn't he?" Dawson persisted.

I shrugged. "Everybody knew bootleggers. They were hard to avoid in those days."

"He have any contacts in the underworld?"

"He may have. Same as the police."

The room once again fell silent. Buster glanced at his watch. As if on cue the screen door to the kitchen squeaked open and banged shut again as the kids came tramping in from the backyard hollering for Mrs. B, lemonade and "tweasure" maps.

Zankich said that he didn't have any more questions and that they had better get going. He thanked us all for our time. Under the circumstances, Swish didn't offer them any squash. Dawson went outside to their car to smoke. Zankich and I strolled out slowly together, pausing in the shade of the porch to let our eyes adjust to the sunlight.

"Nice folks," he said. "No hard feelings I hope."

"You're just doing your job," I said. "But look, McElmon won't like it if a bunch of reporters come around here bothering his wife. I won't like it much myself."

"They won't hear about it from us," Zankich said. "Our skipper wants to keep a lid on this thing for as long as we can. The press is liable to go nuts once they hear about Swann."

He lit a cigarette and glanced around. "Swell place,"

he said. "I wouldn't mind having a little ranch like this myself, where you can grow your own stuff. All I've got is an avocado seed in a glass on my kitchen windowsill, and it's not looking too good. Maybe someday, when I retire. If I get to retire."

"How long you been on the force?"

"I hired on in forty-two," he said. "But then I took military leave. Came back sooner than I expected to. Goddamn medical discharge."

"It's like this: if Harry was still around, he could take care of himself. But he's dead."

"I get it," Zankich said. "He was your pal."

"He was more than just a pal. I wouldn't say he was like a father to me, because he wasn't that kind. But he took me under his wing, and I got to know him better than anyone, I think. There's a lot of stories about him that aren't true. I know Harry Price wasn't any altar boy. But he'd never kill for money. And another thing– if Harry did kill someone for whatever reason, he'd take what was coming to him and see it through. He sure as hell wouldn't hide a body in some makeshift grave."

Zankich looked at me a long time, then nodded. "I'm sure you're right. In my job, though, you find out you don't really know what another person will do when he's backed into a corner. Maybe somebody had some kind of hold over him and he didn't think he had a choice."

"Uh-uh." I shook my head. "Forget that. Harry wouldn't let himself get backed into any corner. He believed people always have a choice. We ran into it all the time with clients who got into trouble because somebody had a hold over them. Harry always advised them to just confess all and take their medicine. It's only the weak or the stupid who let someone yank their strings around, he'd say. Harry wasn't weak, and he sure wasn't stupid."

"A real tough guy type," Zankich said. "I've known a couple like that myself. They both got the bronze star– posthumously."

"Any objection if I do a little investigating myself?" I asked. "I won't step on your toes. Finding Axel Swann's murderer is your job. I don't want it. I just want to know about Harry. If I find out anything you can use, you'll know about it."

"Fair enough," Zankich said. "The truth is, we're short-handed these days. We don't have a lot of time to spend on this case. There's enough pressure to keep up with the fresh ones."

"Any chance I could get a copy of that hotel register photograph?"

"Sure," he said. "I'll have one made and send it over to you."

I gave him one of my cards. Zankich put on his aviator's sunglasses and made his way down the sloping front lawn to the driveway where their car sat baking. He gave a wave as the faded green Ford sedan turned right onto the main road, then was gone, leaving a cloud of dust swirling in the air.

You're not going to find out anything, kid, I could hear Harry's voice jeering. *If I didn't do it, there won't be anything to find. And suppose I did— there won't be anything, then, either. I would make sure of that. No one would know. Not even you.*

CHAPTER 3

I drove straight downtown from the ranch, dropping Bobbie and Edith off on Broadway for their shopping. Then I went on to the main library and spent what was left of the morning and most of the afternoon in the reading room looking through musty bound volumes of old newspapers for details on the Swann case I'd forgotten, or in some cases never knew.

Federal Dry Agent
In Baffling Disappearance

———•———

Police of the missing persons detail yesterday instituted a search for Axel A. Swann, 39 years of age, who, according to his wife Margaret disappeared Tuesday night, leaving no clew to his whereabouts. He met his business associate, Roger de Pietro, for a dinner engagement at Al Levy's Grill, 617 South Spring street, leaving there at approximately ten o'clock. He failed to return home.

Swann, who is a field investigator

for the local federal prohibition enforcement office, was driving a black and yellow Pierce-Arrow phaeton. Police are searching nearby garages for the automobile, which has not yet been found.

Swann is described as five feet nine inches in height and weighing 158 pounds with light blonde hair, blue eyes and a prominent nose. He was last seen wearing a dark blue dinner suit, a sennit straw hat and black patent leather shoes.

By the next day, they were floating the idea that Swann had been kidnapped.

Ransom Plot Suspicion Told

———•———

Federal Agents to Aid Search for Swann

———•———

Dry Agent Missing Two Days

———•———

Business Associate Offers No Clews

The strange disappearance of Axel Swann, federal dry enforcement agent, took a more sinister turn yesterday when police admitted that Swann may be the victim of a kidnapping for ransom plot, of which there has been a recent outbreak in this city.

Police officials would not reveal any further details, and it is not known whether a ransom demand has been received. Swann dropped out of sight Tuesday evening after eating dinner at a café and has not been seen since. Federal authorities have offered to lend assistance in the hunt for the missing man, should local authorities require it. Though officials in charge of the investigation refused to reveal any details regarding possible lines of inquiry, it was learned that the search for the dry agent's whereabouts may lead south of the border. It was also hinted that financial difficulties may have some bearing on the case.

Dinner Uneventful

Mr. Roger de Pietro, attorney and longtime acquaintance of the missing man, who dined with him on the fateful night, could shed no light on the situation. Nothing in their conversation indicated that Swann had any worries or might be planning to absent himself from home for any length of time, de Pietro stated. The two men parted outside the café, with Swann setting off on foot.

Wife Fearful

Mrs. Margaret Swann, the federal agent's uncommonly attractive wife, was near collapse last night and unable to aid the investigation into his disappearance. She expressed fear that her husband is being held against his will, revealing that he had received several phone calls in the days before he went missing from a mysterious man who spoke in "guttural tones."

A large photograph of Swann accompanied this item. Next to it was one of a woman, captioned "Mrs. Margaret Swann." I peered closer at the faded newsprint. The grainy image showed a woman with then-fashionable, pouting cupid-bow lips and dark eyes peering up at the camera from under one of the ridiculous, brimless, bell-shaped hats of the day. They gave her age as thirty-four, but she could have passed for at least ten years younger than that, in a newspaper photograph anyway.

Still more theories were trotted out over the next few days but, while the headlines got bigger, there was little in the way of new information.

DRY AGENT SEARCH
CONTINUES

The hunt for Axel Swann, federal dry enforcement officer, who vanished Tuesday evening under mysterious circumstances, widened yesterday as police officials have been unable to find any trace of him or his Pierce-Arrow automobile.

As it stands, at least four leading theories have been advanced regarding Swann's whereabouts according to police detectives leading the investigation, which began late Tuesday night after the wife of the missing man notified authorities that he had failed to return home from a dinner engagement.

Four Theories

Swann may have been kidnapped and is being held for ransom; he may have met with illness, or been "taken for a ride" by bootleggers, or his disappearance may be related to a rum case, which due to the need for secrecy, he may not have mentioned to his wife or associates. Police officials admit, however, that attempts to prove these theories have not yet met with any success. It is believed that authorities have expanded the scope of the inquiry to the Mexican border.

Last Seen Tuesday

Police have questioned Miss Evelyn Claxby, secretary to the missing man, about his business appointments and any cases he was working on that may have required him to gather evidence out of town. Miss Claxby, it is reported, did not know of any such plans, noting that by all indications her employer expected to be in the office as usual on Wednesday.

PROHIBITION AGENT STILL MISSING

—●—

Suicide Theory Explored

—●—

Missing Man Heavily Insured

The discovery of a sennit straw hat

of the type worn by Axel Swann, federal prohibition agent, at the time of his mysterious disappearance Tuesday night, led authorities to drag the lake at Lincoln Park yesterday afternoon.

Failure to find his body brought relief to the missing man's wife, Mrs. Margaret Swann, who continues to hold out hope that her husband may yet be found alive.

Money Not A Factor

It was learned yesterday that the missing man had insured his life for $250,000 from Guarantee Life Insurance some months previous. Fears that Swann may have taken his own life due to financial difficulties, however, were dismissed by R. E. de Pietro, a business associate who dined with the dry agent on the evening of his disappearance. De Pietro denied emphatically that Swann had any cause for worry with regard to money, nor is he aware of any other troubles. Police plan to examine the missing man's bank accounts at the earliest opportunity.

Numerous Leads

De Pietro and Mrs. Swann, believed by police to be the last persons to see the missing man Tuesday evening, have given every aid to police in this strange case. Investigation of half a hundred bits of information by Detective Lieutenant Ricketts and others have failed to locate the 39-year-old dry agent or the expensive automobile he was driving that night.

Police are said to be looking into reports that bootleggers had threatened to "get" the missing man in revenge for bringing charges against them in federal court.

It went on this way for several more days, with a rehashing of information but nothing much that was really new, until they found Swann's car.

MISSING MAN'S AUTO RECOVERED
——●——
No Evidence of Foul Play
——●——
Police Seek Mystery Blonde

Police yesterday located the distinctive black and yellow Pierce-Arrow automobile belonging to Axel Swann, federal dry agent, missing since last Tuesday, in a public parking garage at 413 South Spring street, a short distance from the café where he is known to have dined on the evening of his mysterious disappearance.

Automobile Unmolested

The vehicle was found in pristine condition, showing no sign of foul play. Detectives now believe he never returned to the auto and are conducting an exhaustive search of hotels and rooming houses in the vicinity with the idea that Swann may have been taken ill or met with an injury that left him unable to communicate with friends or family.

Woman Enters Case

Acting on a tip, investigators are also attempting to locate a young blonde woman who may be acquainted with the missing man, it was learned, although officials refused to elaborate any further on this line of inquiry.

The papers made no further mention of the automobile or the hotel search. If he'd walked north from the restaurant headed for the garage, he'd have passed the Hayward Hotel on the corner of Sixth.

Two weeks into the search, Margaret Swann continued to hold out hope that her husband was being held against his will or in hiding for fear of his life, and offered a reward of a thousand dollars for information leading to his return "dead or alive." Curiously, the police also seemed to believe Swann might still be alive.

SOLUTION CLOSE AT HAND

—•—

Missing Dry Agent Spotted

—•—

Woman Wanted for Questioning

Authorities are now confident that the baffling disappearance of Axel Swann, federal prohibition officer, missing since the fifteenth inst., will soon reach its conclusion. Authorities are investigating reports that the dry agent was seen here in town less than a week ago behind the wheel of a blue sedan, heading south on Main street. Witnesses say he was in the company of a blonde woman, whom police believe may hold the key to the missing man's whereabouts. They have been unable to locate her for questioning.

Detectives are also said to be hurrying to Ensenada, Mexico to investigate a report that a man matching Swann's description was seen there.

Mrs. Margaret Swann, who has offered a reward of one thousand dollars to anyone who can aid in locating her husband, maintains a belief that he is the victim of a kidnapping by bootleggers, though no ransom demand has been made, or is in hiding. She adamantly denied intimations that her husband may have left town voluntarily.

I read through the rest of it, thumbing carefully through the brittle, yellowed sheets, until Swann's trail finally went cold. I wondered if anyone had ever collected Margaret Swann's reward money. I wondered what information Guarantee Life's investigator had been able to find out and whether the claim had been paid.

By the time I left to pick up Bobbie and Edith in front of Robinson's Seventh Street entrance, I had a notepad full of notes, a headache, and, it seemed, a lot more questions than answers. But it was Edith's last night before sailing, so I put all things Swann out of my mind for the time being. When we got home I took a hot shower and a couple aspirin and had a highball out on the deck while the ladies took their turns in the bathroom. Then we took Edith out to a concert under the stars at the Hollywood Bowl and to a late supper afterward at one of the Russian places on the Sunset Strip where they had shashlik and ice cold vodka cocktails and a drowsy-eyed violinist who strolled among the candle-lighted tables playing sad gypsy folk songs.

The milkman was making his rounds by the time we stumbled back to our place. It was on one of the twisting narrow streets, barely wider than an alley, up in the hills above the Strip– a topsy-turvy kind of house where the back faced the front and the bedrooms were downstairs instead of the other way around. From the front it didn't look like much of anything, just a squat, buff-colored stucco rectangle built right on the street. There was hardly any yard to speak of but it had a sundeck that ran the length of it on both levels, overlooking a canopy of eucalyptus and pepper trees and glimpses of the tile roofs of our neighbors' houses, clinging to the sides of the ravine. It was small, inconvenient and expensive, but we'd been lucky to get it, as the realtor kept reminding us. During the day it felt almost like living in a treehouse. At night, the lights of Hollywood and the Wilshire district spreading out below us like a magic carpet were almost enough to make me forget we were paying three times what my bachelor apartment had cost for what amounted to a glorified shoe box.

We'd talked at first of building our own place and had fun sketching out ideas on restaurant tablecloths and looking at photos in the Sunday newspaper magazines. But the price of labor and the shortages of materials had brought us down to earth for the present. In the meantime, though it was only a rental– and a short-term one at that– Bobbie had made the place into a real home. There was a big, wooly sofa and twin armchairs grouped around a low coffee table in front of the fireplace, lamps that looked like lamps, and ashtrays exactly where you wanted them. We bought a radio-phonograph with an automatic changer as a wedding present to ourselves and were building up a little record collection. Beneath the window, Bobbie's growing library filled a small bookcase that Jem and Buster had built for her.

It was a little isolated, but this part of Hollywood had never been all that neighborly anyway, in a drop-in-and-borrow-a-cup-of-sugar sort of way, even back when sugar wasn't rationed.

Edith's trunks had already been carted away to be loaded aboard the ship. Only her hand luggage was still here, waiting packed and ready to go, in the entry hall.

"Anybody for a nightcap?" I asked.

Bobbie smiled, saying she thought she'd turn in and leave us to chat about the Swann case into the wee hours if we wanted to. She kissed us both goodnight and, lifting the hem of her summer evening gown, traipsed off down the stairs to bed humming a popular song of the moment, "Seems Like Old Times."

"I'm so glad I got the chance to know Bobbie these past two weeks," Edith said. "I feel like she's a daughter– or a very good friend, anyway." she added hastily.

"It's okay, Edie," I said. "I know Bobbie's a lot younger than I am."

"You two seem very compatible, even so. It's plain she's crazy about you. And vice-versa."

"Marrying her was the smartest thing I ever did," I said. I mixed up a couple of nightcaps and handed one to Edith. We clicked glasses. "That, and hiring you as a partner."

"I owe that to you," Edith said. "I would never have gotten my license if you hadn't encouraged me."

"Pushed you, you mean," I said. "Anyway, the only reason Harry brought me in with him instead of you is because you're a woman."

Edith shrugged dismissively. "It was just his way."

"It was his loss. You taught me everything I know about the detective business– you and Harry," I said. "But it was mostly you."

Edith tilted her head back like she always did to keep from crying, then squared her shoulders and clasped her hands together.

"Right, so what about this Swann business? What have you found out so far?"

I got my notes and went over all the stuff I'd pulled out of the newspapers.

"The insurance angle could prove interesting," Edith said. "Did their investigator find out anything, and did they ever pay up?"

"I was wondering the same thing myself. I'll try to see the widow."

"As for this former police officer who supposedly got the information about Harry and bootleggers paying to have Swann bumped off– any ideas?"

"Not a one," I admitted. "It might've been someone who worked the case, or it might not. But if he was an ex-officer when they reopened the case in thirty-seven, it would have to be someone who retired or quit by then."

"Frank Ricketts worked the case, didn't he? Do you two still keep in touch?"

"A little," I said. "I'll talk to him, of course, sure. Where that will get me, who knows."

I lifted my glass up to the light and swirled the brandy around, admiring the color. It reminded me of Bobbie's eyes. I felt a little hollow, way down deep in my gut. I'd meant what I said to Zankich. Harry wouldn't kill anyone over a gambling debt. It was funny about that hotel register, though. Frank was a good copper. He would have seen it. If there was anything to it, he'd have asked Harry about it. Harry had never said anything.

"I wish to hell I knew what he was doing at the Hayward that night," I said aloud. "It could have been a divorce case, I guess. But then, why would he keep it to himself? He usually shoved them off on you and me the first chance he got."

"Not necessarily– if the client was someone important and asked him to handle it personally. He'd keep it confidential."

"What ever happened to our old case files?"

Edith shook her head. "I purged everything more than a few years old when we closed the office. Donated them to Arthur's school for their scrap paper drive."

"Probably wouldn't have helped, anyway."

I topped off our B-and-Bs and we sipped them in silence, looking out at the lights, diffused at this hour by a shroud of purple-gray fog. Edith and I had often sat down like this when we'd shared an office, kicking ideas around.

"Did you ever wonder," she said after a while, "whether there was a woman in Harry's life?"

I raised one eyebrow and stared at her. Obviously there had been women– or a woman, anyway– because there was Swish. And ladies were drawn to Harry for whatever reason– whether it was his height, or his air of authority or the threat of danger that surrounded him, it was hard to say. He didn't encourage them in any case, especially what he called "modern women" with their flat, boyish figures and brassy manners, who smoked and pushed in where, in Harry's view, they didn't belong.

"What– that summer? I never saw him with anyone," I said. "Did you?"

"Oh, heavens no," Edith said. "Harry was a man's man, through and through. Women weren't part of his world any more than he could help it." She looked out at the view, sipping her drink and thinking. "I just remember thinking that he'd been acting– well, furtive."

"Harry was born furtive," I said. "If you asked him what he had for lunch he'd say '*Who wants to know?*' and then change the subject by guessing what it was you ate from a stain on your necktie."

"True enough. But this furtiveness was different," Edith said, chuckling. "I certainly don't mean in an 'I'm secretly conspiring with bootleggers to do away with a federal agent' sort of way. I mean furtive like a *man*. I can't even put my finger on it, really. Just– well, little things like hanging up the telephone as soon as I walked into his office, and pouncing on the mail without waiting for me to sort it. It made me think of my husband, right before I caught him with the other woman. Maybe I was overly suspicious. Once a wronged wife, always a wronged wife, and all of that. Maybe I shouldn't have mentioned it. But that was the impression I had at the time."

"I'd take your impression over somebody else's sworn statement any day, Edie," I said, lighting a cigarette. "Sure you don't want to stick around and hang out your shingle with me again? Austin and Shepard?"

"Don't tempt me, Avery. I just might." Edith said, patting my hand. She couldn't keep the tears back this time and dabbed at them with her handkerchief. "Oh, mercy. I'm turning into a regular waterworks in my old age. I'm looking forward to being a lady of leisure, honor bright I am. And you're going to do fine all on your own. Harry picked 'wisely–and worthily.' "

CHAPTER 4

After we had delivered Edith safely to the *Matsonia*, still wearing her coat of battleship gray– the ship, I mean, not Edith, and said our last alohas, I went to see Frank Ricketts.

Frank was the first person I met when I came to Los Angeles. He'd been a city police detective and had helped me when my sister Kit went missing here. It was Frank who had pointed me to Harry. We had a lot in common then– both of us war veterans who'd been in the trenches, a couple of men-about-town with no ties, Frank a bachelor and me happily free from a marriage I'd never really wanted– and became pretty good pals. We'd even had a little jazz trio for a while, performing at charity boxing shows and police Christmas parties and the like, with Frank on the banjo, me playing piano and my lawyer pal Joe Gill on the fiddle.

I hadn't seen a whole lot of Frank these past ten or twelve years, though. There hadn't been a falling out or anything like that. We just more or less lost touch, as old friends sometimes do, after he got married for the second time. I don't think his then-new wife Ruth approved of Frank's buddies, me least of all– a divorced man who drank and played the horses and ran around with loose women. I don't say that the description wasn't fair enough at the time, but I hadn't exactly corrupted poor old Frank.

His first wife, Vera, had been a different story. She was a pistol of a girl. I wouldn't have called her pretty, exactly. If you thought about it, her jaw was too square, her eyes too close set, her legs only passable. But you never had time to think of any of that when you were around her. She was in constant motion, all bouncing bobbed hair and flashing blues eyes, her fashionably boyish hips swaying in abbreviated skirts to some unheard rhythm all her own, and bee-stung lips more often than not parting in laughter. We all wondered, to be honest, how Frank– mild-mannered Frank– had managed to get her.

He met her at the Ace Hudkins-Mickey Walker fight right before the stock market crashed and by Christmastime they were engaged. Frank had been punch drunk with happiness, and like most men in that state, wanted to spread it around.

"Why don't you find yourself a girl and get married Ave?"

"I just got my neck out of the noose. What do I want to stick it back in for?"

I gave him a bachelor dinner at the athletic club– a show followed by a buffet supper at midnight where we'd toasted Frank with real champagne– a gift from Harry. Beautiful blond girls dressed in brief, silver sequin covered costumes and tinseled wigs had wandered through the crowd handing out candy and cigars. There was a jazz band who knew all the latest numbers from Broadway and later, a trio of the chorus girls from the Follies had danced wearing nothing but long pearl bead necklaces.

I could still picture their lovely, slim pale bodies, pert breasts and rounded derrières swaying, and remembered the syncopated cadence of their spike heels on the parquet dance floor: *Tap tap tap, tap tap tap tap, tap tap tap tap, tap tap tap tap, tap tap tap tap– tap tap tap tap tap!*

Frank, as I recalled, had taken one look and turned bright crimson. I'd expected to see him less often after the wedding, as was usually the case when a bachelor friend married. But I was wrong; if anything, I saw him more often.

He transferred out of missing persons to the robbery detail so we sometimes worked together on a case. And Vera had all of us over every week to their cramped little apartment in the south end. She'd make a big pot of spaghetti and Frank would host all-night poker parties. Sometimes we'd all go out dancing or roller-skating. We went bowling and on fishing trips together, and saw all the latest shows. When the weather warmed up there were moonlight swimming parties at the beach and Vera, like the rest of the world, went in for miniature golf, so we took it up too. It was silly, but Vera made it seem fun. Then again, I drank a lot in those days. Nobody had any money, but nobody cared.

Then all of a sudden it was over. After barely three years of marriage, Vera died. It was an accident– she fell down the basement stairs of their apartment building and broke her neck.

It was like Frank had died with her, at first. He didn't eat. He hardly slept. After work he'd go straight back home– a cheap rooming house up on the Hill– and kept to himself, refusing to see any of his old friends. So it was a surprise when he married again after only a year and half or so as a widower. He'd called me up and said he was getting married at the registrar's office that afternoon on his lunch hour and would I stand up for him. The whole thing hadn't taken more than a quarter of an hour. There was no champagne supper this time, just a hastily arranged lunch at a Chinese restaurant across from City Hall, where the only nude cuties were the ones printed on the matchbooks.

Ruth, who worked then as a clerk in the police radio dispatch office, was as different from Vera as Groucho Marx from Harry Truman. Maybe that had drawn him to her, who knows? There was certainly no chance of her reminding him of what he'd had before. It wasn't just that they were opposites in looks– Ruth was pasty and blond where Vera had been darkly exotic– but in personality too. Vera had one, Ruth didn't. Frank would bring her along to ball games and the fights, where her silent, tight-lipped disapproval had a wet blanket effect. I'd hear Frank saying in his gentle way, "But, honey, you said you *wanted* to come." After a while he was always busy on fight nights, and something would come up to keep him away from the ballgames. It got to where I never saw him except professionally, once in a great while. He never even met my second wife, Jean– but granted, that hadn't lasted very long.

We'd written a couple times during the war while I was in the service. Then he'd seen the notice in the papers about me and Bobbie getting married and we'd found a wedding present waiting from them when we got back from our honeymoon– a lamp of pearlescent pink china with a seahorse or a kitten painted on it, I never could work out which. Bobbie sent a polite thank you note and we'd kept it, stashed out of sight but readily accessible, in case they should drop in. But they never did, and Bobbie had accidentally smashed the thing into a hundred pieces when we moved.

I found their place– a little bungalow in Echo Park that had belonged to Frank's mother-in-law. Squatting in the sun on a flat, treeless lot the size of a postage stamp, it looked neat if a little shabby. Across the street, a young woman with a blonde pompadour and a brief, black bra-top bathing suit reclined frog-legged in a beach chair, knitting with a laughing baby in a playpen at her feet while the presumed man of the house, in faded Army suntans and a polo shirt, raked grass clippings into a basket. He glanced up from his work and nodded; she gave me a friendly wave.

In the driveway of the house next to Frank's, two teen-aged boys in grease-stained tee-shirts were blaring a radio and working on the engine of a jalopy; they eyed me with suspicion as I trotted along the concrete walk and up the slightly sagging steps of Frank's porch.

Frank himself answered my knock. He wore slacks and soft-soled shoes and had a sweater draped around his shoulders, though the afternoon was already a warm one. He'd mentioned over the phone that he'd been ill lately, but all the same, I was surprised at how thin he'd become. We shook hands then he had a coughing fit.

"It's nothing. Just my old lung trouble acting up," he said. He stuffed his handkerchief into the pocket of his slacks and ushered me inside. His grin was as easy as ever as he ribbed me about my hair, of which there was less, and my middle, of which there was more.

"Hell, it sure is swell to see you, Shep. I keep meaning to call you up but then I get busy with one thing or another. You know how it is."

The living room was hot and airless, and it didn't look like much of what I'd call living was done in it. Something about the room's unrelenting tidiness reminded me of an Army barracks on inspection day. It was papered in an ugly, faded brown floral, with an overstuffed yet hard looking sofa and chair set of taffy-colored mohair placed around a beige floral print rug. A row of small porcelain ducks were arranged just so along the mantle of the tan brick fireplace.

There was the sound of a throat being cleared from the hall doorway behind us. I turned and there was Ruth, looking much as I'd last seen her only more so. The years hadn't softened the sharp lines of her figure— she was even thinner and more angular. She wore a drab flower patterned housedress and flat sandals that looked as if they were made from old rubber tires. Her thin, brownish-blonde hair hung in wispy curls around her shoulders. She stood with her arms akimbo, her lips pursed in a thin line, and stared at me, unblinking.

"Oh there you are, honey," Frank said. "You remember Ruth, don't you, Shep?"

"Of course, sure," I said, nodding. Ruth didn't nod back. I guess she remembered me, too.

I declined Frank's offer of a drink, knowing that, Ruth being teetotal, he probably meant lemonade. He looked at his watch. "Lunch is just about ready, isn't it, honey? Let's have it outside on the patio, how 'bout it? That way I can show it off to my pal."

Ruth stared at Frank now, blinking rapidly. "*Outside?*" she repeated, as if Frank had suggested we shimmy up a tree and eat lunch there.

"Sure, why not?" he shrugged.

"Suit yourself," she said.

I followed Frank through a dull Nile-green kitchen that smelled of yellow soap, and down the steps of the service porch to a narrow slab of gray concrete that butted up against the rear of the house, bare except for a card table and two metal folding chairs. Beyond it was a scrub lawn with a clothesline on a pulley strung across its length at the back, and a dirt path leading to the side of the garage where a few tomato plants were struggling to grow, limp from the heat. Frank gestured to one of the chairs and sat down in the other.

"Laid this thing myself six months ago. Not a bad job if I do say so, eh?" Frank said, indicating the patio. "I might put in a barbeque next. I got the plan for one out of *Sunset*."

We chatted a bit, catching up. I knew from his letters that he'd retired from the police force with his twenty years just after the war started. He'd been a private in the last war; the Army hadn't wanted him in this one, he said, because of his lung, but he'd taken a job as a guard at a defense plant. Since the war ended he'd been working as a night watchman in a metal works. Ruth worked part-time in the bookkeeping office of The Broadway department store.

He asked after Buster and Swish and the kids. I brought him up to date, and told him about Edith going off to Hawaii. He wanted to know all about Bobbie.

I took a snapshot of her from my wallet, in shorts and a sweater and a little yachting cap, posing with the marlin she'd caught on our honeymoon, and passed it to him.

He gave a low whistle. It wasn't directed at the fish. "You always did get the pretty girls, Shep. A redhead, you say? I'm partial to them myself."

I remembered then that Vera had been a redhead.

"Well, maybe someday I'll make it to one of your weddings," he added, sounding a little hurt.

I told him how it had been a whirlwind wedding, with only the McElmons and the few close friends we'd been able to assemble on short notice. "And anyway, you're out of luck," I grinned. "I'm all through with weddings."

Frank laughed good-naturedly. "That's what you say now. Hell, you might've at least given me the chance to throw a bachelor's party for you. Remember the one you gave for me? We were lucky it didn't get raided."

"By who? Half the force was there."

Frank sat back in his chair, crossed his arms, and gave me a fixed look. "Okay, now we got the small talk out of the way, let's get down to brass tacks," he said. "You didn't come over just to gab about old times."

"Well, in a way I did," I said.

I told him about Swann's bones being found and our visit from the detectives, leaving out for the moment the allegations about Harry. Frank listened in silence.

"Well, I'll be damned," he said when I'd finished. He shook his head slowly. "I always figured he was dead. Still it's a shock, I'll say."

"What made you so sure he was dead?"

Frank shrugged. "Certain quarters were pushing the idea that he'd run off on his own. But if he'd been alive I'd have picked up his trail. I ran down every lead, followed up on tips from every crackpot who claimed to have seen him. There was no trace of him."

"Who was pushing it?"

"Oh, I dunno. The feds were working the case too, though they mostly stayed out of it. And the homicide boys had their hand in."

"Like who?"

"Well– there was Cyrus Law for one."

"He'd be retired now too, I guess?"

"Who, Law? He was gone long before me."

Something in Frank's tone told me he didn't hold this Cyrus Law in the highest regard.

"What did you think of the bootlegger angle?" I

asked. "Anything to it?"

"Sure– there were rumors. That he was a kidnap, or was taken for a ride by eastern bootleggers who wanted to muscle in here. It made sense to me, given what Swann did for a living and his reputation. For what it's worth, the wife thought so. She was sure they were holding him somewhere, or that he was hiding out from them in Mexico. But I didn't work that angle myself. That was for the smart boys in homicide, with all their underworld contacts. They didn't think there was any connection so…" He shrugged and made a swatting motion in the air with his left hand.

"Did you ever hear anything about big-shot bootleggers paying someone to get Swann out of the way?"

"What's that? Hell no. Where'd you get that?" He gave me a sharp glance. "Why are you poking around in this case anyway, Shep? It's police business."

"What about Harry? Did his name ever come up at all?"

Ruth came barging out with our lunch on a tray then– a couple of dry-looking sandwiches on white bread with a slice of ham so thin you could read through it, a handful of potato chips and junior-sized glasses of lemonade. She set it down on the card table with a bang.

Frank reached into his billfold, took out a bill and handed it to Ruth. "Run down to the market and get us a couple beers will you, honey?"

Ruth shook her head. "You know as well as I do the doctor said–"

"I said I want a beer," Frank snapped.

Ruth pursed her lips and directed a narrow-eyed glance at me. Then she turned on her heel and went back into the house. She came banging out again a moment later wearing gloves and a hat, with her handbag slung over her arm, and disappeared around the corner of the house without a word.

When she'd gone Frank leaned across the table and squinted at me.

"Now what was that you said about Harry? Where would you get the idea he had anything to do with it?"

I repeated what we'd heard from Zankich and Dawson. "I figured they would have come to see you already."

"No one's been to see me about a damn thing," Frank said. "It's bullshit, of course. Forget it. You know Harry wasn't mixed up in this."

"He was at the Hayward Hotel that night, though," I prodded. "His name's in the register."

"So? What of it?" Frank shrugged.

"What about Swann being seen at the Hayward?"

Frank made a dismissive gesture. "You mean that kid– the bellhop? I interviewed him myself. He might've seen Swann there sometime, but not that night. He was only after the reward money Swann's wife put up for information. They came out of the woodwork then."

He crossed his arms and stared out across the back of the patio, seemingly lost in his memories.

"I always thought that pal of Swann's had something to do with it," he said after a little while. "The one he had dinner with that night. We only had his word for it that Swann went off by himself after they left the restaurant."

"What made you doubt his story?"

He shrugged again. "Just my gut. He was a dodgy son of a bitch. Some parts of his story didn't quite ring true. Why'd he call over to Swann's later that night, for one thing? He never would say."

"What motive?"

"Seemed to me he had designs on his pal's wife," Frank said. "I went to see her a few times while I was working on the case. Swann going missing like that left her in a bad way. Everything– all their credit and the bank accounts– was in his name. She couldn't pay the bills or do anything. I took her some groceries once or twice. She was a nice lady and cut up about her husband being gone. I had to talk to the wives of a lot of missing men in my time, and I could tell crocodile tears from the real thing. Hers were genuine. That pal of Swann's was always there, hovering around. Or maybe he was just after the money."

"So was Swann well off, then? The papers couldn't seem to make up their minds."

"I'm talking about the insurance money. Swann's life was insured to the hilt. Say the pal is in love with Margaret. He gets Swann out of the way. She collects a quarter million, then he marries her."

"But he'd want the body found in either case, wouldn't he?"

"There could have been some snafu with his plan," Frank grumbled. "I can't say. I never got the chance to follow up. I had a hundred other leads to chase down. Then the brass decided Swann was probably alive, and I got transferred over to robbery anyway. So that was that." He pulled his sweater closer together and stared past me at the tomato plants. "But the fact is they *did* get married."

"Who did?"

"Swann's pal and Margaret. After she had Swann declared legally dead. It was in the papers."

Ruth came back then with our beer. It was slightly warm, but we drank it anyway. Frank talked about his vegetable garden and his fruit trees. Before too long, I said I had better get going. He walked me out front– around the corner of the garage, not back through the house again. The man across the street was setting up a lawn sprinkler while his wife stood by, bouncing the baby on her hip.

"Don't be a stranger," Frank said as I got in the Buick. "Maybe we could go to the fights or something one of these days, just you and me."

"That's a good idea," I said, handing him one of my cards. "Call me up sometime."

When I got home, Donny was sprawled out on the living room rug, busy with his coloring book and crayons. Bobbie was in the kitchen, a blue-flowered apron over her shorts and shoulder-baring top, singing along to some nonsense song on the radio about shoo-fly pie as she placed a pie of her own into the ice-box. The kitchen smelled of vanilla and was cheery, with roses from Swish's garden in a little vase on the red and white dinette table and brightly colored Mexican print curtains that Bobbie had made out of tea towels she'd brought back from our honeymoon trip. I wrapped her up in my arms and squeezed her tight.

"What's that for?" she laughed. "I mean, I like it, but is something wrong?"

"Uh-oh. The honeymoon must be over if I hug my wife and she asks me what's wrong."

Bobbie chuckled again. "It's just that there seemed to be a particular urgency in that hug."

"I'm just glad you're you, and that I'm me, and that we've got each other," I said, pulling her close again. "It's too hot to cook. Why don't we take the kid and drive down the coast, maybe find someplace on the water for dinner?"

"I have no idea what brought this on, mister," Bobbie said, stripping off her apron, "but you'll get no argument from me."

CHAPTER 5

Mr. and Mrs. Roger de Pietro were listed in the phone book. They lived in an apartment on Durant in Beverly Hills not far from my office. The building, set well back from the street, resembled a Normandy castle in miniature. At the curb, a uniformed driver leaned up against the enormous fender of a gray and silver older model Rolls Royce, his nose buried in the *Daily Racing Form*. A canopy-covered brick walkway lined with hibiscus shrubs led up to the front doors. I followed it, spoke into a little telephone for a few seconds and was buzzed into a white marble lobby where a curved staircase with a white painted wrought-iron rail took me to the de Pietro's second floor apartment.

A Filipino houseboy answered my knock.

"Avery Shepard for Mrs. de Pietro."

"What about?"

"Say Guarantee Life Insurance."

He took my card and had me cool my heels in a drawing room papered in black and white toile. A pair of needlepoint arm chairs and a blue silk tufted love seat in the style of some Louis or another were grouped around a marble fireplace with a large gilded mirror mounted over it. Perched on an ebony grand piano, a parian statuette of Una and the Lion gazed serenely across the room at a Meissen shepherd boy, who frolicked on a marble-topped table alongside a silver candelabrum and a tidy stack of auction catalogues. Floor-to-ceiling windows framed with pink silk drapes looked out over the street.

"Mr. Shepard?" a voice behind me said. I turned and saw a nurse in a white uniform. She was about thirty-five, with a bland, professional expression and black hair drawn back in a severe upsweep. "Mrs. de Pietro can see you for a few minutes."

I followed her into a bedroom. It was stifling, and had the usual medicinal odor of a sick room. The walls were painted an apple green, with a white ceiling and moss green carpet. There was an inlayed Italian secretary in one corner, a Venetian style sofa upholstered in green and white striped satin placed at an angle next to it. The double bed was empty. A hospital cot had been set up next to the window, with a lamp table next to it, its surface cluttered with pill boxes, glass vials and tissues. Under a red silk spread lay the wasted form of the woman who had formerly been Margaret Swann.

The face staring up at me was so altered from the photograph in the newspaper that it might as well have belonged to someone else. She had hollowed-out eyes and translucent, waxy-looking skin drawn over concave cheeks, with silver-gray hair splayed out across the pillow.

"She has good days and bad days," the nurse whispered. "She's pretty dopey right now, so I'm not sure what you'll get out of her."

Margaret's blue eyes seemed alert enough, however. The guided me to a low slipper chair next to the bed.

"I wondered if I could talk to you about your late husband, Mrs. de Pietro. Axel Swann."

She looked up at me and nodded. "We were waiting…" she said, "…it was wrong of me."

"Did Mr. Swann ever mention anyone who might have wanted to harm him?"

"I thought there was….another," her ravaged voice became barely a whisper, "…man…"

"A man? Do you remember his name?"

"No, no, not a man..." Margaret said peevishly. She closed her eyes. I started to think she might have gone to sleep but just as I was getting up, her eyes opened again and looked around wildly. "I'm sorry, Axel! Forgive me!"

An angry male voice rang out from behind us. "What in blazes is going on here?"

I hadn't heard him come in. His footsteps were masked by the deep pile of the carpeting.

He couldn't have been five feet tall, a dapper little man in his late fifties with black patent-leather hair and a well-tended Adolphe Menjou mustache. He wore bedroom slippers and a navy blue silk foulard dressing gown, with a pale blue silk cravat at his throat, prewar Hollywood style. His hooded brown eyes and prominent hooked nose gave him more than a passing resemblance to a bird of prey. He stood with arms crossed, glowering at me.

"Who are you?"

"Avery Shepard." I passed him my card.

"Who gave you permission to come in here and annoy my wife?"

"I'm sorry, Mr. de Pietro," the nurse piped up, shooting daggers at me with her eyes. "He said it was about the insurance. I thought it was important."

"Never mind, Elsie." De Pietro went over to the bed and took Margaret's hand. "I'm sorry about this, my darling. I'll just see this Mister...uh, Shepard to the door."

We went out into the small foyer. A round table in the middle of the room held a vase of pink roses along with a pair of men's pearl-gray gloves, a panama hat and a program from the Del Mar Turf Club.

De Pietro still held my card between slender, manicured fingers, pondering it with pursed lips.

"If you are representing Guarantee Life, then you may assure them we have no intention of pursuing the matter any further," he said.

"They didn't send me," I said.

"Oh?" he stared at me, blinking and waiting.

"Detective sergeants Zankich and Dawson have been to see you?"

"Yes– yes, they have. They told us about poor Swannie. You're not affiliated with the police?"

"I'm conducting a private inquiry," I said. "I was hoping to ask Mrs. de Pietro about a couple of things."

"That's out of the question. She's far too ill, as you saw for yourself."

I nodded. "Maybe I could talk to you?"

De Pietro hesitated for a moment then sighed. "Very well. Won't you come through to the loggia?"

I followed him past a pair of folding Chinese screens into a dining room that opened onto a covered balcony. We sat down at a glass-topped garden table of painted wrought iron. The houseboy appeared with coffee on a silver tray. De Pietro took some for himself and offered me the same. I shook my head.

"It must've been a shock to your wife to hear that her late husband's bones had been found after all this time," I said.

"I'm not sure she even realizes what's happened. She's doesn't know what she's saying most of the time. The doctors sent her home. They say there's nothing more they can do for her, just make her comfortable. Comfortable!" De Pietro sipped his coffee from a bone china demitasse cup then sighed again. "To tell you the truth, in a way I'm almost glad Margaret isn't able to understand all this. It used to upset her to no end whenever the papers dredged it all up again."

"She believed her former husband was still alive?"

"The police seemed to believe it too. She held out hope that he was. Certainly the insurance company did, though as we now know that was just a ploy to keep from having to pay Margaret."

"Guarantee Life never paid?"

"Oh, eventually. Margaret had to fight them in court for every penny."

"They sent an investigator out to look into the matter, didn't they? He worked with the D.A.'s office here?"

"Yes, that's right. Indeed. I'd forgotten. They did send someone. That was after Margaret put in her claim. She had to have Swannie declared dead, as a legal formality."

"She thought bootleggers were behind his disappearance?"

"In the first place, yes. She was convinced they'd kidnapped him and hidden him somewhere. There was a lot of that sort of thing going on at the time. When nothing came of that, she thought he might have been hurt, or was hiding out of fear. Deep down, perhaps, I think she must have known he was dead after seven years had passed. But I don't think she ever accepted it– in her heart."

"Did Guarantee Life say what came of their investigation?

"They claimed to have information that Swannie had been living in San Vicente, El Salvador, under the name Andrew Sawyer. It was a false name he used sometimes in his work. He had a lot of them. It meant nothing. They said they'd tracked this Sawyer from there to Guatemala City, and then on to Havana, where they claim his trail was lost. There was a lot of talk about them reopening the case, but nothing ever happened. The company reached a settlement with Margaret. She only got a fraction of what the policies were worth."

"Did you have any ideas of your own about what had happened to him?"

"I?" He blinked rapidly. "Well– I suppose at first I believed as the police did, that he might have been kidnapped. Swannie was, after all, a fairly well-off man. But when there was no ransom demand– well, it hardly seemed likely. Then I started to think…that is, I thought it might be possible that what they said was true– that he had taken himself off someplace on his own."

"Did he say anything at dinner that night that gave you that impression?"

"N-no. Nothing definite, that is," de Pietro shook his head. "He seemed in fine spirits, everything considered."

"Considering what?"

"Just– the usual pressures– you know."

"Financial problems?"

"No– no. I was a lawyer. I handled Swannie's investments personally. No money worries at all. The police checked up on all of that. Although I did wonder–" he broke off abruptly and picked up his coffee cup, clutching it so hard I was afraid it might crack.

"You wondered…?"

"If he wasn't being blackmailed," de Pietro blurted. "In the year before he went missing, he'd taken out a large sum of money in cash from his bank. I don't know what he wanted it for and he didn't say."

"Did he gamble? Play around with women?"

De Pietro grimaced. "Certainly not! Swannie was very much a homebody and a devoted family man," he said indignantly. The hooded eyes, however, looked troubled. He stared past me at the trees framed by the arched spandrels of the balcony, apparently lost in thought. I didn't say anything. After a while he sighed and went on. "I wouldn't normally have thought so, but it's a fact he hadn't been himself lately. Though I dare say others who didn't know him as well as I might not have noticed."

"You and Swann were old friends?"

"We were at school together," de Pietro nodded. "I put it down to his time of life. Men often do odd things at middle age, they say– take up new– er– interests. I sometimes think he planned to confess the whole sordid thing to me that night at dinner but changed his mind."

"What sordid thing was that? That he had a mistress?"

De Pietro winced at the word. "Yes. It's possible. I managed to keep it out of the papers, for Margaret's sake, but he apparently was visiting someone quite regularly at a hotel. It occurred to me that one of his enemies could have found out about this– *liaison* if you will– and was using it against him. That's how these– hoodlums– operate, isn't it?"

"Did he have a particular enemy that you knew of?"

"Well– no one specific. But a man in his position is bound to have them I should think. It seemed a reasonable assumption at the time that perhaps the strain had become too much for him, and that he had taken himself off to Central America or wherever– he and some woman. I am ashamed now for having thought it of him, and poor Swannie in his grave all along."

He looked and sounded genuinely grieved; if it was an act, it was a good one.

Traffic noise rose up from the street. I could hear the rhythmic metal *swoosh-swoosh* of garden sheers in motion, and the gentle splashing of a fountain somewhere below.

"You called him up that night, after he left the restaurant– what was that about?"

De Pietro's mouth opened but no sound came out at first. He looked shocked. "Why I– I can't say that I recall. I was worried about him I suppose."

"What for?"

"Well I– that is, he'd seemed nervous. I wanted to check that he got in okay."

"You said earlier he'd seemed in fine spirits."

"Indeed, but as I also mentioned, I had the impression there was something weighing on his mind that he wished to tell me, and he did not do so." De Pietro put his cup back in its saucer and folded his hands. "Well, then, Mister...er, Shepard...I have a business appointment I must attend to, so if there is nothing else...."

The Filipino houseboy appeared at his side as if out of thin air and started collecting the coffee things onto a silver tray.

"Just one more thing." I said, keeping my tone light. "How well did you know Margaret Swann before your marriage?"

De Pietro's affable, vague expression vanished. "Why,

I hardly knew her at all," he said in a clipped tone. "And to tell you frankly, what I did know I didn't much care for. I thought she was one of those social butterfly types, spending money by the fistful, never without a bunch of people around her. But we were together quite often while I was putting the estate in order. Once I got to know Margaret, I realized I'd misjudged her. I was quite wrong, indeed. In fact, I came to admire her very much. I wasn't the only one. Perhaps if the police officer assigned to the case had spent more time looking for Swannie than flitting around Margaret, they'd have caught the fiend before the trail went cold." The hooded eyes met mine with an icy stare. "Now if you please, Axel Swann's disappearance has plagued her long enough. She became quite bitter and started to drink too much, I'm sorry to say. It's robbed her of her health. He will rest in peace, finally. I'd appreciate it, out of respect for what are surely to be my wife's last days on earth, if you and everyone else would leave us alone and let this matter drop once and for all."

CHAPTER 6

Leaving de Pietro, I went downtown to see an old reporter pal of mine, thinking he might be able to give me some inside dope on Swann. Stubby Vargas had worked the police beat during the so-called dry years and was a walking authority on crimes and criminals. He could rattle off names and dates and other details like it happened yesterday. During the war he'd taken off to serve in the Signal Corps but was back now working as a sports editor for his old paper.

It was housed in an unremarkable long, low building of sandy brown brick. The ancient rattletrap of a cage elevator groaned and wheezed its way up to the third floor, where a gimlet-eyed brunette paused long enough in her task of trying to unstick a typewriter key with a pencil eraser to point me in the right direction. The newsroom as usual smelled faintly of sweat and sour paste, cooking grease and burnt coffee. Sunlight flooded in through the familiar bank of windows, filtering across the clusters of desks where a couple dozen reporters in shirtsleeves were hunched over typewriters or had telephone receivers jammed into their ears. A cloud of blue smoke hovered overhead. A skinny office boy with a broom almost taller than he was darted around sweeping up scraps of paper from the worn gray and white speckled linoleum floor.

I found Vargas tucked away in a corner at a desk that, like its occupant, looked as if it had seen better days but still had a lot of good use left in it. Half hidden by stacks of copy paper and file folders, he was slumped in a swivel chair thumbing through a tattered armed services edition of *The Poems of Carl Sandburg*. A red necktie in a print of bright yellow and white splotches like cockeyed fried eggs flopped loose outside his vest. He grinned as he looked up and saw me, took off his gold-rimmed bifocals and ran an ink-stained hand through thinning brown hair that had retreated about two inches from his forehead since I'd first met him.

When did all my friends get so old? I thought. Vargas was looking at me like he was wondering the same thing.

"Well, well," he said. "You have the look of a man in need of a favor."

"Is it that obvious?"

"No, but that's the only thing I can figure that would drag you down to this dump these days. Well, if it's passes to the fights you're after, it just so happens I've got two left for Friday."

"I'll take them— but that's not it."

"So, pull up a seat and tell papa all about it. I guess I can spare you ten minutes."

The guest chair was buried under more bulging file folders and a box of carbon papers. I shifted them to the floor and sat down across from him.

We chewed the fat a while about this and that: the upcoming Rams charity game, the sub-par pitching of the Angels so far, whether Sugar Robinson had a shot at the welterweight title.

"Keeping yourself busy?" I said, nodding at the book.

"I was just looking up a quote while I waited for a phone call," Vargas yawned, glancing up at the clock. "Something about 'new and old darlings of destiny.' "

"You ever miss the crime beat?"

He snorted. "Miss it? Do I miss having to crawl through a bathroom window into a hotel where there's a week-old corpse with its throat slit? Or trampling into houses where the father had just killed his wife and three babies with a hatchet? Sure, I miss it. Look at that bunch," he said with a nod indicating the newsroom at large. "Can you picture any of that clean, healthy, polite, hard-working bunch doing stuff like that? They're okay kids, I guess, even if they do make me feel like I ought to be in a rocking chair, nursing my rheumatism. Still, it's a helluva raw deal– while I'm off getting my ass shot at, they swoop in and get all the plum jobs."

"I thought you were in Florida?"

Vargas narrowed his eyes. "I thought *you* wanted a favor."

I asked if he had covered the Axel Swann story.

The puckered lines of Vargas' brow smoothed out again. "Yeah, I covered it. Tried to anyway. The cops more or less made chumps out of us."

"How's that?"

"By tossing out a different motive every day, for one thing. It was all just smoke and mirrors. They never meant to solve that one." He leaned forward and gave me a sidelong glance. "Why are you interested? Is there something up with the Swann case?"

I ignored his questions. "What do you mean it was never meant to be solved?"

Vargas kept a steely eye on me, but settled back in his chair and lit a cigarette. "That's how they operated, the cops. They either shut a story down completely by not coming across with any information, or else they smoked us out by giving out too much information. You know– false leads, stringing us along. Throw in an unknown blonde and the hint of sex and we'd be off to the races. It works for a little while. But then nothing ever comes of any of it. After a while the fickle public gets bored and forgets all about it, and we move on to the next big thing."

"Why do you think it was? That they didn't want the case solved, I mean?"

"I had some ideas. Kicked them around a little. They didn't get me anywhere, except to the morgue, almost," he said. I stared at him. "It doesn't take a genius to figure out it had to be somebody who had enough pull with the cops to make it worth their while, bringing the curtain down on a murder investigation.

"You thought it *was* murder, then?"

"Never any doubt about it, to my mind." He squinted at me through a gray haze of smoke. "Hell, Shep– you didn't believe any of that bullshit they were peddling about him running off to Mexico or wherever it was? Take it from me, Swann never left this town."

I stared at him, feeling like a heel for not telling him how right he was about that.

"You're saying you think the cops hushed it up?"

"Well, they'd have had help from the D.A. Maybe the feds too. Swann might have been the sweetheart of the W.C.T.U. and all, but not everybody in his department practiced such dedication to the job."

"Frank Ricketts worked that case," I said slowly. "He wouldn't go along with a thing like that."

Vargas' placid brown eyes met my angry gaze. "Put your hackles down, Shep. I don't mean Frank. He was a good copper. Why do you think they had him chasing his tail through the whole thing, interviewing grandmas that couldn't recognize their own face in a mirror who claimed to have seen Swann around town, and off looking under rocks for him in the desert?"

I nodded in grudging agreement. "Okay, but I talked to Frank recently. He didn't mention anything was wrong about it."

"He wouldn't, would he?" Vargas said, blowing a perfect smoke ring. "Coppers always rally around one of their own. No one likes to be a rat. You can bet they know who the bad apples are, all the same. Just like us newspapermen. There were plenty in this town happy to write whatever their pals in the department wanted them to."

The office boy came around with his broom. Vargas made an impatient gesture.

"Never mind that now, kid. Go get us some coffee. And I don't mean that slop that's been on the hot plate all morning." He flipped a coin into the air. The boy caught it and scurried away.

"Know anything about a guy named Cyrus Law? A homicide cop?" I asked.

Vargas pressed his chin with his thumb. "Not a whole lot. Weasely type. Wore bow ties. I could never get a bead on the guy. On one hand he was a good detective— he caught the Pillowcase Bandit, the one that killed a bank guard. But he had a nasty side, too." He gave me a long once-over. "Law worked on the Swann case— had to resign not long after that as I recall."

"Why– because of Swann?"

"More like all his sins catching up with him, I think. Beat up one prisoner too many, probably. They filed it under 'conduct unbecoming an officer.' The new chief of police wouldn't have wanted any more scandals on his watch."

"Any idea what Law did after that?"

"Last I heard he was in your line– confidential investigations, discretion guaranteed, that sort of thing," Vargas said. He narrowed his eyes. "There *is* something up with Swann, isn't there? You working for the widow? She still think he's hiding out?"

"What did you mean about your ideas almost got you killed?"

"Be that way, then," Vargas sighed and flicked his cigarette ashes into the lid of an empty typewriter ribbon tin. "Okay, so I asked myself– who had that kind of pull and would want Swann out of the way? It had to be somebody interested in one of the big rum-running outfits, at the wholesale end of things. You know– with contacts in the Canadian shipping companies, and their own ships to haul the stuff. That kind of set up involved a big operation. There weren't too many around here who could do it."

"For instance?"

"That, my friend, was the sixty-four dollar question. They hardly ever caught the really big fish– the ones who actually ran the whole works. If it'd been a couple years earlier, I might have said Tony Cornero or Charlie Crawford. But Tony was doing time in the federal pen by then and Crawford's influence wasn't what it was, since he didn't have his pals in the mayor's office anymore. I got it into my pea brain that Angus Taggart was a possibility."

"I thought Taggart's line was gambling. Harry used to say he was a gyp artist."

"Sure, that's how he started out– running some of the big casinos for the Crawford outfit. His inroads into the booze racket aren't as well known, but he was a big operator, alright. Maybe wanted to be bigger. I happened to be on the spot once when he got arrested on a liquor beef."

"How'd you swing that?"

"It happened the year before Swann went missing. Me and this police detective I knew, Cap O'Leary, were riding up the coast to Venice late one night. The fog had rolled in over the highway, so we weren't exactly setting any land speed record. We were just coming up on Palisades Del Rey beach club, when all of a sudden he pulls over on the inland side and elbows me to hush up. He's staring off across the road. At what, I didn't know. I couldn't see a damned thing myself on account of it's pitch black. There's not another car on the road. The only sound is the lap of the waves. But we sat there real quiet and then I hear something– a boat motor idling. And I see it– this flash of light. And just then, the mist clears out and there in the moonlight, goddamn me if there isn't a speedboat sitting there about a hundred yards off shore with its lights out. We can also see now that there's about a dozen people down on the beach and a dory up on the sand with three of four big, beefy types unloading sacks of booze out of it onto a big two and a half ton truck parked there with its bed facing the water.

O'Leary whispers he's going down to the beach club

to use their phone to call Venice division. They must've had a lookout, though, 'cos the next thing we knew, a flare went off up on top of the bluff and all hell broke loose down on the beach. The guys that were unloading the dory dove into the water and swam out to the speedboat, and off it went. The other people were running every which way, swearing and yelling.

So O'Leary gets his service revolver out of the glovebox and asks me if I had my gun. We all had them back then on the crime beat. Police badges, too– remember? It was the only time I was ever glad I did, even if I didn't end up having to use it. He says we're going down on the beach to capture the truck and bring in anyone who hadn't got away. Like hell we are, I said. But right then a big black Packard touring car came shooting out onto the highway and passed us, heading north. Like a shot, O'Leary took off after it. We were doing forty-five, maybe fifty. I thought his old heap was gonna fall apart. But we caught up to them and headed them off just before they turned up the Culver road.

The driver, he was dressed up like a Jap fisherman, and next to him was Taggart. While I held my gun on them, O'Leary leaned in and pulled a blanket off the back seat and there's about thirty sacks of booze, still dripping wet. O'Leary told Taggart he's under arrest for possession and transporting liquor. Taggart just laughed and said it was all a big mistake. Claimed he was coming from a private party at the beach club and the business with the speedboat had nothing to do with him. Here we had him dead to rights with the goods and he tried to bullshit us."

"So what then?" I asked.

"O'Leary flagged down a motorcycle cop and had him go back and guard the liquor truck. Two hundred and forty cases. We escorted the Packard to Venice and O'Leary turned the pair of them over to the chief of detectives for booking. Taggart's lawyer showed up and sprang him before I was done calling in my story. That was some scoop. If I hadn't been there, I'd have missed it."

"So he just walked?"

"It was a little misunderstanding, Taggart said. Some prewar liquor from his own collection that he'd taken to the party. He got a fine for transporting and that was that."

"What about the stuff on the truck?"

"They couldn't connect Taggart with that. The truck was registered in another name. O'Leary couldn't swear he actually saw Taggart on the beach. He became an ex-cop after that."

"Fired?"

"Yeah. Not for the Taggart pinch officially. They found some trumped-up reason to bounce him. Four months away from retirement. They let him come back after a while so he could get his twenty years in and qualify for his pension— stuck him behind a desk where he couldn't do any damage and gave him some papers to shuffle. He worked for the D.A. for a few years after that."

The office boy came back with our coffee in paper cups. I waited until he went away again.

"Did you ever hear anything about bootleggers trying to organize?"

"All in good time. Who's telling this story— me or you?" Vargas said, sipping his coffee. "So getting back to my ideas, after I started asking questions, word came through underworld rumor that Taggart was thinking of organizing. Gambling, hooch, women, all of it under his control. He wanted the big time bootleggers to start getting their stuff through him instead of dealing with the wops."

"Why should they? Sounds like a good way to get killed."

"Sure. But there were a lot of palms that needed greasing to get their stuff up from the beaches, and to be able to operate around town once they got it here. You had to look out for the D.A.'s booze squad and the sheriff's deputies in the county, the vice boys and the beat cops in the city limits, and the feds, who could go anywhere they want. The wops didn't have any pull. That's where a guy like Taggart could be useful– if he could guarantee protection, they might go along with him. Say Swann got in the way of that. He'd have to go."

From the newsroom came the sounds of phones jangling frantically, the clack of typewriter keys, the steady hum of voices punctuated now and then by someone shouting "Boy! Boy! Copy!"

"How do you know your source was on the level?"

"All I can say is there must've been something to it because as soon as I started writing about it, somebody called me up and threatened to throw a Chicago pineapple through my window if I didn't stop poking my nose in," Vargas said grimly. "You've got a point, though. I couldn't get anybody to confirm the rumors. I talked to all the top bootleggers I could find– the ones who hadn't blown town already, that is. Old Dutch Meagan, Harry Winslow, Frankie Parma, Eddie Durance. None of them would talk. Who could blame them? Seems like anybody who might've known anything about Swann got dead fast."

"Yeah?"

Vargas shrugged. "Maybe I'm just talking through my hat. But it looked to me like there were a lot of bodies turning up of all of a sudden– people who were supposed to have been informants."

"Like who?"

"Well, there was Mike Higgins, for one. He was a smalltime bootlegger and hijacker with an arrest record as long as your arm– everything from public drunkenness to attempted murder– but he almost always walked. Until he got shot by a cop."

A vague memory stirred at the back of my mind. "Are you talking about Alibi Mike?"

Vargas nodded. "Yeah, some of the papers did used to call him that. He tried to break into a liquor warehouse one night. Only it was bad luck for him a vice cop named Nick Lundy was waiting for him with a machine gun."

"Dead?"

"Yeah." Vargas stamped out his cigarette. "So maybe Higgins had it coming to him. I'm not saying he didn't. But there was something funny about that whole business."

"And you think he might've had information about Swann?"

"There were rumors. The cops denied it. They said they didn't know anything about him being any informant. Lucky break for somebody, his getting shot like that, if he was."

"Did Lundy say how he knew Higgins was going to be there that night?"

"Our old friend, Anonymous Tip, told him Higgins might try to pull something. Higgins' wife wasn't having it, though. Kay, her name was. At the inquest she said she thought a cop probably put Higgins on the spot. What a gal! You shoulda heard her. Lundy was up on the stand telling how he had to kill Higgins in self-defense, that Higgins pulled a gun on him first. He said Higgins had a reputation as one of the worst gunmen in the city. Kay, she stood up and yelled *'Yeah, and so's your old man!'* at him. He deserved it. Self-defense, my ass. Lundy was a trigger-happy son of a bitch and nothing but a brute. He slugged me one time."

"What for?"

"I did a story about him roughing up a bootlegger suspect in the holding cell. It was the truth. He and that Law were cut from the same cloth. The other papers wrote about him like he ought to be handed a medal. Good old Indestructible Lundy, the big hero who ran eastern gangsters out of town with his trusty machine gun. If you ask me, he was nothing more than a hired thug with a badge, and if he ever ran an eastern gangster out of town it was because people like Gus Taggart didn't want the competition."

"You think Lundy was on Taggart's payroll?"

Vargas shrugged. "Maybe, maybe not. All I know is he jumped ship and retired as soon as the new mayor started cleaning up the department in thirty-nine. Along with the guy who was chief of police at the time of the Swann case, and the chief of detectives, too, as a matter of fact."

The phone on his desk rang shrilly.

I stood up. "I owe you, Stub. You know, if something did come up with the Swann case…"

"Forget it," Vargas said, waving me off. "Nice seeing you, old pal. Shoo yourself out, will you?"

CHAPTER 7

That night after supper, when Bobbie and I had done the washing up together and Donny was in bed, I went over all I'd learned the last few days and tried to make sense of it.

Frank thought Swann's pal de Pietro might have had something to do with the disappearance, for love or money or both– Margaret Swann had stood to collect a small fortune from Swann's insurance policies. "Dodgy" Frank had called him. I'd agree with him there. De Pietro hadn't impressed me much in our interview, either. It had thrown him, my asking about that phone call. He'd known, too, exactly what I was getting at by wanting to know how well he'd known Margaret before they were married. But my gut told me de Pietro was no murderer.

Zankich and Dawson thought bootleggers had wanted to organize and had paid someone to get rid of Swann. Vargas had more or less said the same thing, but his information had it that it was Taggart who was trying to organize and wanted the bootleggers to come in with him. Vargas thought the police had helped hush the whole thing up, for a price. It didn't seem that big of a stretch to me.

The only problem with either theory, though, was that the booze racket in Los Angeles never did organize itself like Chicago. Maybe the sunshine and wide open spaces had a pacifying effect. Silvery-haired old Charles Crawford was the closest thing to an Al Capone we'd had here– an ex-saloon keeper who controlled vice operations through a syndicate and had a lot of friends at City Hall. The syndicate ran gambling clubs and bookmaking rackets, brothels and dance halls, speakeasies and swanky nightclubs through fronts, none of whom had any obvious ties to Crawford. They operated without interference so long as the right people got their protection money. If the Anti-Saloon League or the W.C.T.U. squawked too loudly about the liquor problem in the city, the police obligingly went out and made sweeping raids. After the excitement died down, the syndicate-backed joints would quietly open up again while their rivals stayed padlocked. At least, that was how Harry explained the system to me.

All I know is, I never saw any barred doors where you needed a password to get in, and the bartenders didn't make any pretense of serving booze in teapots like they do in the movies. The joke around here was, if you wanted a drink, all you had to do was go into certain cafés and look thirsty. If you didn't know where to go, just ask the nearest policeman.

I made a list of names Vargas had tossed at me:

> Angus Taggart – booze operation?
> Old Dutch Meagan – bootlegger
> Harry Winslow – bootlegger
> Frankie Parma – bootlegger
> Eddie Durance – bootlegger
> Nick Lundy – ex-cop. Taggart?
> Mike Higgins – shot by Lundy. Connection to
> Swann?

I used to see Taggart around town but didn't know much about him beyond a few scant details from Harry and what I read in the papers, which usually referred to him as a wealthy sportsman– newspaper talk for persons with unlimited income of indeterminate source. Unlike most of that type, Taggart lived modestly and dressed like a tent-revival preacher in dark suits three or four sizes too big for him that looked like they had come from a mission barrel. His gambling casinos, though, were supposed to be the biggest and plushest in town, including one on the entire top floor of an office building not two blocks from City Hall. Sucker joints, Harry called them. *Think they lay out all that jack for window dressing so the house can lose?'*

Taggart always laughed off any reports that he was a gambling boss. "I'm retired, boys," he'd say in interviews from the links of his country club, insisting that golf was his only vice.

Old Crawford had been gunned down in his office, less than a year after Swann went missing. An ex-deputy D.A. prosecutor confessed to the crime claiming it was self-defense, and had been acquitted. The remnants of the syndicate carried on for a few more years, until Los Angeles went in for real reform. Taggart and others had reportedly left town and in due time opened legal gambling halls in Las Vegas, Nevada.

I thought about what Vargas had said about Mike Higgins, and wondered who Higgins had worked for– had he been in a position to know anything about Swann? I added Kay Higgins to my list with a question mark.

Dutch Meagan, Harry Winslow and Frankie Parma I had never heard of but a phone call to a friend of mine on the local parole board got me the information I needed: that they were either dead or in prison or had otherwise not been around here for at least fifteen years. I drew a line through their names and put a star next to Eddie Durance.

Eddie I knew. A young, brash, good-looking Italian, he had been Harry's bootlegger– and mine, when I could afford him, which wasn't often in those days.

Never part of the Crawford syndicate, he'd run his operation alone, headquartered in an import grocers on West Sixth Street. Behind dusty bottles of olive oil and shriveled salami were banks of phones to take orders; out back he had a fleet of fast cars with burly, tough-looking drivers ready to make deliveries and collect the cash. Stock on hand was stashed in the basement of the building next door to his; he showed me the set up once. There was a tunnel, accessed from Eddie's basement by a hidden staircase. He had a warehouse somewhere else in the city where most of his supply was kept, along with the trucks he needed to haul the stuff up from the beaches.

Eddie usually delivered Harry's orders to him personally, because he liked Harry, and more often than not would stay on for a friendly game of cards. He and I were about the same age and I liked him okay but we never became pals. We bumped into each other once in a while at the fights or shows, but outside of Harry's, he and I didn't exactly travel in the same circles. It had been fashionable for a time to rub elbows with bootleggers, or so some people thought. I never did. It wasn't fair; I realized it even then, but that's how it was. You told yourself bootleggers were a necessity, like dentists. You could fool yourself into thinking you weren't breaking any laws by buying the stuff, even if by doing so you kept the bootleggers– who were– in business.

Not that Eddie thought of what he was doing as a crime, or of himself as a criminal. As he saw it, he was supplying a product that a large percentage of the population wanted but couldn't have due to a generally unpopular law, that in fact, he was doing us all a favor by providing booze that was the real McCoy so we wouldn't poison ourselves to death with watered down rotgut of unknown origin. *'It's just a business– a service,'* he'd say. *'What the hell's the difference between what I do and the cobbler or the baker?'* I could see his point. But I never heard of any cobblers or bakers settling their differences with machine guns.

I don't mean to say Eddie was violent. Tough, for sure. Ruthless, probably. I remember he'd been hauled downtown for questioning in connection with a shooting death in what the papers called a bootlegger's war. He hadn't been charged, though, and I never heard of him being involved in any other killings. But then, conveniently, I hadn't looked too deep into Eddie's business dealings. In any case, Swann's disappearance hadn't done him much good that I could figure– his set up on West Sixth and his liquor warehouse had been raided that fall. Eddie himself and several of his associates were arrested and charged with conspiracy to violate the federal prohibition law.

I ran into him once not long after that, when he was out on bond. It was at a party in the roof garden on top of the Bendix Building. Eddie was standing off by himself, looking as if he didn't have a care in the world, in a beautifully cut tuxedo that clearly wasn't a rented number like mine. He had one patent leather-clad foot up on the parapet and was staring out at the twin spires of St. Joe's and beyond to the hulking steel skeletons of half-built skyscrapers. He offered me one of his custom-made silver-tipped cigarettes and we stood there for a little while smoking in silence.

"You maybe mighta heard I ran into a little trouble," he said finally.

"It was in the papers," I said.

"Guess Harry will have to get himself another bootlegger."

I stared at him. "Is it as bad as all that?"

Eddie grunted. "Maybe I go free, maybe I don't. I do, maybe I don't start up again. It'd be a lot of trouble. And for what? I pay, and they shut me down anyway. They even take my car. Ten grand I just pay for that car. My business– it's the same one I have these six, seven years now. So I ask myself– what changed?"

"They've got a nice new mayor up at City Hall," I said. "He doesn't like crime."

"He picked a funny place to be mayor of then," Eddie said.

He looked out at the neon lights blinking white and orange, green, blue and red from other rooftops. Somewhere off to the north, a beam of pink light cut a swath through the night sky.

"Things ain't so easy anymore," he went on after a while. "Not like they was in the old days. This town was wide open then."

"It isn't now?"

"Hell, no. Not for me it ain't. What the hell– maybe I quit the racket. Prohibition's almost all washed up, anyway."

"You think so?"

Eddie shrugged. "Wanna bet on it? But what's it to me if it is?"

Out of the corner of my eye I caught sight of a blonde, a stunner in an orange velvet coat, trimmed in ermine, walking around looking forlorn. Eddie saw her too. He flipped away his cigarette and offered me his hand. "I guess I neglected my girl long enough. Be seeing you, Shepard."

But we didn't see each other again. To everyone's surprise, Eddie pleaded guilty to the charges against him and got two years in the federal penitentiary at McNeil Island.

The next time I heard of him was about a dozen years ago or more, when I'd read that he had an interest in one of the gambling barges anchored off the coast at Santa Monica. The D.A. and local police had long made a big show of trying to get the ships shut down, but the fact is they'd been operating for years. Eddie made the news when his ship broke loose of its anchor during a storm and sank. It was lucky that no one was aboard at the time. The state stepped in and did finally close the ships for good not long after that, and Eddie disappeared from the headlines again.

It took me a few more phone calls to find out where he hung his hat these days. It was nearly midnight before I got the information: he'd just bought a gambling casino in Las Vegas.

CHAPTER 8

From the window of the big Skymaster I watched the brown-beige colored sand coming closer and closer. I hadn't been to Las Vegas since before the war, when my second wife Jean and I were married. We'd stayed at the new Hotel El Rancho resort out on the highway and hadn't seen much of the town. From the air I could see a lot of new buildings had cropped up since then, like small islands with only a little patch of lawn and the azure rectangle of a swimming pool separating them from the jack rabbits and chaparral. The railroad track and a slash of gray-white highway cut through the open desert, stretching endlessly toward the jagged purple-red mountains. We passed low over the shimmer of green that marked the business section and circled north, where factory buildings and housing tracts were laid out in neat rows like shoe boxes.

Stepping off the plane onto the tarmac, I felt a blast of blistering air. It was as if I'd opened an oven door and got kicked in the chest by a kangaroo. We had heat in Los Angeles, but this heat you could almost reach out and grab hold of. The sky was pure blue and perfectly cloudless. Women, bare-armed and gloveless, tugged at their clinging skirts. Men in light colored slacks and open-collar sports shirts whipped sunglasses out of their chest pockets and put them on. I felt like a used car salesman in my dark blue business suit. A hot used car salesman who needed a tall, cool drink and a shower. Both would have to wait.

An outfit called the Lucky Cab Co. with the phone number 7-11 painted on its side ran me out to Eddie's place, about a fifteen minute ride south from the airport, past an assortment of fairly unremarkable auto repair garages and gas stations, motels and nightclubs. It was off by itself surrounded by more buff-colored sand and sagebrush just north of downtown.

The cab swung into a half-circle driveway marked at either end with pillars of white painted brick topped by oversized brass coach lamps. In neon script, a signboard facing the street read:

THE OASIS
HOTEL CASINO
COCKTAILS DINING DANCING
SWIMMING POOL
AIR CONDITIONED

The main building was low-slung and modern, painted a blinding white with dark green shutters. Above the flat roof, large white neon letters stood out against the desert sky, spelling CLUB OASIS. Underneath it in smaller letters were the words HOTEL CASINO. The parking lot, off to one side fronting the highway, could have accommodated a modest race track. It was about half full of automobiles, many of them expensive makes and new looking. Beyond it were two rambling, L-shaped buildings separated by a broad green lawn inset with palm trees and a lot of lush, tropical shrubbery that I was pretty sure didn't grow natural in the desert. A hand-lettered wooden sign mounted on the grass said LOU SHELDON WELCOMES YOU! ENJOY YOUR STAY!

I peeled myself out of the cab and went into the lobby, which was pleasantly cool thanks to the conditioned air, as advertised. It was all done up in the latest version of Sunset Strip swank, with a lot of mirrors, walls painted in shades of coral and cocoa brown, and furniture upholstered in smoky blue leather. There was a fireplace at one end, going full blast for some reason; next to it were telephone booths and a gift shop, and a barber shop just beyond. Across the back wall, ceiling-high French doors opened onto a concrete terrace with a sparking swimming pool in the center of it.

Branching off in the other direction, a cocktail lounge and the wide-arched entrance to the casino beckoned enticingly. Both looked to be doing a brisk business. I could hear the tick-tick-tick of a wheel of fortune; the mechanical whir of slot machines followed by the metallic whunk of coin hitting coin; the click of the ball bouncing around a roulette wheel; the slam of the die against backboards. Above the din, the droning of the stickmen– "Plaaace your bets, please, ladies and gents!... Nummmber two, black!... Gone Awaaay!... Deeealer wins again!" – mingled with the hum of voices, laughter and the tinkling of the lounge piano.

A sunburned man wearing huarache sandals and a sports shirt that matched his Hawaiian print swim trunks came plodding in from the pool terrace and made a bee line for the casino, coins jingling in his hand. People came and went from the lounge: women in pastel slack suits or bare-backed sundresses, men in variations of Hollywood casual: slacks with vivid hued sport shirts– tieless– with or without a herringbone or check-patterned sports jacket, soft-soled loafers and snap-brim panamas if they wore any hat at all, and both sexes in western-style cowboy shirts and boots.

Wading across an ankle-deep expanse of green and gold patterned carpet to the registration desk, I asked the clerk where I could find Eddie Durance. He picked up the receiver of a white telephone and mumbled something into it. I must have gotten the nod at the other end because he hung up and told me I'd find Mr. Durance in his office, Bungalow

A. I went out the way he indicated, through the French doors onto the pool terrace. Green and yellow umbrella tables, captain's chairs and plump-cushioned chaise lounges, most of them occupied, were arranged around the spotless white concrete surface. A voice crackled over a loudspeaker, paging someone to the telephone. Waiters in maroon trousers and white mess jackets sallied around serving tall, iced drinks from silver trays. A dozen or more swimmers were splashing around in the pool. Women in florid two-piece suits sunbathed around its perimeter, watching over the tops of their sunglasses as a hairy Adonis with rippling muscles and abbreviated trunks strutted around on the diving board before plunging in. Bare-chested men– fat, trim, pink, white, red and bronzed– were sprawled out on the chaise lounges watching the women, or sat in the shade of the umbrellas with cigars clenched between their teeth playing cards. Behind them, large, sharp-eyed sentinels in dark business suits with bulges under their arms loitered at a discrete distance, watching everyone.

I came to a sign at the head of a walkway that pointed me in the direction of Bungalow A. A woman got to it just as I did– a deeply tanned blonde in a skintight strapless white bathing suit with a short, bright red Mandarin-style beach coat thrown over her shoulders, her eyes shielded by a pair of white leather-framed sunglasses. I was about to yield the right of way to her when she suddenly lurched forward. I caught her just before she fell on her face.

"Whoopsie," she said.

I made a corny joke about women always falling into my arms.

"S'ese damn shoes," she slurred. Leaning one hand against my chest for support, she bent down to unbuckle the ankle straps on a pair of white kid-leather sandals with sky-high cork heels, and stepped out of them with a happy sigh. "Thas' better," she said. Then her brow puckered with worry. "But *he* hates for me to go around barefoot."

"I'll never tell," I said.

She gave me a cockeyed grin and, grabbing the sandals by their thin straps, traipsed off along the brick path that according to the sign led to the residential section.

I walked in the opposite direction until I came to Eddie's offices, a white stucco, green shuttered building with a pair of oversized air conditioning units on the roof. The front door was locked; I pushed an electronic buzzer and was admitted into a central reception hall with a round desk in the middle of it and offices to either side.

The desk was occupied by an attractive girl of maybe twenty-five, with dark eyes, a pert, freckled nose and a cap of dark brown feathery curls, dressed in a dusty pink man-tailored suit. She held a gold ball-point pen in her left hand and was busy jotting something down in a leather-bound book; she looked up at once and flashed me an engaging smile.

"You're Mr. Shepard? Mr. Durance is expecting you. I'll let him know you're here."

I heard Eddie before I saw him. From within the office to our right came the sound of his voice. I was surprised that I recognized it right off– deep and unaccented, with a slight gravelly timber to it now. He was bawling somebody out with it in terms that might have made General Patton blush. I glanced over at the girl. She didn't seem to take any notice as she marched up to the door and knocked.

There was the sound of a telephone receiver being slammed into its cradle, followed by another profane tirade. Then the door opened, as quietly as if it had been blown ajar by a gentle breeze, and Eddie stood in its frame.

He was shorter than I remembered, and even the expert tailoring of his suit couldn't hide the fact that he'd grown stoutish. He was still quite good-looking, though, with the same Roman coin features– hardened a little now– and changeable blue eyes in a deeply tanned face. His black hair had gone gray at the temples but there was plenty of it. He had on a charcoal-gray suit and a black dress shirt, a white silk necktie with his monogram embroidered on it in the same shade of white, and square-toed black leather oxfords, handmade probably. Eddie had always been particular about clothes, I remembered, though he had often accused me of the same thing. We both used to go to Harry's tailor, Abe Schneiderman, an aristocratic old gentleman who'd operated out of a third floor loft on West Seventh before he was discovered by the film stars.

Eddie's naturally grim expression brightened when he saw me. "Hell– Shepard, is that really you?"

I admitted that it was.

"I almost didn't know you without that pompadour of yours," he said. "How the hell are you? You're looking good, for an old man."

"You too."

We shook hands and he introduced me to the girl. "This is Sandy. She's the entertainment director around this place. Brings in the talent for the floor shows and all that sort of thing."

"How do you do?" Sandy said with another flash of the engaging smile.

Eddie gave her backside an appreciative once-over as she walked back to the circular desk, then waved me into his inner sanctum.

It was a large room dominated by a massive, glossy desk made from a thick slab of some exotic wood. Desert scenes rendered in oils were mounted on one cream-colored wall above an angular, white leather sofa. Venetian blinds covering the corner windows threw patterned shadows across a pale blue broadloom carpet.

There was someone else there ahead of me, a man a few years younger than either Eddie or me, with a pink, cherubic face framed by thick, black wavy hair parted down the middle. His brown check-pattern sports jacket had western-style stitching at the shoulders and he wore blue-gray slacks with a hand-tooled leather belt around a trim waist, and a rust-colored, hand-painted tie depicting a gold miner's pick and shovel.

"You know Lou Sheldon?" Eddie asked, gesturing to the man. I shook my head. "Shelly used to work for me in the old days, running liquor. I lost touch with him for a while, then I find out he's out here, getting himself a nice little foothold before the big rush. He got a line on this place coming up for sale, and let me in on it. He knows all about managing the place, don't you Shelly? Shepard and me go way back."

"How'd ya do?" Sheldon said. His voice was smooth and well-modulated, with the hint of a Southern drawl to it.

Eddie pointed a finger at the telephone. "I wanna meet with that cocksucker– person to person. Take care of it, will you?"

"But, Eddie, I really think it'd be better if–"

"Never mind," Eddie said almost playfully. Whatever heated exchange he'd had before I came in, he was over it now. Eddie, as I recalled, had always been a bit of a hothead that way. "Just do it, will ya, Shelly."

"Sure, Eddie." Sheldon picked up his hat, a high-crowned leghorn panama, and moseyed out.

Eddie strode over to a well-stocked drinks cart. "Have one?" he asked, picking up a crystal decanter. "It's the good stuff– the McCoy," he added, just like he used to in the old days.

My throat was so parched I'd have accepted bathtub rotgut and liked it. I nodded and he mixed us a couple of scotch highballs. Eddie belted his down and went back to the cart to mix himself another. That was new, for him; Eddie had never been much of a drinker when I knew him. I used to kid him about it being bad advertising for his product.

"*The hell with you, Shepard,*" he'd say. "*The undertaker don't sample his own product, do he?*"

We chatted a while in a casual way, catching up. He had married again recently, too, it turned out, and not long after that bought the Oasis. He still had a house in Los Angeles but lived in Las Vegas more or less full time now.

He'd gone to Mexico after he got out of prison, he

said, and ran a casino down there on the beach until the government outlawed gambling and took over the property. It was after that that he'd come back to Southern California and got into the floating casino business.

"I was making more money off that gambling ship of mine than I ever did in the rackets. And it was a hundred percent legitimate, no matter what the goddamn laws said about it. We were outside the state's jurisdiction, and sure as hell outside the authority of the county of Los Angeles," Eddie said, shaking his head. Then he grinned. "I read where Tony Cornero's got himself a new ship. There's talk going around if he makes good, they might try to get another fleet of 'em going again. Not for me. I'll pass."

"Looks like you're doing well," I said.

"Yeah, not too bad if I do say so," he said. "We're booked solid here every week. They'd sleep on the dice tables if we let 'em."

The telephone on the desk rang. Eddie lifted the receiver and murmured a few words into it then hung up and freshened up our drinks.

"It's been a helluva long time, Shepard," he said. "I haven't seen you since I dunno when. I'll never forget that blowout you threw for Frank Ricketts— and all those cops slurping my champagne one night and gunning for me the next. How is old Frank, anyway?"

"Not so good. His old lung trouble is bothering him."

"He oughta move out here. Be good for his health," Eddie said. "He'd fit right in, that's for sure. This place is lousy with ex-cops."

He'd been sorry, Eddie went on, to hear about Harry's passing.

"I never thought I'd see it. Matter of fact, I had a bet with the old bastard that he'd outlive me," Eddie said. "I guess I know where I gotta go to collect it, but it may take me a while."

"I'll pay it for him," I said. "Harry wouldn't like it said he ever welshed on a bet."

"No," Eddie said, eying me keenly. "Harry always paid."

We looked at each other: me trying to figure out how much he might know and how far I could push him. What Eddie was thinking, I couldn't guess.

"As a matter of fact, it's kind of on account of Harry that I came out here to see you."

Eddie leaned back in his chair and crossed his legs. "Oh? How's that?"

I told him about Swann's skeleton being found with a bullet hole in the skull, watching his reaction closely. His surprise struck me as genuine.

"No shit," he said, shaking his head slowly. "Imagine old Swann turning up like that. I'd have laid six, two and even that he was lying low somewhere, living it up." He took a gold cigarette case out of his coat pocket and offered me one out of it, taking one for himself. "But, anyway, what does any of that old business got to do with Harry?"

Eddie listened in silence while I told him about the visit from Zankich and Dawson.

"Who are these guys, these cops?" he scoffed when I'd finished. "A couple of rubes? Burns me up, them bothering Harry's kid like that."

"I don't think much of it either. That's why I'm looking into it. Do you remember seeing Harry in town the night Swann went missing?" I asked, watching him. "At the Hayward Hotel?"

Eddie took a drag of his cigarette. "What the hell would he be doing at the Hayward Hotel?"

"That's what I want to know. He was there. His name was in the guest register."

"So what? If that's all they've got, tell them to go fuck themselves. It's nothing to do with Harry and you know it."

"They seem to think someone paid him to bump off Swann."

Eddie's blue eyes flashed me a pained look before again assuming their usual impassive expression. "I take it this someone is supposed to be me?" he said lightly and turned away, occupying himself with adjusting the slats in the venetian blind. "Oh well. I get it. They think they can make me the goat because I was in the rackets. Hell, I'm a legitimate businessman now. They try to drag my name into any of this, I'll see their asses in court, alright, only I'll be sitting on the other side this time."

"They didn't ask us anything about you, specifically."

"Damn right they didn't," Eddie snapped. He stared past me. Some of his cigarette ashes fell onto the blue carpet. "Maybe that's why somebody's been following me around. Goddamn cops. You can always spot 'em."

"Did you have any dealings with Angus Taggart in those days?"

"Hell, no. What would I need him for? I got my stuff from the wops."

Eddie had never considered himself an Italian, I remembered. *'My ma's French,'* he used to say.

"Is there anything to the rumor that the bootleggers were trying to organize around that time?"

Eddie came away from the window and plopped down in the leather chair behind his desk. "Organize? You seem to know more about it than I do, Shepard. Sure, I guess some of the boys might've been talking about it. The town was being flooded with booze— mom and pop homebrew shit. It was cutting into our bottom line. There was some talk going around about how we ought to organize as a way to squeeze out the competition, bring prices back up. I didn't want any part of it. I like being my own boss. And anyway, that's all it amounted to— talk. Nothing ever came off."

"Why was that?"

He shrugged. "Too many cops, maybe. Everybody had their grubby hand out, from the cop on the beat on up the line. That's what I like best about it out here. The gambling's legal. You don't have to pay anybody off. I never could stand for shakes. Speaking of that, would you believe the feds slapped me with a bill a while ago. You wanna know what it was for? Back taxes on the liquor stock they took from me before I went away. Said I owed 'em for an import tax or some bullshit. Can you beat it? Now you tell me who's running a goddamn racket."

"Was there any talk of getting Swann out of the way?"

"There were plenty of 'leggers who would've been glad to see the back of Swann. But I didn't have any beef with him, myself. He was an okay sort, for a federal. He didn't try to shake you down. Not like most of those bastards. Anyway, even if I did want him gone, I wouldn't need to hire it done. I could take care of my own beefs. You ought to remember that."

Eddie's telephone rang again. He grabbed up the receiver and barked into it. "I said hold my calls...What? Oh yeah? I wouldn't be so sure if I was him." He glanced up at me. I turned away and squinted at the desert paintings on the wall like they were *The Rake's Progress* until I heard Eddie slam the receiver back into its cradle.

"So is the third degree about over with?"

"Just a couple more things. Did you ever have a guy named Mike Higgins working for you– Alibi Mike?"

"That lousy mick?" Eddie sneered. "If he'd worked for me, would he have gone after my loads the way he did? Hell, I wouldn't have had a rummy like him on my crew. They talk too much."

"So there's nothing to the rumor that he was a police snitch?"

Eddie didn't answer. He stamped out his cigarette in an onyx ashtray with THE OASIS stamped on it in gold paint and looked down at the floor, his mouth a grim line. "Higgins was nothing but a goddamn hijacker. There were times I mighta shot him myself and he'd have had it coming to him," he said finally. "But what happened to him shouldn't have happened to a dog. That bastard Lundy didn't have to shoot him."

"You know if he might've worked for Taggart– Lundy I mean?"

Eddie stared past me, his eyes hard. Then he got up and poured himself a drink, without any pretense of a mixer this time. "I couldn't say for sure what their deal was back then," he said, "but he does now. He's head of security over at Taggart's place. You ought to get a load of Taggart, Shepard. Funniest damn thing you ever saw. He wears these fancy western getups and parades around like he's Roy fucking Rogers, rubbing elbows with the yokels. You'd think he was running for mayor or something."

"He still runs a casino here?"

"You bet he does. Just opened a big new place downtown. He hasn't got a hotel though. Scuttlebutt is he's looking to build one way out on the highway, along the county strip. Everyone's looking to build out there. Me, I say they're crazy. For one thing, airline travel's gonna be a big deal in the next few years– you watch. All the suckers coming out from the airport have gotta pass by my place first. Whatta they wanna drive miles all the way out there for? When I get this place all fixed up the way I want it, everybody's gonna wanna stop at the Oasis, take my word on it. Problem is, the feds got this goddamn freeze order on new construction."

I knew all about that. With both living quarters and building materials in short supply, the Civilian Production Administration had clamped down on non-essential commercial construction in order to concentrate on building houses for veterans.

"Even if you do get the okay to build, you might as well forget trying to get your hands on the supplies you need," Eddie went on. "And if you do manage to find the stuff, it costs a fortune. Prices are through the roof and the quality's shit."

I nodded. Bobbie and I had quickly come to the same conclusion when we looked into building a place of our own.

"Only person around here with enough cash and pull in the right places to do anything now is fucking Siegel," Eddie said with some bitterness. "He manages to get everything *he* needs."

"Who's he?"

"*Bugsy* Siegel? Even you must've heard of him."

I said I knew the name. Benjamin "Bugsy" Siegel was either a wealthy sportsman or a gangster of some importance in the New York mob depending on which paper you read and how gullible you happened to be. He'd been held in Los Angeles on murder charges before the war but they'd had to let him go after the star witness against him fell out of a hotel window. I remembered reading that he'd been arrested on bookmaking charges a couple of years ago, but I hadn't heard anything about him lately.

"Yeah, well Siegel's building some sort of motel court and casino out on the highway way out there," Eddie said. "Or was, anyway. The feds aren't so sure his project was underway before the freeze order like he says it was. They might even shut him down."

"You don't sound brokenhearted," I said.

"I should care? Serves the motherfucker right for trying to shove his goddamn race wire down my throat," Eddie said, grinning. "Shelly says we gotta have a horse race book on account of it brings in the daytime trade, and when people get bored between races they wander over and gamble at your tables. But Siegel controls the race wire around here, so if you want a horse race book, you gotta have his race wire. That means you do all the work of running the thing and he gets all the dough. How does that square? I say to hell with him and his race wire. I'm turning 'em away as it is, and this isn't even the busy season."

"I guess that may change when Siegel's place opens and Taggart builds his hotel," I said.

"You mean if, not when," Eddie said. "And so what if they do? It's nothing to me." He shrugged. "There's plenty of suckers to go around. You get a chance to look over my place?"

I said I hadn't so he grabbed his hat, a broad-brimmed, gray senator type, and offered to give me the nickel tour.

Eddie seemed as excited as a kid as we walked back the way I'd come, pointing out all the improvements he'd made or wanted to make as soon as the government lifted its restrictions. The heat seemed to invigorate him

He'd shut the place down for a couple months in the spring while the guest rooms and restaurant-showroom were being remodeled. It had only just reopened last month and was proving a huge success, he said.

"Of course, it's not done yet by half, but there's only so much you can do with the feds breathing down your neck all the time," he said. "Not if you wanna do things on the square."

We crossed the still-crowded pool terrace to the lobby entrance. A man built along the lines of a jeep, with a massive, bald head, a short thick neck and a broad, flat nose opened the door for us and fell in to step alongside Eddie.

They must have a factory around here where they manufacture these guys to order, I thought.

"Manny here works security for me. He was Kid Herman in the ring. Ever see him?" Eddie said over his shoulder as he stalked toward the casino.

For a short man who was far from slim, he moved swiftly and gracefully, as if on ball bearings. His eyes had a flinty hue as they darted around, watching everything.

A dozen brand-new silver slot machines lined part of the far wall, nearest the lobby entrance. Customers, mostly women, stood at all but one of them, feeding coins into their slots and yanking the metal arm with a practiced motion. In the middle of the room there were four green felt dice tables and about a half dozen poker tables, three roulette wheels, and chuck-a-luck birdcages. All were in play. Off in an alcove they had a wheel of fortune going, a pair of bearded men in checked shirts and cowboy boots watching it with spellbound concentration. Waitresses in abbreviated skirts with kid-leather half-boots like the carhops wore circled the floor dispensing drinks.

The employees, from pit bosses to floor men, cashiers

with their folded green aprons, even the stickmen whose eyes never left the dice, seemed to snap to attention under Eddie's gaze. Several of the customers looked up at him with curiosity, as if sensing that he was somebody important. The din of the room grew louder.

Eddie stood there taking it all in for a few minutes, his granite features expressionless. Then he motioned to me with a slight movement of his head and I followed him back outside to the pool terrace.

The sky was still a perfect Prussian blue but the light had changed; the sun, just starting to sink behind the jagged line of red-brown mountains to the west, gave it a softer, champagne-colored hue. Eddie surveyed the bathing beauties as he fished a cigarette out of his gold case and lit it.

"How long you in town for, Shepard?"

"Just overnight," I said. "I catch the first flight home in the morning."

He looked at his watch, a Movado– also gold. "Well, how about having dinner with me and my wife, then? The food's good here, and we can talk some more about old times."

I shrugged. I had to eat. And what the hell– I might even learn something useful.

"I'm game if I can go like this," I said. "I didn't think to bring anything more formal."

"Hell, this is Las Vegas. You're lucky if they even wear jackets," Eddie said, shaking his head. "We'll meet you in the lounge in say, half an hour?"

I nodded and toddled off past the splashing bathers into the lobby.

CHAPTER 9

Since I had time to kill, I found the one-chair barber shop and got a shave while a shoe-shine boy did the best he could with my brogues, which were covered with sand. Then I headed for the lounge and ordered a scotch highball. I drank it at the bar, enjoying the air conditioning.

The piano player was still tinkling away in the corner. He was on to "Personality" now. He wasn't bad, I decided. Or maybe the heat was starting to affect me.

A couple came stomping in, snapping at each other.

"But I was feelin' lucky, Margie, I tell ya. I woulda won it back if you hadn't a made me—"

"...lost half a month's wages already."

Other people drifted in and out. Two women with a lot of jewelry and no escorts, divorcees in waiting maybe, sat alone at small tables near the piano; women in slacks; men in sports shirts; young couples passing through on their way to the dining room.

After about ten minutes, the dark haired woman I'd met in Eddie's office came in, bare armed and bare legged, looking chic and cool in a short, black dinner dress and strappy gold sandals. Her hair was arranged in an upsweep, secured with a gold clip of some sort. She paused at the door, and seeing me, came strolling over.

"Hello, again," she said, swinging herself onto the barstool next to mine. I caught the scent of her perfume—White Shoulders. "It's Sandy, remember? Mr. Durance invited me to dinner. I think I'm meant to be your date. You don't mind, do you?"

The bartender came over and stood at expectant attention.

"Can I get you a drink?" I asked.

"Thank you. Dubonnet cocktail, please."

I ordered another scotch and water for myself while I was at it and we took our drinks over to one of the little tables, a quiet one in the corner away from the piano.

"Have you been to Las Vegas before?" she asked.

"Once. In 1941," I said.

"Not in a hurry to get back, I guess?" she smiled. "I've been here a couple of years myself. It took some getting used to, but now I wouldn't live anywhere else. Except Paris, maybe."

"What brought you out here?"

She laughed, showing even, white teeth. The gold sequins outlining the deep V-neckline of her dress twinkled in the soft, indirect lighting. "Believe it or not, I thought I could be a singer. I got over it pretty fast. Frankly, I stink. But I'm great at recognizing talent when I do hear it. I found him playing in a little hole-in-the-wall on La Brea, back in Hollywood."

She nodded at the piano player, a thirtyish man in a white dinner jacket who could have passed for Frank Sinatra's older, well-fed brother. He caught Sandy's glance, winked, and launched into "That's For Me."

I noticed that she'd emptied her glass.

"Have another?"

"No thank you. One's my limit during business hours."

"Is this business hours?"

She laughed. "It is when you have my job. I'm out 'til four or five seeing everybody else's shows. I don't mind. It gives me my mornings free to go for a gallop across the desert and work on my tan."

"When do you sleep?"

"I don't," she grinned. "I've learned to catnap during the day, like Mr. Durance. He says you knew him back in the bad old days. So tell me, did he ever shoot anybody?"

"You'd have to ask him," I said.

"I have. He never gives me a straight answer, either."

I glanced up and saw Eddie coming our way, dressed up in a white shawl-collared dinner jacket and white-on-white dress shirt. On his arm was my tipsy blonde from the pool path earlier.

She had changed into a long, chartreuse green, paisley printed dinner gown with a bare midriff and a slit that showed off her legs up to the knee as she walked. She'd remembered to put her shoes on— ankle-strap sandals with a peep toe. In her ears were gold button earrings with matching cuff bracelets on each wrist. A cocktail ring with a gobstopper of a diamond sparkled on her left hand. Without the sunglasses, I saw that she had wide, pale blue eyes with high-arched, over-plucked brows and a round, thin baby face, heavily made up.

Eddie introduced us. She was Cathy. If Cathy remembered meeting me before, she didn't give any sign of it. After we nodded to each other, Eddie led the way to the dining room down a glassed-in breezeway, pointing out his cocoa-brown padded-leather walls and hand-blocked drapes like a proud parent.

The restaurant-showroom was situated in an L-shaped wing with wide plate-glass windows at one end that looked out over the now floodlit pool terrace, where even at this hour bathers still frolicked in the water or played cards under the umbrellas. There were views beyond it to the rugged purple mountains. The dining room was done up in the same soft desert colors as the hotel lobby and casino. Horseshoe-shaped booths upholstered in dusty-blue leather ringed the perimeter, while random tables set for two or four, softly lit by nightlights and dressed with spotless white linen tablecloths, were arranged around a good sized dance floor. At the back of the room was a stage, occupied at the moment by an eight piece rhumba band.

As Eddie had predicted, most of the male diners hadn't dressed for dinner; like me they wore business suits or sports jackets. Some were in their shirtsleeves. At least none were in their bathing trunks. A tuxedoed maître d' showed us to a corner booth with a good view of the whole place, clearly Eddie's usual spot. He and I sat across from one another at either end of the booth with the girls on the inside, both acting as if the other wasn't there. Sandy looked around at the other diners, nodding to some. Cathy watched the dancers out on the floor, shrugging her shoulders more or less in time to the music. A waiter came by and went away again with our drinks order. I glanced over menu.

"We got anything you want here," Eddie said. "New York sirloin, lamb chops, roast beef, you name it. We even got lobster flown in every day from the east coast."

I settled on a charbroiled T-bone steak with mushrooms and shoestring potatoes. The food, when it came, was as good as anything you could get for three times the price at a Sunset Strip nightclub, especially considering we were in the middle of a desert. All the same I'd rather have been eating hot dogs with Bobbie and Donny at Gilmore Field like we'd done yesterday afternoon, even if it meant watching our team, the Stars, lose again.

Eddie and I chatted some about the old days. Between bites of prime rib with sliced tomatoes, he told a funny story about his early bootlegging career, when he had almost been caught by a customs agent out at Fish Harbor while loading cases of whiskey onto his truck. He'd escaped by jumping into the water and swimming out to the jetty.

"Did you shoot them?" Sandy asked.

"Hell, sweetheart, they were shooting at me," Eddie said. "That little swim cost me seventy-five Gs by the way. Not counting the price of the suit I ruined."

He launched into another yarn from his gambling ship days, of the time he'd missed his footing stepping into a water taxi and plunged into the sea, ruining yet another new suit.

"I guess that's why I like it out here," he said, lighting up a cigarette. "It's dry."

Sandy and I laughed.

"So did you–" she began.

"Eddie and me, that's how we met," Cathy Durance interrupted, joining in the conversation for the first time. She'd mostly been knocking back rum and cokes and pushing her dinner of spaghetti and meatballs around her plate with her fork. "I had a job on his boat."

"Ship, baby," Eddie said. "It was a ship, not a boat."

"Well whatever it was, I worked on it. I got five bucks a night for being a– whadda ya call it, Eddie? When you're nice to the men so it makes them wanna keep gambling some more?"

"A shill, baby," Eddie said. He grinned at me. "We sure don't need 'em here."

Over a dessert of chilled watermelon, flown in from somewhere no doubt, the conversation turned back to the Oasis and Eddie's big plans for it.

"If you can believe it, Shepard, here where we're sitting was the casino when I took this place over, and where the casino is now was the showroom," he said, shaking his head. "The schmuck who built it, the guy Shelly got it from, was some bandleader from Hollywood who thought he was running a hotel and nightclub, with a little gambling as a sideline. Here you got legal gambling, and people are tripping over themselves to shove their money across your dice tables, and the jerk treats it as a goddamn sideline. No wonder he went bust. First thing I did is move the casino over there so you get the foot traffic coming in from the lobby, and bumped the back wall out here to make this the restaurant showroom. Now you can watch the show from the pool, too.

There was only so much I could do, though, without getting the feds up my ass about the freeze order. But someday we're gonna put a second floor in here and have the dining room all glassed in, with stairs coming down there so the ladies can make a grand entrance– like this," he said, drawing it out on a napkin. "You got a view of the pool here, and mountains on all three sides– see?"

He had to have poured a mint into the place already, I thought. His sign budget alone must have set him back a few thousand. But he seemed to know what he was doing.

The man I'd met earlier, Sheldon, stopped by our table. He hadn't dressed, but he'd changed his checkered shirt for a white one with a tomato-red string tie. He leaned over and whispered something to Eddie.

Eddie frowned and waved him away. "We'll talk about it later."

Sheldon hopped off to the next table and shook hands with the people there, laughing and chatting.

"Look at Shelly. How he's loving it all," Sandy murmured, watching him. "You'd think he really ran this place."

"Doesn't he?"

She looked at me levelly. "Everybody knows this is Eddie's place. That's his problem. One of them anyway," she added with a pointed glance at Cathy.

Cathy was still picking at her dinner and humming along with the music. When the current song came to an end, the stage went dark for a moment. Then a spotlight fell on a tiny woman standing center stage in an off-the-shoulder midriff top and long ruffled skirt with a slit up to her naval. The band struck up a slow bolero beat and the woman began to croon the introduction to "Yours."

"Eddie– Eddie! That's our song they're playing!" Cathy said breathlessly. She dropped her fork and tugged at Eddie's sleeve. "C'mon and dance with me, honey. It's been so long."

Eddie hesitated for half a second then tossed his

93

napkin down and slid out of the booth. Cathy scrambled out and led him by the hand toward the dance floor, hips swaying.

Sandy watched them go. When she turned back to me there was a wistful look in her eyes. "Do you know how to rumba, Mr. Shepard?"

"I can take a hint as well as the next guy," I said, mashing out my cigarette. "Would you like to dance?"

"I thought you'd never ask."

We made our way onto the crowded floor near the Durances. I caught a glimpse of Eddie. He wasn't half bad as a dancer. His granite face seemed to soften and for that moment, it almost looked as if he was enjoying himself. Suddenly Cathy lost her footing and with a flash of tanned legs, fell to the floor, landing solidly on her rump.

The band played on, oblivious, while dancers nearby stopped to stare. Diners around the perimeter craned their necks, trying to see what the fuss was all about.

Eddie, his jaw clenched so tight I thought it might snap, reached down and hauled Cathy to her feet.

"Let's go," he hissed.

"But the song's not done yet," Cathy said.

"It is for you, baby," Eddie said.

He steered her back to our table, one arm around her waist, Sandy and I following in their wake. The whole thing happened and was over in less time than it takes to describe.

"Time for the hay now, huh?" Eddie said. His voice was gentle but his mouth was still a thin, grim line. He collected Cathy's bag from the table and handed it to her.

"I gotta go to the powder room."

"You can wait. You'll be home in five minutes."

"But I can't hold it."

Eddie sighed and glanced at Sandy, who'd been watching Cathy with a mix of repulsion and amusement.

Sandy sighed. "I'll take her."

"I can take myself," Cathy said, raising her chin. She lurched off in the general direction of a lighted sign marked

LADIES ROOM. Sandy went after her.

Eddie and I wandered back through the lounge and went outside. The night had turned balmy. A slight breeze had kicked up, but it was a warm wind. Through the lighted windows of the restaurant, we could see the busboys in white coats clearing tables and couples whirling around on the dance floor. The pool had emptied, finally; white neon lights spelling out LOBBY, CASINO, and COCKTAIL LOUNGE were reflected in its smooth surface. Above us, the desert sky was midnight blue and completely starless.

Eddie fumbled in his coat pocket for the gold case and lit a cigarette. He stood staring out at the lights glimmering across the pool. It reminded me of the time on the Bendix roof.

"I really wish I knew what Harry was doing at the Hayward that night," I said.

Eddie just shrugged and went on smoking.

Lou Sheldon came ambling up out of the shadows. "Eddie, there you are. The thing's true. I just got off the phone. It's all gonna come out tomorrow unless– well, you'd better go and talk to him tonight. In person. I kind of told him you would."

"He can go fuck himself," Eddie said, grinning at Sheldon. "I may have a few things to say to him later, when I'm good and ready."

"He's not kidding around."

"Neither am I."

"But Eddie–"

"But nothing."

I felt like a third wheel, listening in on their conversation.

"I guess I'd better get going," I said. "Good seeing you again, Eddie. Thanks for the dinner. And the help earlier." I handed him one of my cards. "If you think of anything I can use, call me up."

Eddie looked at the card for a second then slipped it into his pocket. "If I were you, Shepard, I'd forget all this

Swann business. You and I both know Harry didn't have a damn thing to do with it."

"I know he didn't. I just want to be sure the cops know it, too."

I reached out my hand. "You always were a stubborn ass," Eddie shrugged, grinning. We shook hands. "Come back sometime and stay a while. On the house. Bring the wife. Or don't."

I was heading across the lobby to the phone booths when Sheldon caught up to me, panting. "I'll run you out to your hotel, Shepard," he said.

"I can get a cab," I said.

"It's no bother. Eddie said to. His car's right out front."

"Fine. Suits me," I said.

A bellhop scurried past, trailed by a drooping couple in rumpled traveling clothes. Sheldon paused to shake their hands, scribbled something on a card and gave it to them.

In the circle of the driveway, lit up by yellow and green floodlights, another bellhop was loading bags into the trunk of a dusty red convertible Cadillac with a blonde in pink behind the wheel. She raised one arm and waggled gloved fingers at Sheldon. The parking lot had filled up. From the shadows, lone men and a few couples were strolling across the lawn, on their way to dinner or the casino. Red and white lights flashed by from cars passing along the highway. The neon of the Oasis sign cut a swath through the otherwise dark sky.

Eddie's Chrysler sedan– brand new, with wood-paneled sides and a shiny blue paint job– was parked in a place of honor next to the lobby doors. I ran my hand over the sleek hood. My Buick was almost six years old. I'd put in an order for a new one, but the dealer had been suspiciously vague about when I might actually see delivery of it. *Eddie must have some terrific pull,* I thought.

Sheldon slid behind the wheel but didn't start the motor right away.

"The problem with Eddie is, he won't see reason," he muttered. "He wasn't exactly welcomed here with open arms. This is still a small town, for all it's grown lately. I told him you gotta make nice with the yokels, try to blend in. But he don't listen. Now lookit the mess we're in. The city commission's pulling our gambling license tomorrow."

"What's that mean?" I asked.

"It means we got to shut down the casino."

"Why would they do that?"

"They're saying Eddie didn't declare himself as a partner when he took over this place, so the license issued in my name is a fraud."

"I'm sure Eddie will sort it out," I said. "He always did. Anyway, you've still got the hotel and restaurant. He says they're booming."

"They operate in the red, Shepard. The only way we can afford to offer the rooms and meals and all of it at the prices we do is because the loss is offset by what the casino takes in. It's a come-along. Without the casino, we'd be in the hole inside of a week. Eddie's almost tap city as it is. You know– broke."

Sheldon maneuvered the big car out onto the highway and drove south toward the lights of the downtown section. There wasn't much to see– a motel court, a couple of all-night garages, a market. On the other side of the road were the railroad tracks. Beyond them there was nothing but blackness as far as I could see.

"He's gambling too much. He oughta lay off," Sheldon went on. "If he'd quit with the dice and dump that broad he's with we'd be okay again. He just ought not to have married her, that's all. She's bad luck. It was soon as she came around everything started going south for him. She starts working for him on the ship and what happens? The thing got wrecked."

"That's pretty hard on the girl, isn't it?" I said. "It was hardly her fault."

"She's a jinx," Sheldon muttered. "He almost got rid

of her once, after she shot him in the leg. But he took her back again. He's too sentimental for his own good– that's his trouble. I told him not to. But you know Eddie– he always does whatever he wants. You're an old pal of his. You could talk to him. Maybe he'll listen to you."

"It's none of my business," I said.

Sheldon fell into a moody silence. He switched the radio on, twisting the dial until he found a station playing hillbilly music. I was sorry I hadn't taken the taxi after all.

At the train station, we turned left onto the main thoroughfare, if that's what you'd call it. It looked like they had taken all the neon of the Sunset Strip and squeezed it into two short blocks. Huge signs, some taller than the buildings themselves, advertised cafes, liquor stores, cut rate drugs, cocktail bars, horse betting parlors, and gambling halls in lurid shades of red, blue, green and yellow, all of it flashing and winking like mad. The brightly lit gambling halls had large, chromium-framed plate glass windows that opened right onto the street. I could see customers at the green felt tables, the rows of shining slot machines, the white shirts of the dealers. The sidewalks, lit up by jutting marquees, were jammed with people strolling. Sheldon slowed to a crawl as some of them darted out from between parked cars to try their luck on the other side of the street.

"Which one is Gus Taggart's place?" I asked.

"His is up the other end of town," Sheldon said. He turned off at the second corner and pulled up in front of my hotel.

"Nice meeting you," I lied. "Thanks for the ride."

The hotel, at three stories, was practically a skyscraper here. I took my key and went straight up to my room, stripped and took a shower. Afterward, still dripping, I put in a long distance person-to-person call to Bobbie. Hearing her voice, chatting about normal, everyday things– she'd taken Donny shopping for school shoes and they'd gone to an early show afterward– cheered me up. After the operator came on to say our three minutes were up, I sat at the desk for a few minutes and jotted down some notes on hotel stationary. Through the window in front of me, I could just make out the outline of the jagged mountains in the distance.

I stretched out on the bed and closed my eyes. Even nude, it was still too hot to sleep. After about half an hour of tossing, I gave it up. I got dressed again and went downstairs to the bar and ordered a cold beer with an ice water chaser.

The bar looked out into a casino that took up most of the hotel's ground floor. Its mirrored wall reflected a row of slot machines off to one side and a dice table positioned down the center of a long, low-ceilinged room. Sheldon was hunched over the end of it, his back to the plate glass windows that looked out onto Fremont Street. He had his hat pushed back on his head and his eyes were trained on the pair of dice in play. I could see his lips moving but his words were swallowed up by all the racket.

A tall figure hulked at his elbow, puffing on a cigar and watching the dice idly– a man with iron gray hair worn in a crew cut and tiny, pin-dot eyes shadowed by bushy, gray brows, with fleshy jowls that bulged above the neck of a blue and white checked shirt. He unclenched his cigar and gestured with it as he spoke.

Neither man looked at the other; they seemed altogether an unlikely pair. All the same, I had the impression that they were deep in conversation.

'Seven the winnah!" the stickman called out.

The big man plugged the cigar back into his mouth and scooped up some chips. Dropping them in his pocket, he stalked off toward the street doors without another glance at Sheldon.

Sheldon's shoulders drooped. He started to turn away, then seemed to think the better of it and came back to the table with a haggard expression.

CHAPTER 10

After a night of fitful sleep, I showered again, dressed and had a shave in the hotel barber shop, then ventured out in search of breakfast.

Unlike the Sunset Strip, which usually looked deserted at this hour of the morning, Fremont Street was already hustling, if it had ever stopped at all. But it had a tired, washed-out feel. The low buildings, their neon signs unable to compete with the brilliant morning sun, looked faded and a little shabby. The wind I'd heard howling and lashing against my windows all night had deposited a layer of dust on all of the parked cars. Cowpokes and gamblers, red eyed from staring at cards all night, staggered squinting from the casinos, shirts wrinkled and sweat-soaked. Ordinary people strolled past, going about their business.

The sun was warm but not yet scorching on my back as I wandered up the street and found a coffee shop with twelve counter stools, eight booths and six slot machines.

I glanced through the local paper while I had my meal. There was a damning editorial piece on the third page about the late invasion of what it called an "undesirable element" to Las Vegas. It didn't mention Eddie or the gangster Siegel by name, but the implication was clear.

I was having a second cup of coffee when I noticed

the people sitting in the booth two booths away in front of me– a silvery-haired old man, a little boy of maybe twelve and a woman. She had her back to me, but as she stood up I saw that it was Eddie's girl, Sandy. She was dressed for riding in a fringed suede jacket, dungarees and cowboy boots. The boy clambered out after her.

"See ya, Pop," he said.

The old man nodded after them, then settled back into the booth and tucked into his steak and eggs, spreading his newspaper out on the table in front of him.

I recognized him as Angus Taggart, though he'd aged quite a bit since last I'd seen him. As Eddie had mentioned, he was kitted out like a Hollywood cowboy in a red and blue embroidered shirt and a yellow neckerchief around his throat. His broad face was deeply lined now and pale, the hollow cheeks blotched with purple veins and a bulbous nose almost as red as his shirt.

The waitress came by to take the order of a family of five who had just come in and were crammed into the end booth across the aisle– a father in dungarees, a mother holding a little one on her lap, and two small children, a son and daughter.

"I'm hungry!" the girl blurted.

"That bacon sure smells good!" the boy said. "Can we have some, Ma?"

"Hush, Jerry," the mother said.

The father ran his finger down the side of the menu with a frown and ordered hot cakes for three and a glass of water.

"The kids need some milk, Herm," the woman said in a loud whisper.

"They can have milk later," Herm muttered. When the waitress had gone he took out a billfold and looked through it before shoving it angrily back into his pocket.

Taggart glanced up from his paper and motioned the waitress over as she passed him.

"Look, Sally, bring those babies some cow juice, will

you? And some more food for all of them— meat, coffee, the works," he said. "Put it on my tab. Tell 'em the cook mixed up their order or something, so his pride don't get in the way of their stomachs. You'll fix it up somehow, won't you hon?"

"Sure I will, Mr. Taggart. It's awfully sweet of you."

"Not a bit. Just pray the fool don't gamble away the rest of their money," Taggart said. "But he will, of course."

I looked at my watch. I had a few minutes before I had to leave to catch my flight. I paid for my meal and introduced myself to Taggart.

"Sit down, sit down. What's on your mind, son?" he asked in the hearty, yet vague way of a politician addressing a constituent.

"It's about Axel Swann," I said. "They found his bones in Los Angeles lately."

"Yes, I believe I did hear something about that," he nodded. "Violent town, Los Angeles was then. Even worse now. Glad I left when I did. In Las Vegas we've no crime to speak of. A man's as safe on the streets here as he is in his own home. 'Course, things are changing now. Lot of new people moving in to our little town. Well, that's progress for you." He glanced down and grinned at his paper which, I noticed, was open to the editorial section.

"What do you know about bootleggers trying to organize before Swann went missing?"

The gaunt cheeks shook as he laughed. "By God, but I like your nerve, son. When I was running nightclubs, of course I had some business dealings with what you might call bootleggers. They were impossible to avoid. Can't say it gave me any insight into their inner workings, though."

"Did you ever have a guy named Mike Higgins working for you?"

"I employed so many people, Mister— Shepard was it? Can't expect me to remember them all. I'm an old man."

"I thought you might remember this one," I said. "He got shot by a cop name of Nick Lundy. I guess you remember him."

"Of course. Why, Nick's a good employee of mine." Taggart's watery blue eyes met mine. "The department needed men like him in those days to stand up to the hoodlums. They could use men like that again out there, I hear."

The waitress came out with a tray of milk and coffee on one arm and plates of hot food– crispy bacon, a steak, eggs, and hash– in the other, and delivered it to the people across the aisle.

"…terrible sorry. Must have been some sort of mix up in the kitchen," she was saying as the mother and father protested. "Certainly not. It's our mistake. You may as well…"

A shadow loomed over Taggart's table. I looked up. It was the man I'd seen talking to Sheldon at the casino the night before.

"Speak of the devil," Taggart said. "Nick Lundy– this is Mister– uh– Shepard from Los Angeles. He and I was just talking about your bravery."

"Oh yeah?" Lundy looked me over, his tiny, black eyes expressionless. "You a cop?"

"Private. I used to work for Harry Price."

"Not old Hatrack Harry? Now there's a name I ain't heard in years," Lundy said with a twist of his fleshy lips.

"Shepard was asking about that unfortunate incident years ago with the Higgins lad."

"There's a rumor he may have had some information about Swann before he was shot," I said.

"Lemmie tell you, what a guy like Higgins knew about Swann you could put in a book the size of my thumb," Lundy said, holding up the appendage for my inspection. "He was a two-time loser looking at going away for a long stretch. That's how come he pulled a rod on me." He dismissed me and turned to Taggart. "I got the car out front, boss. We gotta hustle if you wanna get over there by nine."

"Ah, well. So many demands on my time these days. Nice talking over old times with you, Shepard," Taggart said, wheezing to his feet. Lundy handed him a ten-gallon Stetson off the peg outside the booth and the two of them went out.

I caught a taxi straight to the airport and made it just as they were announcing the flight.

As it turned out, I needn't have rushed. We were boarded and buckled into our seats but the plane made no move to take off. Five minutes, then ten, ticked by while we just sat there, broiling on the tarmac. There was some sort of commotion behind me, and at last one final passenger came lurching down the aisle. She wore a black suit under a white shorty coat that she held clutched at her throat, with a white turban and large black sunglasses. An alligator handbag was slung over her free arm. It was Eddie's wife, Cathy Durance. A stewardess helped her to her seat and strapped her in. Cathy turned her face to the window and the plane taxied off at last toward the hazy purple mountains.

Bobbie was waiting for me in Burbank when we landed. I wasn't expecting her; she hadn't owned a car before we were married, had never learned to drive one until Buster taught her this summer, and was still a little nervous behind the wheel.

"You didn't have to come out," I said.

"I guess I know the way pretty well," Bobbie said. "Besides, I missed you. Donny's been having a ball watching the planes land and take off."

"Your mom used to build 'em here, pal," I said, ruffling his curls.

"She did?" Donny looked up at Bobbie, wide-eyed.

"Well, I had some help," she laughed.

Cathy Durance tottered by. The big, bald, flat-nosed gorilla I'd met at the Oasis— Manny, Eddie's bodyguard or whatever he was— was waiting for her next to a dusty black prewar Cadillac with Nevada plates. Las Vegas was three hundred miles away; he must have driven all night to get here.

Bobbie turned to stare at Cathy. "Who was that? A movie star?"

"Nope," I said as I opened the passenger door for her. "That's a gangster's wife."

"Really?" Bobbie said, craning her neck to try to get another glimpse of Cathy.

The gorilla was helping her into the Cadillac. He closed the passenger door then slid behind the wheel. The Caddy sped away.

CHAPTER 11

I had taken an office again lately, on the second floor
of a modern building on Sunset at the western outskirts of
the Strip only five minutes from home. It said Beverly Hills
on my business cards. That may have been stretching it
somewhat, but not by much. It was close enough, anyway,
that I could justify charging Beverly Hills rates.

Paul, my part-time operative, was at the front
reception desk flirting with Grace, my secretary, when I
walked in. A wiry ex-Army sniper, Paul worked as a process
server when he wasn't doing jobs for me. He brought in an
expense report for my approval and gave me a rundown of
the cases he'd been working on– the kind that made money.

Grace brought in a list of my calls and the mail. Then
she and Paul went across the street for lunch. I returned a
couple of phone calls and looked through the stack of bills
and advertising circulars for the latest thing in spy cameras–
smaller than a package of cigarettes; the Dainty Didy Baby
Laundry– citywide and suburban delivery; Redi-Cut Homes
for immediate delivery– ask the veteran who owns one.

My mind kept drifting back to Mike Higgins. I hauled
out the telephone book and turned to the listings for Higgins,
running my finger down the page until I came to the Ks. It

was a longshot. His widow had probably remarried and changed her name, or moved out of the area. She might not have a telephone. I sighed and started dialing. I'd gotten through to the first two names– neither was the Kay Higgins I wanted– and was getting no answer at the third when I heard high heels clattering up our stairs from the street.

No one else used those stairs but us; the talent agent on the penthouse floor had his own private entrance. I shrugged. It was probably Grace coming back early from lunch. But Grace had been wearing flats, I remembered. A customer maybe, although we didn't get a lot of walk-in trade. The heels clacked into the reception room and stopped. I held the telephone receiver away from my ear, waiting for whoever it was to say something. Nothing happened. I could see the shadow of a figure behind the pebbled glass of the connecting door. I went around my desk and yanked the door open. Cathy Durance practically fell into my arms.

She still wore the dark glasses but had changed into a yellow slack suit with her monogram embroidered in green, and high-heeled green snakeskin sandals.

"So you are here, then," she said.

"Yeah– we were on the same flight this morning," I said.

"Oh," she said. "I tried calling you up but the line was busy. So I thought I'd just come over. I got your card from Eddie. He doesn't know."

"Where *is* Eddie?"

"Why, he's in Las Vegas. *You* know."

"Is there something you wanted to see me about?"

"Aren't you a detective? Well, I wanna hire you."

"To do what?"

She seemed wobbly again so I led her over to the guest chair across from my desk and sat her down.

"I think Eddie's tryin' to get rid of me," she said in a whisper, looking over her shoulder.

I went to the window that looked out over the street

and glanced through the slats of the blind. The black Caddy was parked crookedly at the curb. There was no sign of the gorilla.

"You're alone?"

"Uh-huh. I slipped out while Manny was taking a nap. Eddie sent him out here in the car with my suitcases, but he's really here to spy on me."

"I'm not sure I follow, Mrs. Durance," I said. "If you're afraid of Eddie, you ought to go to the police."

"I'm not afraid. I just wanna know if he's really gonna divorce me."

"Why should he want to divorce you?

She took the dark glasses off and blinked at me. One of her eyes was ringed with purple.

"Eddie give you that shiner?"

"We had a big fight after you left. I've got a bruise where he kicked me, too. He said I embarrassed him at dinner in front of– of you and everybody."

She might be telling the truth. Or she could've got it falling on her face. Eddie had seemed so patient with her that night. But some men turned brutish behind closed doors. Neither was hard to imagine in his case.

"He started to divorce me once already."

"Was that before or after you shot him in the leg?"

She stared at me with wide blue eyes. "That was just an accident. Eddie knows I didn't mean to do it. He never even filed the paperwork. But he says he's gonna go through with it this time. And I know he sees other women. Shelly brings them to his bungalow. They don't think I know anything about it. But I do."

"So, why don't you divorce him? It's easy enough in Nevada."

"But I don't want a divorce. I love him," she blinked. "And he loves me, too. He always says we were meant to be together. He always liked me, right from the start. He hired me, even though he knew I wasn't eighteen like I said I was, just so he could be around me. He used to say 'What am I going to do with you, Jailbait?' or 'You're drivin' me crazy, Jailbait.' That was his nickname for me– Jailbait. But he never even laid a hand on me. He finally had to send me away because he liked me too much. But he missed me too much, too. So he found me again and we got married. I was old enough by that time. Just about anyway. 'I guess we're stuck with each other, Jailbait,' he said. And he gave me this," she added, extending her arm. A bracelet of gold links with a large, thin disk attached to it dangled from her thin wrist. "See? It says 'Forever, Eddie.' "

"Look, Mrs. Durance–"

"Cathy."

"Cathy– sometimes men say things. They may mean them at the time. But it doesn't always work out. Anyway, if he hurts you, maybe it's for the best if the two of you do split up."

"Oh, but he didn't mean it. He was just upset. He's got a lot of worries right now. He doesn't think I know about that, either. I know lots about a lot of things. If he left me, I don't know what I'd do. I'd kill myself or something."

I sighed. "What is it you think I can do for you, Cathy? I'm a detective, not John J. Anthony."

"Can't you find out for me if he's got another girl lined up to take my place?"

I shook my head. "No. I'm sorry. I don't take domestic cases." It was a fib. They were our bread and butter, as a matter of fact. But I wanted no part of this particular domestic case.

"You mean you won't help me?" Tears welled up in her blue eyes. Mascara started to run in black streaks down her cheeks.

"It's not so much won't as can't. Look– I'm here, Eddie's in Las Vegas."

It took a while to get her to listen to reason. I gave her my handkerchief and waited while she fixed up her face, then escorted her downstairs and put her in her car. Sunset baked in the sun, the heat rising up from its crack-lined surface. Horns blared as the Cadillac made a U-turn in the middle of oncoming traffic and fishtailed up the boulevard toward the bridle path, out of sight.

That evening after supper and after Donny was in bed, Bobbie and I had a glass of wine out on the sundeck. The lights of Hollywood glowed red and white all around us. The damp air smelled of cool earth and lupine and eucalyptus. Through the open sliding glass doors to the living room, dance music played softly on the radio. Critters rustled around in the underbrush. From far below came the wail of police sirens and even more distant, the roar of the midget racing cars at Gilmore.

The telephone bell jangled.

It was her– Cathy Durance. I recognized the slurred voice. The words were hard to make out. She took some pills, she said. She wanted to end it all, this time. I heard the phone receiver drop to the floor.

"Cathy? Cathy! Answer me!" I shouted. There was no answer. "For Chrissake! Cathy? Goddamn it!" I slammed down the receiver and grabbed the telephone book from the shelf under the hall table, flipping through it to look up Eddie's local phone number. It was a Bradshaw exchange. I dialed it and got a busy signal. Bobbie came in to see what the shouting was about. I told her while I dialed the Hollywood Receiving Hospital from the list of emergency numbers she kept on a pad next to the phone. She calmly read out Eddie's address to me and I repeated it to the operator. They promised to send an ambulance over right away. I tried Eddie's line again; it was still busy.

"Are you going to go down there and find out if she's okay, Ave?" Bobbie asked.

"Why should I?"

"Because– well, because that poor girl's in a bad way. I know what it's like to feel as low as she must have." Her gentle brown eyes smiled up at me. "And someone was very kind to me, when I needed it."

"That was different," I said. "You weren't– you aren't– anything like her."

It was no use. I was going.

I found my car keys. Bobbie met me at the door with my hat and gave me a lingering kiss.

"I'll wait up for you," she said.

I parked under one of the scrawny looking pepper trees across the street from the emergency hospital, a small tile-roof building of sunbaked yellow brick on Wilcox next to Hollywood police station. There was an ambulance in the courtyard; inside I found a nurse who told me they'd just brought Cathy in. I'd have to wait. So I flipped through some magazine back numbers and waited.

Ambulance drivers came in and tried to make time with the nurses. People with pinched and drawn faces came in and sat in the other chairs. Sirens wailed out in the courtyard.

After about an hour, a doctor came out. The ambulance drivers had found Cathy sprawled across her bed in her nightgown, the telephone and some empty pill boxes on the floor next to her. She was out cold. They'd brought her in and he'd pumped her stomach. It showed a lot of alcohol, but no sign of sleeping pills.

"Not a thing wrong with her. My guess is that she'd had too much to drink, that's all." the doctor said. "We'll be sending her home in a little while. She's awake if you'd care to look in on her."

"No, that's okay," I said. "Thanks, Doc."

I avoided Sunset on the way back, instead threading my way through the dark, quiet streets. Bobbie had fallen asleep on the couch with the lamp on and a *Reader's Digest* lying open across her belly. Her eyes fluttered open and she smiled at me.

"Darn it, I really tried to stay awake. Guess I'm not

much of a night owl these days," she said. "So how is she?"

We went into the kitchen and ate leftover strawberry-rhubarb pie in front of the open icebox while I told her what the doctor had said.

"It's like I said, she's screwy. A dipso, for sure– maybe other things too."

"I feel sorry for her," Bobbie said. "What kind of life can that be– married to a gangster?"

There were a lot of girls like Cathy in Hollywood. It seemed to specialize in them. Pretty girls, treated as expendable by brutish men who lavished them with furs, jewels, money, and cars, until one day, they didn't.

I shook my head. "I don't understand it myself.

Bobbie put the dishes in the sink and stood behind my chair, nuzzling my neck. I felt my pulse quickening. "Ready to hit the hay?"

"Y-yes." Bobbie said. "But let's not go to sleep right away– hmm?"

CHAPTER 12

Grace poked her head in my office the next morning to tell me I had a long distance call from Las Vegas. It was Eddie.

"Manny told me what you did for Cathy, Shepard," he said. His voice sounded flat, exhausted. "I just wanted to call you up and thank you."

"I didn't do anything. There was nothing wrong with her."

"Yeah, well, you couldn't have known that, could you? This isn't the first time she's pulled something like this. Only the time before, she really did take all those pills. She drinks too much, that's her trouble. I tried to get her dried out, years ago. Sent her to one of those places— a rest home, you know? It worked— for a little while. Anyway, I owe you. Anything I can do for you, just ask."

I thought about my new Buick. Probably Eddie knew people who knew people who could get it delivered to me within the hour.

But I had a reputation for honesty in this dishonest town, and was proud of it. And I didn't especially want to be beholden to Eddie. *'Once you let them do favors for you, they get to thinking they own you,'* Harry would have said.

"You could tell me what you know about Gus

Taggart trying to organize the big bootleggers right before Swann went missing," I said.

Eddie swore at his end of the line. "So you still won't let go of that old business? I told you, there's nothing in it. Thanks again about Cathy," he muttered and slammed the line down at his end.

I'd finished calling up all the K, Kay, Katy, Katie and Katherine Higgins listings out of the phone book and finally got through to one Kay Higgins who admitted having once been married to a Michael. She was a stenographer for a fur company now and I reached her at work. She'd been suspicious at first and refused to answer any questions. I managed to talk her around and she agreed to meet me during her lunch hour.

I drove downtown into a stinging smog. The stuff had shown up here a few years ago and was supposed to have gone away after the war ended but no one had told that to the smog, which still hung over the city like an old Army blanket, dingy and gray from age. The air held the faint rotten egg odor of sewer gas.

I waited for Kay in the elevator lobby of the Cutts Building on Hill Street. She was right on time, a trim, pale, efficient-looking woman of forty or so in a black silk office dress, with brown eyes and graying blonde hair worn in a artfully arranged topknot.

"Mr. Shepard?" She offered me a gloved hand. Over the telephone she had sounded icy and aloof. In person, her voice had a more congenial tone. She glanced at her watch. "Do you mind if we eat while we talk? The Owl here has a grill. I have to be back upstairs by one thirty on the dot."

"Whatever you like."

There was an entrance to the drugstore from the lobby; elbowing through the usual lunchtime throng, past glass counters crammed with colognes and dusting powder, cold cream and sun tan lotion, a floor rack of paper-backed novels with garish covers, and displays of electric fans, we climbed the stairs to the mezzanine where there was a short wait for a booth in the fountain grill. I took up a menu and glanced over the specials.

"What do you recommend?"

"Going someplace else," Kay said flatly. "But I haven't got the time. The powers that be decided that the ideal time to sell fur coats is when it's a hundred degrees outside. I'm simply rushed off my feet." She looked at her menu. "Oh well. The chicken pie won't kill you."

We ordered two of them, and coffees. Kay fished around in her bag for a cigarette, and I lit it for her.

She looked at me, still wary but curious, then grinned. "I guess I wasn't too friendly earlier."

I grinned back at her. "I've had warmer receptions. In court, from the opposition's lawyer."

"It's just– a detective calling me up about Mike– well, it brought back some bad memories, if you don't mind my saying. Tell me, what kind of trouble is he causing me now?"

"It's nothing like that, Kay," I said. "I'm trying to find out about a prohibition agent who went missing back in 1930. Mike may have known something about it. Did you ever hear him mention a guy named Axel Swann?"

She shook her head. "The name sounds kind of familiar, but I can't really say for sure."

"What about Eddie Durance, or Angus Taggart?"

Kay sipped her coffee. "Oh, I remember Mr. Taggart. He was very kind. He gave us some money once, when Mike got shot– he was hurt and couldn't work."

"Was Taggart his boss, then?"

"I don't know. He might have been. I can't say for sure. Mike never talked to me much about his work– not that I ever asked him to. It was easier not to know what he got up to. I'm sorry I can't be more helpful." Kay put down her cup and looked up at me. "The truth is we hadn't been on the best of terms lately. I finally got fed up with his boozing and waiting his supper for him all hours of the night, and his crook friends hanging around all the time. I kicked him out."

"So you were split up at the time?"

"Briefly. We made up," Kay said with a wry smile. "He came around begging me to take him back, swearing on his poor old mother's grave he'd quit the booze and turned over a new leaf. I fell for it, alright. Maybe I was only seeing what I wanted to, but he *did* seem different. He wasn't drinking, that much was true, anyway. So I took him back. And then what happens? He goes and gets himself shot breaking into a government warehouse." She sighed. "Poor Mike! He never could catch a break."

"At Mike's inquest you said you thought a cop put Mike on the spot that night. What gave you that idea?"

"Because that's what Mike said. That he was going out to meet a copper."

The waitress brought our food and refilled our coffee cups.

"A cop, you're sure? He mention any name?" I asked when we were alone again.

She shook her head.

"Did you ever see him with any cops?"

"There was one of them who used to come around the house a lot, bothering us. Cyrus Law. I remember the name because Mike thought it was a funny name for a cop."

"What did Law want with Mike?"

She shrugged. "They argued a lot. They got into a fistfight once."

"Did Mike know Nick Lundy before?"

"Not that I know of. At least, I never saw him around." Kay's eyes flashed and for a moment I had a glimpse of the girl who'd yelled '*So's your old man!*' at a police officer in court. "As if I could ever forget that dead-eyed lug. Lundy shot my Mike in cold blood, I just know it."

She blinked back tears. I patted her hand.

"Look, Kay– could Mike have been a police informant?"

Kay raised her eyebrows. "Mike, a snitch? I don't believe it." She jabbed at the crust of her pie with her fork.

"He could've been, I suppose. I wouldn't know. The person you really ought to see is Mike's old partner, Jake Barnett. He was with Mike the night he– when Mike was killed. Jake came and told me about it afterward."

"So where can I find this Barnett?"

"He was working as a bartender in some joint. I've got the address for it in here somewhere." She fumbled around in her bag. "The last time I heard from him was about six months ago. He's out on parole– he did a stretch for robbery a while back. Here it is." She handed me a matchbook advertising the Hi-Ho Cocktail Lounge on Western Avenue. Steaks & Chops. Short Orders. Gaiety. Entertainment.

Kay gave me a sidelong glance. "He goes by the name of Jack Burkett now. Tell him I sent you. He won't thank me for putting you on to him. But you seem like an alright guy."

"You're alright yourself," I said.

She sighed. "It was a rough and tumble life we led, Mike and me. I broke a beer bottle over his head once, he made me so mad. Things are a lot nicer now, you know— more settled. I've got this job, some money put by. And you know what? I'm bored stiff. Life's funny."

"Is that why you never remarried?"

"I like my name. Why shouldn't I keep it?" Kay tossed her head and turned to the window, watching the crowds jostling along outside on the dirty sidewalk below. A streetcar went by, nearly colliding with a pickup truck turning from Seventh Street. She looked back at me with a little half-smile. "Maybe I still love the jerk. Who knows?"

After Kay had taken her leave of me, I paid the check and went in the back to the phone booths. Cyrus Law had an advertisement in the yellow pages under Detectives. WE SOLVE YOUR PROBLEMS. CONNECTIONS THROUGHOUT THE WORLD. His offices were in the Fay Building. I left the car where it was and legged it the four blocks.

The directory in the dimly-lit lobby showed a lot of

vacancies. There was an assortment of quack cure-all pushers and quack evangelists, accountants and lawyers with a string of letters after their names, watch and handbag repairers. Finding Law on the fifth floor between the Golden State Finance Exchange and the Osbourne College of Short Methods, I pushed the call button for the elevator.

"You look like a sportin' fella," a voice with the burr of old age and tobacco said.

I looked over in the direction of a handsome marble staircase and saw a withered old man at the newsstand, no bigger than a ten-year-old boy, with a pink, nearly bald head and deep lines in the corners of his bright blue eyes.

He beckoned to me with a gnarled, arthritic hand. I went over. The nameplate on his dusty counter said he was Pop Quinn. "Need a racing form today?"

"No thanks, Pop," I said.

"Oh well. It was worth a shot," he shrugged. "Don't get many live ones come through this joint anymore."

"Been here long?"

He glanced up at the clock on the wall above the elevators. "Not really– only since seven."

"I was thinking more in terms of years."

His face contorted as he emitted a high pitched cackle. "I knew what you meant, sonny. I was just funnin' ya. Yeah, I had this here stand thirty-eight years. A guy named Fay used to own this place. He give it to me. I used to ride the nags before that."

The elevator dinged for me. It was an automated one. I slid the door open and got in.

"I wouldn't waste my dough on that Doc Walden's hair restorer treatment, if that's what you're here after," Pop called after me. "It's the bunk."

On the fifth floor, I threaded my way back to Law's office suite in the middle of the building near the south side and entered a small, windowless reception room where Law's secretary, a blonde with long red-tipped fingernails and a tight green sweater, took my card. Her desk was bare except for two telephones and a square of waxed paper with the remains of a ham sandwich on it. There was a covered typewriter on a rolling stand near her elbow, a row of steel filing cabinets along the wall, a hard-backed wooden guest chair and not much else.

"Have you an appointment?"

"No. I was just in the neighborhood."

"I'll see if Mr. Law is back from lunch," she said in a tone that let me know my odds weren't very good, and disappeared with my card through the connecting door. Through the pebbled glass I could see her shadow cross the room and return.

"Mr. Law will see you, Mr. Shepard," she said, making it clear she didn't care much for the idea.

Law stood behind his desk, an enormous hunk of Grand Rapids walnut placed at an angle in the rectangular room. He was in his late sixties I'd guess, with a prominent forehead and a broken halo of brown hair clinging to an otherwise bald dome. Deep-set gray eyes peered coolly at me from behind round, horn-rimmed spectacles. He wasn't a big man— I had about four inches and at least thirty pounds on him— but looked lean and wiry. He wore tan and white wingtip oxfords with cream-colored flannels and a blue double-breasted jacket, a pale blue shirt and a yellow polka dotted bow tie.

The office had a veneer of solid respectability, with faded Wilton carpets and sets of gilded tomes in glass-fronted cases. The oak-paneled walls were hung with a series of gun dog prints and framed photographs of a younger Law shaking hands with long-ago mayors and chiefs of police. Though daytime, the lamps were already on as only a murky gloom filtered in from the light well window.

Law invited me to sit. He plopped down in his own swivel armchair, unwrapped a two-for-a-quarter cigar and lit it.

I told him I was a former partner of Harry's. He'd

known Harry, Law said. His voice had the twang of a native Texan, softened by decades spent in Southern California.

"He and I butted heads a few times when I was on the force. Now that I think about it I do remember hearing that Price had got himself a sort of protégé." He pushed my card around on the glass surface of the desk. "You must be doing alright for yourself. Beverly Hills. Nice district. Well, the business sure ain't what it used to be. Don't even really take brains nowadays. You just need yourself a telephone."

Law, I noticed, like the girl, had two of them. I had been lucky to get the single line I had.

"Well now, there something I can help you with, Shepard?"

The gray eyes didn't change expression when I asked him about his work on the Swann case. "That brings back some memories. I'll say it do. So it's true then— they found his grave at last? Yes, I know all about it. I've got my methods. You have yours, too, I expect."

"I heard about it from a police detective sergeant who thinks Harry might have had something to do with it."

Law paused with his cigar in midair. "Now where in the world I wonder would he get a notion like that?"

"I was hoping you could tell me," I said. "You never heard anything like that when you worked on the case?"

"There were all sorts of rumors swirling around back then, son," Law said. "All our best information at the time suggested Swann had up and left town on his own— mebbie had a gal with him, mebbie not. Everything pointed to it. Them finding his body puts a whole new light on things, for sure. They have to go over all that old ground again. Think they'll find something we missed and be the big heroes who solve the famous Swann case. They won't. Not unless they were to get a mighty big break."

"So you didn't think there was a bootlegger angle behind Swann's going away?"

Law raised his eyebrows at me. "I didn't say that. There were some indications that a rough element was trying to move in from the east and set up their rackets here. We rounded up a bunch of Bugs Moran's boys here that summer, matter of fact. Could be some of them convinced Swann it would be healthier for him someplace else, I thought at the time. Turns out I was wrong."

"Did you ever hear that bootleggers had paid someone to get rid of Swann?"

He shook his head. "Wouldn't have believed it if I had. Things didn't operate like that here."

"Then there's nothing to the idea that bootleggers here were trying to organize like Chicago?"

Law leaned back in his chair and tipped his ashes into a brass stand. "Pure bullshit, son. The 'leggers here wouldn't have stood for any Al Capone taking over."

"How about Gus Taggart?"

"Why, what about him?"

"He was trying to expand his liquor operations, wasn't he?"

"Who says Taggart had liquor operations?"

I shrugged. "Seems to be common knowledge. A detective named O'Leary arrested him once for transporting and possession."

"You mean old Paddy O'Leary? Now that name does take me back, I'll say! Well, he's a fine one to accuse another of a liquor rap. As I recall he got kicked off the force for a drunk driving accident. Liked a bit of a nip. Didn't we all— though it may be said some set more of a store by it than others. Ah, well. Seems silly, now we've drawn a veil over that chapter in our history. I had a sworn duty to uphold the law but that don't mean I had to like all of them."

"You left police service not too long after the Swann case started. Resigned— isn't that right?"

Law chuckled. "My being made to go was a political maneuver, son— strictly political. The new mayor, the new chief of police, they didn't want anybody around they thought might be loyal to their predecessors, and that's a fact. The previous chiefs I served under didn't have any complaints about my work."

"You knew a hijacker named Mike Higgins?"

"Sure, sure. That is, I arrested him so many times, I guess I did get to know him. Tried to talk some sense into that boy, but never could."

"He may have had information about Swann but was shot before he could talk. Was he a police informant?"

Law's gray eyes had a shrewd expression. "Now that's an idea. His life wouldn't be worth a plugged nickel if his underworld friends knew he'd turned squealer. Well, Michael was clever, but not too smart."

Law's secretary opened the connecting door and stopped short. "Oh– pardon *me*, Mr. Law. I didn't realize you were still in conference."

I stood up and said I had better be going anyway.

"You ever get tired of going it alone, Shepard, I can always use a good fellow around here in my credit department. The rubber check racket is booming, if you didn't know it. The latest is people going to Las Vegas from here and paying off by check. Then they stop payment on it once they get back home, seeing as how the casinos have a tough time collecting on a gambling debt."

"I haven't heard that one," I said.

We shook hands. I nodded to the secretary and left them.

On the way back to the office I swung by the Hi-Ho to try to see Jake Barnett, alias Jack Burkett. It was near Melrose, a beer and saxophone joint with nightclub pretensions on the ground floor of a two-story building that had been newly made over with luminous white stucco and glass block, all outlined in pink and green neon, of which there was apparently no shortage. In the far reaches of the half-lit barroom, a string of chorus girls were going through their paces on a tiny stage to the accompaniment of a jukebox record. A man of about fifty with jowly, unshaven cheeks and a once-white apron tied around his thick middle watched them as he listlessly wiped down the handful of tables scattered around a postage stamp-sized dance floor.

A man with black, center-parted hair and a pencil mustache was behind the bar, tending to the late lunch customers occupying the wooden stools in front of it. I asked if Burkett was working, shouting to be heard over the blaring boogie-woogie beat. The barman shook his glistening dark head.

"Never heard of the cat, pally. I just come on here a month ago. You could ask old Smitty there. He's been here a long time— longer 'n me anyhoo," he added, nodding at the older man, who flung the wet rag into a bucket and shouldered through a swinging door at the back of the room. A blast of grease and other cooking smells escaped before it pivoted shut behind him. My stomach, still uneasy after that drugstore lunch, gave a lurch.

Smitty didn't strike me as the talkative type, but I was game. I cut around to the alley behind the place and found him slouched against the kitchen door, smoking a cigarette.

"Know where I can find Jack Burkett?" I asked.

"Who?"

"He used to be a bartender here, about six months ago."

"Whadda ya want with him?" Smitty asked with a blank stare.

"I'm just looking for him."

"Copper?"

"Private," I said.

"You *look* like a copper," he sneered.

"Do you know where he went to work after he left here?"

"Maybe. Cost ya."

"How much?"

"Fiver."

"That include all federal taxes?"

"Huh?" Smitty's mouth gaped open like a codfish. "Look, copper, do ya wanna know where he is or don'tcha?"

123

I opened my wallet and handed him a fin.

"Burkett's at another joint over on Vine," he said as he folded the bill and shoved it into the pocket of his grubby apron. "The Rumpus Room."

I found the Rumpus Room, which was not substantively different from the Hi-Ho except it had pink stucco with blue and white neon. They'd had a Jack Burkett working there but he hadn't been around for at least three months. He didn't leave a forwarding address.

CHAPTER 13

That evening was another warm one with no hint of a cooling breeze. We left the bedroom windows open and could hear the crickets, and the owls up in the palm trees, and the faint rumble of traffic rising off Sunset down below.

Bobbie was sleeping soundly next to me. I lay there only half dozing, thinking about the Swann case.

The bedroom was well suited for thinking. It had soft, soothing blue-gray walls and big glass doors that opened onto the sun deck and looked out over the canyon. I'd told Bobbie she could have it as frilly and furbelowed as she wanted; somehow she'd managed to make it feminine and pretty without making me feel like I was sleeping in a chocolate box. There was an oversized bed, custom ordered, with a headboard covered in a tropical print fabric and a tailored spread of the same stuff, with a night table and lamp on either side. On the opposite wall was a set of his and hers chests of drawers in a modern bleached wood. The one really frou-frou note was Bobbie's organdy-draped dressing table against the window.

All at once the stillness was shattered by a loud bang and the sound of metal gnashing against metal. It seemed to have come from out on the street above us.

Bobbie jerked awake and sat up, clutching the sheet

up to her breasts in alarm. "What on earth was that?"

A car horn started to blare steadily as if someone was holding it down.

"Stay here. I'll go and see," I whispered.

I slipped into my bathrobe and dashed up the stairs and out the front door. A black Cadillac with Nevada plates was parked sideways on the street in front of the house, with its nose buried in our garbage cans. I ran around to the driver's side. Cathy Durance was slumped over the wheel.

"What in the hell do you think you're doing?" I yelled over the noise of the horn. She didn't move. I pushed her away. The horn went quiet. Cathy moaned and fell over across the seat.

I hauled her out of the car and lifted her up. She weighed next to nothing. She was dressed like she'd been out for the evening in a short black cocktail dress with a silver fox fur chubby draped around her bare shoulders. Her breath reeked of booze. At least she was breathing. I carried her into the house. Bobbie, having slipped into her nightie and a robe, met us at the door, a look of astonishment on her face.

"Meet Cathy Durance," I said.

"Is she hurt?"

"I don't think so, honey. I'm pretty sure she's just passed out drunk. She might've bumped her head on the steering wheel, but I don't think anything's broken. She'll be okay once she sleeps it off."

I placed Cathy's prone form down gently on the living room sofa. One of her pumps had fallen off. I went back outside to look for it as Bobbie headed to the kitchen to make some coffee and get a warm cloth for Cathy's head. I found the shoe on the floor of the Cadillac and brought it with me into the house.

"I guess I ought to call that tame gorilla of Eddie's— the guy who's supposed to be watching her– and let him know where she is so he can come get her," I said.

"I think she might need a doctor, Ave," Bobbie said in a calm, even voice. "There's blood on her. I didn't see it at

126

first because of her dress. Look— right here. See it?"

I knelt down and looked. Cathy's side just below her rib cage was damp with blood and the fabric of her dress had a small ragged tear in it that might have been made by a bullet.

"Christ! I think she's been shot."

I ran to the hall cupboard and grabbed some towels then wet a facecloth under the faucet of the bathroom sink. After handing the lot to Bobbie, I went back into the hall and phoned for an ambulance.

When I hung up, Donny was standing at the top of the stairs in his pajamas, rubbing his eyes.

"Som'fing woke me up, Ave."

I swore under my breath, furious with Cathy for having dragged us into this, whatever it was. I scooped the little boy up in my arms.

"Sorry about that, pardner." I said. "It's nothing to worry about. A friend of ours just stopped by. She's sick, so we're going to send her to the hospital. We'll try to keep it down from now on so you can get back to sleep."

I carried him downstairs to his blue and red room and put him in bed.

"Sometimes mom lets me listen to the radio to help me go to sleep."

"Think it'll help you tonight?"

Donny nodded, his eyelids already starting to droop.

"Okay, pal," I said. I switched the radio on and turned the volume down low then tucked the covers around him. "Your mom will be along to check on you in a little while. You try to get some shut-eye, huh? You're going to visit with your dad tomorrow."

" 'kay. G'night, Ave."

Bobbie was busy ministering to Cathy, holding the compress against the wound in her side and murmuring soothing words to her.

"She came to but then passed out again," Bobbie said. "She was calling for Eddie. Is that her husband?"

I nodded. "I'll go wait outside for the ambulance."

The sky was dark with only a sliver of moon. I went in the garage and got my flashlight out of the Buick and used it to look inside the Cadillac. Cathy's bag was on the seat. I picked it up and could tell by the weight of it that it didn't contain a gun. I looked anyway and found nothing but the usual junk. Shining the light, I felt around on the floor, the back seat, the glove compartment– all empty.

Before long I heard the wail of a siren and the sound of the ambulance chugging up the hill, gears grinding. I waved my flashlight to guide it.

We slept late the next morning. After breakfast I went to see how Cathy was doing. They'd transferred her in the night from the emergency hospital to Cedars of Lebanon; she must have been stable enough to make the move, at least. The stern, sturdy-looking nurse hovering around outside her door regarded me warily and referred me to the doctor.

The doctor wasn't in his office, but I found Eddie Durance waiting in a little ante-room, half asleep in a hard wooden chair. Manny the bodyguard must have called him, as I'd figured he would.

Eddie came instantly alert at the sound of my footsteps. There were deep lines under his blue eyes and the chiseled granite face was haggard and unshaven. His charcoal-gray suit looked rumpled.

"I caught a charter flight out last night soon as I got the news," he said.

"Have they said how she's doing?" I asked.

"She's going to be okay. They stitched her up. She took a bullet to her side but it didn't hit anything vital. Jesus Christ!" he ran a hand through his thick hair. "What the hell happened?

I told him my little part of the story, and how the police detectives had taken statements from me and Bobbie last night.

"They were mainly curious to know what the lady was

coming to see me about and couldn't quite bring themselves to believe I had no idea."

"What did you tell 'em?"

"As little as possible," I said. "I didn't see what else I could do but call them. She was in a bad way. The doctor would have to report it, anyway."

He nodded. "I appreciate that. They've already been to see me, asking a bunch of dumb-shit questions. How the fuck should I know why someone would take a shot at her? We don't even live here anymore. I haven't been in the rackets in close on twenty years. Someone shoots my wife and they act like we're the criminals."

A passing nurse peered in and gave us the shush finger.

"So she was shot *at*, then?" I asked, lowering my voice. "I thought maybe...."

Eddie nodded again. "Yeah. The cops say she told the doc she did it herself, but they been all over the car and didn't find a gun. For now they say they're treating it as attempted murder, but I dunno. I don't trust the bastards." He rubbed the palms of his hands over his eyes. "Someone's got great goddamn timing. I got business back in Vegas. I oughta be there for it."

"You mean about losing your casino license?" I said. Eddie stared at me. "Sheldon mentioned something about it when I was there."

"Fuck Shelly! He tells me don't worry, he'll handle it. Jesus Christ! The guy couldn't handle his own mother." He sank back into his chair and closed his eyes with a sigh. I almost felt sorry for him.

"You want to get a cup of coffee or something?" I asked.

"No, that's okay." Eddie shook his head dazedly. "I'm gonna run home after a bit, soon as I see the doc. Thanks though, Shepard. For all of it. That's twice now I owe you— you know?"

CHAPTER 14

When I got back to the house, Bobbie was putting sandwiches together at the kitchen table. Through the window above the sink, I saw Donny riding his tricycle around on the concrete patio of the service yard.

"Bob late again?" I asked. "I thought he was supposed to have picked the kid up by now."

Bobbie's normally gentle brown eyes snapped with anger. "He called and cancelled– again. The baby's sick, or so he says."

Bobbie's ex-husband, after battling Bobbie in court over custody of Donny most of last year and the start of this one, lately seemed to be taking less of an interest in the boy, especially now that Bob had a new family. I personally thought we were well rid of him, but minded for Donny's sake.

"Poor kid," I said. "How about I take him with me after lunch and we he-men do the marketing? He'll like that. Have you got a list?"

"I do, and right now Bob is at the top of it," Bobbie said. She grinned. "But you probably meant a shopping list."

An hour later I was maneuvering a push basket around the brightly-lit aisles of the Thriftimart at a slow crawl, munching on a large, economy-size chocolate bar while I shopped. Donny trotted along at my side, busy with his own candy. A Lana Turner lookalike with very blonde hair and long legs on display in tiny white shorts paused in her inspection of canned soups to smile at me and asked Donny if he wasn't getting to be a big boy.

Donny gave the question some serious thought. "No," he said finally.

We threaded past the showy displays of pears and grapes, tomatoes and cucumbers, and shelves full of paper towels and furniture polish, boxes of crackers, flyswatters, dish cloths, breakfast cereals and tins of coffee, until I had most of the stuff on Bobbie's list plus a few things that weren't.

"We're just about done here, buddy," I said. Donny took no notice of me. He had stopped at the end of the aisle and was gaping in wonder at a towering display of dog food with a picture of a scrappy black and white pup on the label.

I edged around him to the back wall and was trying to find where they'd hidden my brand of beer when out of the corner of my eye I noticed two guys swinging toward us from opposite directions. They looked like walking advertisements for a menswear specialty shop. One was short and wide, wearing a pair of dark glasses balanced on a long, needle-like nose and a noisy red and pink floral patterned short-sleeved sports shirt that just about matched his ruddy complexion. The other one was taller, at least six feet, with a hulking build. He was dressed in tan slacks and a two-tone green sports jacket and had a snap-brim panama pulled low over a broad forehead. A hunch told me they weren't here to do their weekly marketing. I made a move toward Donny but I wasn't quick enough. Short and Fat, light on his feet for someone his size, got there first and blocked my path with the push basket while Big and Tall tried to pin me up against the counter. I craned my head away from his bulk and saw Short and Fat idling next to Donny, who was too enthralled by the dog pictures to pay any attention to him.

"You got a cute kid there and a pretty little wife at home, Shepard," Big and Tall hissed in my ear. "You oughta not to go getting involved in things that are none of your business."

"Fuck you," I growled back.

One of his hands was in his jacket pocket. It might have held a rod but white hot anger made me reckless. I gripped his free wrist and twisted it until he cringed.

"Threaten my family again and six guys will be walking slow with you," I said.

I let go of him and he socked me in the gut. It made me double over a little but I didn't go down. Two aisles away, an elegantly coiffed lady of about eighty was casting a critical eye over the bakery counter's homemade pies. If she had glanced over at us, it probably just looked like I was laughing at a good joke. Suddenly Big and Tall eyed Short and Fat, who shrugged, and the two of them wandered off as casually as they'd arrived.

I left our basket where it was and grabbed Donny up in my arms. We bolted past an unoccupied checkout lane, out the spick-and-span tile entrance and onto the sidewalk. A black coupe was speeding off, heading east up Sunset. They were going in the opposite direction of the house but that didn't mean anything.

Still clutching Donny, I dashed across the street to a drugstore and called Bobbie. I told her to lock all the doors and stay away from the windows and to not answer if anyone knocked.

"Okay," she said, trying to keep her voice steady.

As I had the night before with Cathy, I felt calmed by Bobbie's composure in an emergency. She knew I wouldn't be calling like this if it wasn't serious, that I would explain all when I could, and didn't waste time asking me questions now.

"We're both fine," I said. "Pack a few things for the two of you. We'll be home in a few minutes."

The Buick was parked out in back of the market. I

put Donny down in the front seat then jumped behind the wheel.

"Can I step on the starter, Ave?" Donny asked.

"Maybe next time, pal," I said. I pulled out onto Laurel and swung left onto Sunset

"You forgetted our groc'wees," Donny said. I glanced over and saw a worried expression in his brown eyes that were so like Bobbie's, and cursed those goons all over again.

"I just remembered Mr. and Mrs. McElmon want you to come out to the ranch this afternoon and stay for a few days."

The little guy brightened at that, then his brow furrowed. "We din'nit pay for the candy."

"It's okay," I said. "They'll put it on our bill."

"But Mom says we're not suppos'ta take any'fing we din'nit pay for."

I swerved around a florist's delivery van and made the hard right onto our street. The Buick groaned but gamely leapt up the hill.

"You mom's absolutely right, pal. She always is. I'll bring 'em the money after I get back tonight."

"You aren't staying wiff us?"

"Can't, pal, I gotta work. I'll come out and see you every chance I get, though."

Bobbie had an overnight bag ready when we pulled up in front of the house. I hugged her, then loaded it into the trunk and glanced around.

Living on a Hollywood hillside has its disadvantages, but as a defense position it couldn't have been more ideal. Those medieval kings had known what they were doing alright, building their fortresses up high. Here there was only one practical way up, and I could see anybody coming from a long way off.

"I didn't know if you'd need this so I brought it along," Bobbie said, flashing me the inside of her shoulder bag. It was my gun from the shelf in our closet, wrapped in a handkerchief, and a box of ammunition. I tucked the gun into my waistband and telephoned Paul.

"Drop what you're working on. I got a stakeout job for you," I said. "You'll need some armament."

I gave him the particulars and hung up. The three of us went outside and piled into the Buick. Bobbie sat close to me on the front seat, holding Donny on her lap. In a low voice I told her what had happened.

"Do you think this has anything to do with Cathy Durance being shot?" she asked when I'd finished.

"It's one possibility," I said.

I went over all my recent cases in my head but couldn't think how any of them would provoke someone into sending thugs to warn me off. That was more in Eddie's line. But whether the business I was supposed to keep out of had to do with what happened with Swann sixteen years ago or more current events, I couldn't yet say.

The weathered green shingles of the McElmon's barn roof came into sight. I turned into the driveway. Buster was coming down the lane with a wheelbarrow full of firewood, Jem and Kit at his heels. His handsome face widened into a surprised grin of welcome that quickly turned to concern. The kids ran up to the car, chattering.

"Well, here's Bobbie and Donny come to stay with you," I said.

Swish appeared on the front porch in a red and white striped playsuit and her hair up in braids. She waved and called to the kids to bring Donny and come into the kitchen for some Cokes out of the icebox.

I brought Buster up to date on the case while we walked up to the house.

He frowned. "Maybe we should just forget the whole thing, Ave," he said. "Let the police handle it, after all, if it's dangerous–"

"We don't know for sure that's its anything to do with Swann. But if it is, it just makes me more convinced than ever that Harry isn't mixed up in it at all."

"I don't understand," Bobbie said.

"Well, because Harry's dead," I said. They both stared at me. "If someone's warning me off the case, it suggests the person involved is someone who's still alive." I put my arm around Buster. "I'll stick with it a little longer. I'll be careful."

Swish met us at the back door and ushered us out to the shade of the terrace. She and Buster went back in the house to get some cold drinks.

"I want to go home with you, Ave," Bobbie said when we were alone.

"Uh-uh." I shook my head. "I've got to figure out what's going on. Until then, I want you to be safe."

"I am safe– with you," she said, slipping her hand into mine. "You remember, you told me how Swish didn't seem like herself when Buster was away in the war? And you said they just weren't right without each other? Well, that's how it is with me, about you. I know it sounds silly. I mean, we haven't been together anything like as long as they have– but that's how I feel."

She looked up at me and met my eyes with her warm brown ones. I squeezed her hand.

"I just want to keep you safe," I said.

"I never felt so safe before than with you."

I kissed her on the forehead. "I guess it's settled then. I know better than to argue with a redhead. Do you know how to use a gun?"

Buster and Swish came out with a drinks tray and a plate of cheese straws. To Mrs. B there was no crisis so great that it couldn't be improved by cheese straws.

"Bob tried to teach me to shoot before he went in the Army, but I don't know if I could hit the broad side of a barn," Bobbie said.

"Let's go down to the barn and see," Buster said.

Mrs. B kept the kids busy in the kitchen making cookies while the four of us walked down the lane to the big barn with its peeling white paint. For a target, Buster set up a beer bottle on the stump of an orange tree.

I loaded my gun and handed it to Bobbie. "Here, honey. Just grip it here and look straight ahead and aim– like this."

Bobbie squeezed her eyes closed, aimed, and fired. The bottle shattered with a ping. Bobbie opened her eyes and stared in surprise as Swish and Buster whooped and applauded. "Did I hit it?"

"Hell, yeah, you sure did," Buster said. "We'll have to start calling you Annie Oakley."

"Did I really do okay, Ave?"

Bobbie looked up at me with shining eyes. There was worry there too, but her jaw had the determined set to it that I knew meant her mind was made up.

"Sure, baby– you're a natural," I said.

I just hoped she would never need to prove it.

CHAPTER 15

The late afternoon sun was at its hottest as I stood panting in front of Eddie Durance's blue painted front door, reached by a zig-zagging concrete staircase of exactly thirty-two steps.

His place was over off West Pico near the Hillcrest Country Club. It didn't look so much like a house as an ocean liner about to sail down the quiet street, all blindingly white stucco and rounded corners, porthole windows and curving steel railings of gunmetal gray. It sat close to the street, built into the sloped lot, discreetly screened from the tile-roof villas on either side by overgrown cypress hedges and bougainvillea shrubs. Palm trees from across the way were reflected in Eddie's windows.

Manny answered my knock and ushered me in to a sunken living room where modernistic sconces flanked a black lacquered liquor cabinet, stark against an ivory colored wall. In the center of the room was a chrome-legged sofa and a pair of matching white leather easy chairs arranged around a circular, blue-mirrored coffee table. It had all the warmth and personality of a high-tone tonsorial parlor.

Eddie was stretched out in one of the chairs with a leather document case across his lap, studying some legal forms. He'd shaved and his suit had been pressed, and he looked altogether less haggard than he had this morning. I waved off his offer of a drink.

He listened intently while told him about my strange run-in at the Thriftimart, his lips practically disappearing into a thin line. His eyes took on the flinty blue of a roof tile and looked almost as hard.

"Tell me again what these two sons of bitches looked like?"

I repeated the description of Short and Fat and Big and Tall.

"Where's your wife and kid now?"

"The kid's safe. My wife's at home. I've got someone watching it."

"I can call some people. I'll find out who these cocksuckers are and who sent 'em."

"Now look, Eddie– if you've got any idea what it's all about, I want to know. Now."

He glared at me. "You think I had anything to do with this? That I would send people around to threaten a guy's family– your family? For fuck's sake."

"It was you who told me to forget about the Axel Swann case." I glared back at him. "You know I wouldn't drop it until I clear Harry."

He swore and fumbled with a cigarette, then leaned back in his chair. The muscles of his face loosened and the angry expression in his eyes faded. He looked all at once older.

"You ought to know better than to talk like that, Shepard. I only meant to save you the trouble. What I mean is, the Swann thing hasn't got anything to do with Harry."

"You said that before, too. You talk like someone who knows who it does have something to do with," I said. "Look– I came to you with this instead of the cops because I thought we might be able to help each other out. I've got people threatening my wife– my kid– and you still won't tell me anything."

Eddie got up and paced around. "I told you I'd take

care of it," he snapped.

From the next room, I could hear the telephone bell jangling.

"I gotta take that. I'm expecting the doc to call about Cathy," Eddie said. He stalked off, up the couple of steps to the hall and went into a room just beyond the front door.

A car horn honked from out on the street somewhere. I glanced out the big front window and saw a black Mercury convertible had pulled up to the curb down below. A young man in the uniform of a Driv-yer-self outfit got out from behind the wheel and went around to the back of the car to open up the trunk.

Someone came down the curved staircase from the second floor and into the hall. It was the girl from Las Vegas, Sandy, dressed in white pedal pushers with a red and white striped blazer-type jacket and leather thong sandals. She had a handbag slung over her shoulder and was carrying a small raw leather overnight bag.

"Oh, hi there," she said brightly as she caught sight of me. "It's Mr. Shepard, isn't it? I flew out with Eddie this morning. It was so late, he let me spend the night here. Wasn't that sweet of him? I guess my rent car's here so I'll be off now." She looked around. "Where *is* Eddie? Isn't he here?"

I told her he was on the telephone. "I'll just leave him a note, then," she said, fishing around in her handbag. She brought out a leather notepad and jotted something down with her gold ball-point pen, then tore the page out and handed it to me. "An act I'm thinking of getting for us is performing tonight at the Domino Club. I'm hoping to get Eddie to come and see them. They aren't going to be cheap, so I think he ought to see what he's paying for. You're welcome to come too if you like."

"How do you know Angus Taggart?" I asked.

She blinked for a second then shrugged. "I'm not sure I do know him, even if he is my father. Anyway, I hope you decide to come. If so, I'll see you later."

The Driv-yer-self attendant met Sandy at the door and took her bag. He placed it in the trunk of the Merc and they drove off.

Eddie came back a little while later. "That was the doc."

"How's Cathy doing?"

"They think she can maybe come home in a day or so," he said.

"Is she able to say who shot her?"

"She's sticking to the story that she did it herself." He shrugged impatiently. "The laws must believe it– the doc says I can come pick up her car from the lot there. I guess those assholes don't need it anymore."

I gave him the note from Sandy. He read it and a half-grin came over his face. "That broad. She's something else. Always thinking of business. I bet she even takes notes in the hay."

"Did you know she's Angus Taggart's daughter?"

"Sure, I knew about it," he shrugged. "They aren't close, from what I hear. She never met him before she moved to Las Vegas a couple years ago. He's got himself a new wife not much older than Sandy." Eddie looked at me. The blue eyes were placid again. "Look, Shepard, I've got a bunch of stuff I gotta take care of, but I'll look into that matter we were talking about first thing. Why don't you– uh, meet me later at the Domino Club on Sunset and I'll have some news for you?"

He'd posed it as a casual suggestion, but it came across more or less as an order. I said I'd be there.

Driving home in the early twilight, I stopped to talk to Paul. He was parked down the hill from us in a seemingly unoccupied gray Dodge coupe with a dented right fender. The street had been quiet, he said. I told him to go and have his dinner and come back in a couple of hours. Then I went on up to the house to see Bobbie. We held each other close for a good long time.

Afterward we had our supper out on the sundeck, listening to the birds calling to each other through the trees and watching as the lights of Hollywood and the Wilshire district came on.

The McElmons had called to check how things were here.

"Donny's having a grand old time, they said, so we don't have to worry about him," Bobbie said. "Buster dug up an old wagon wheel in the back forty so the kids were out there all afternoon looking for the other three."

We spent a normal evening– as normal as possible under the circumstances, that is. It got chilly enough for a fire so I lit one and we stretched out on the sofa in front of it. Bobbie read her book and listened to the ball game with me. When the time came, I showered and changed clothes to go out and meet Eddie.

Bobbie brought the gun in from the coffee table for me to take along.

I shook my head. "I won't need it. Not that *you* will. No one is going to get past Paul. But I'd feel better leaving you on your own, knowing you've got it." I hesitated. "Look Bobbie, if anything ever did happen to me–"

"Ave!"

"–which isn't going to be anytime soon, but if it did, you should know we've got some bonds, and we're part owners of a parking garage downtown. Brings in enough a month so you and Donny won't have to worry. Joe Gill handles our money and all of it. He'll fix everything up."

Bobbie shuddered. "I don't like this talk, Ave."

"There's something else you ought to know." She looked up at me, waiting. "What you said before, about how it is for you when we're apart? It's like that for me, too."

We kissed goodbye.

"You'll be careful, won't you?"

"I'm not taking any risks, don't worry," I said. "I'll honk three times when I come home so you know it's me."

CHAPTER 16

The Domino Club was on the south side of Sunset. Like most nightclubs on the Strip, it wasn't much to see from the outside– just a dinky, flat-roofed stucco box covered in neon with an awning out over the sidewalk and a couple of neatly-clipped shrubs in matching pots flanking the door. I coasted down the inclined driveway a few minutes after ten; a lot attendant materialized from the shadows. He arm-wrestled me for the Buick and accepted a dollar for doing me the favor of driving it a few feet to a vacant parking space.

The inside was, as usual, much bigger than it looked, with a spectacular view of the lights of Hollywood and Beverly Hills down below. I'd been to the place before when it was called something else. Someone had spent a lot of money on redecoration since then. Smack in the center of the main room was a circular black patent-leather bar ringed by matching padded stools. The ceiling was laced with blue neon, held up by glass columns lit from within by soft lights that changed intermittently from pink to blue. Down half a flight of pink-carpeted stairs was the showroom, with zebra-stripe upholstered booths around the perimeter and three tiers of tables leading down to a tiny dance floor and a stage where a pair of comedians were warbling a naughty parody of a popular song to howls of laughter. I hoped for Eddie's sake they weren't the act Sandy had in mind.

I didn't see either of them seated anywhere in the showroom, nor were they to be found in the smaller, more intimate lounge in the basement, where a jazz trio that sounded worth listening to was performing a Fletcher Henderson arrangement for an indifferent crowd. I went back upstairs and leaned against the round bar near the entrance to the check room, where I'd be able to see Eddie come in. The bartender growled at me that if I wanted to take up space, I had better order something.

I supposed they had to pay for all that decoration somehow, but I didn't feel like forking out three dollars for a beer so I wandered outside to the sidewalk where I could breathe the fresh carbon monoxide and wait for Eddie for free. The doorman and another of the lot attendants were shooting the breeze. Since I wasn't anybody special, they took no notice of me.

"...skinflint only tipped me half a buck."

"I hear his new picture's a flop."

"...even better lookin' in person. You oughta see those gams!"

"She's okay I guess. Ava Gardner now..."

"...practically hadda roll him outta here."

"Oh, good evening, Miss. Prentiss. Nice to see you."

The traffic roared by on Sunset, horns blasting, brakes squealing, engines backfiring. I hadn't been there long when I noticed a black Cadillac careening down the hill from the west, weaving in and out of the far right lane. As it came closer, I could see it had Nevada plates and that Eddie was behind the wheel.

His driving's almost as bad as his wife's, I thought.

I waved but the big car rolled on by without slowing, missing the turn to the driveway. It jumped the curb with the front wheels and came to a stop about a hundred yards away in front of a long-vacant art gallery.

Eddie made no move to get out. I walked toward him with the strange sensation that I'd done this before– walked up to this car in the same way. I had– the other night, with

Cathy. And just like that other time, I found the driver half slumped over behind the wheel.

"Eddie?"

He groaned.

Reaching through the open window, I shook him by the shoulder of his white jacket. He groaned again and fell back limp against the seat cushion. A stain was spreading across the bosom of his white-on-white dress shirt, red as the carnation in his lapel. I wrenched the door open. Eddie's eyes fluttered and half opened. He looked at me dazedly.

"I'm shot."

"Where?" *And me without my gun,* I thought.

"Back there...at the corner."

"Did you see who did it?"

Eddie only groaned and tried to clutch at his side. His eyes closed again.

There was a racing form folded on the seat next to him. I snatched it up and used it to try to stop the bleeding. I blasted the horn twice and the parking attendant came running.

He peered over my shoulder at Eddie. "Your pal sick or something, mister? Holy shit, that's– it's– he's Eddie Durance!"

"Never mind who he is," I said. "He needs help. Get an ambulance– now."

The lot attendant dashed off to go call for one. I kept the thin paper pressed against Eddie's wound. It was already soaked through.

A crowd was starting to gather around us on the sidewalk, talking and smoking. The doorman came over to say the ambulance would be here soon then tried to shoo the curious mob away.

A woman shoved past him, calling out, "Eddie? Eddie?"

It was Sandy, in a form-fitting white strapless evening dress with a matching wrap, dainty as a cobweb, covering her bare shoulders.

"Mr. Shepard– Avery? I just got here and–" She glanced inside the car and gasped. "Oh my God! Eddie! He's hurt! What happened to him? He isn't–?"

"Give me your wrap," I said.

She took it off and handed it to me. I tied it around Eddie's chest.

"He's been shot," I said.

"Shot? What–? Who–?"

I turned to look at her. Her eyes looked glazed and her mouth hung open slightly like a person in shock.

"Get in," I said. "He can't wait anymore for the ambulance to get here. He's losing too much blood. I'll bring him in myself."

Sandy slipped in to the passenger side seat. I skooched Eddie over to the middle and climbed behind the wheel.

"Keep that wrap on him."

We took Fountain, past stately apartment houses and refined homes. Eddie groaned now and then. Sandy pressed her shawl against his shoulder and murmured things to him, sniffling.

I pulled the Cadillac straight into the courtyard of the Hollywood Receiving Hospital and honked. A couple of attendants in white coats ran out and took him away.

They'd moved Eddie to Cedars of Lebanon in the night, where he'd been rushed into surgery. By the time I went to see him in the morning, the doctors had pronounced him critical but stable. He'd been shot just below his right shoulder. Another bullet had grazed his ribcage. He was scheduled for another operation in the afternoon.

Manny's hulking form was perched on what with him looked like a child's chair outside the door to Eddie's room holding his big, bald head in his palms. He looked up at me with a gloomy-eyed expression. I guess it doesn't look good for your employment record, when you're a bodyguard, if both the people you're supposed to guard take a bullet.

A couple of other men were waiting around outside the door, too. One was smoking in front of a NO SMOKING sign. He looked as if he could toss Manny around like a rag doll. The man with him was smaller, only about six three, with red hair and a broad, freckled face. They crossed their arms and squared their shoulders as I walked up.

They identified themselves as Watts and Sangor, police detectives from the vice squad.

"Who're you?" Sangor, the larger of the two, challenged. I told him. "Oh. The shamus. You the one hauled him in?"

I said that I was.

"What was this shooting all about?"

"I have no idea," I shrugged. "I wasn't there. I found him after he was shot. Why don't you ask Durance?"

My head still felt groggy. Most of the Strip was county territory, the sheriff's jurisdiction. I'd given a statement to a deputy at the scene last night, after driving Eddie's car back to the Domino Club. I'd sent Sandy home in a taxi from the Receiving Hospital; there was no point bringing her into this thing. It had been close to midnight before I could get away. Our hilltop had been quiet all evening, according to Paul. I'd taken over the watch from him for the overnight hours.

"We thought of that all by ourselves, shamus," Sangor said. "He's not talking. These tough guys and their goddamn code of silence. They always think they can handle everything themselves. Why do they gotta come here and use my town for a shooting gallery?"

"Somebody shot his wife the other night. I suppose that's her fault?"

"We dunno. She won't talk to us either. Keeps insisting she shot herself. Maybe so, but I'll tell you one thing, General Motors must've been getting in some practice making tanks when they built that Cadillac of hers. Damn thing's got about as much armor plating as one, anyway. And you know what? We found a thirty-two bullet down inside the passenger door panel. Durance has a thirty-two revolver

146

registered to him."

I shrugged. "So do a lot of people."

A passing nurse gave Sangor a withering glance; he dropped his cigarette to the floor and stepped on it with a size fourteen brogue.

"That all you've got to say about it, shamus? Let me guess– client confidentiality?" Sangor sneered. "Which of the Durances are you working for– him or her? Or both?"

"Who says I'm working for either one of them?"

"Well, it's funny how you seem to be Johnny on the spot whenever one of them is getting shot at," Sangor said. "If you know anything, you'd be doing everybody a favor by letting us in on it– Durance included."

Watts ran a hand through his already tousled hair and grinned at me. "Why not level with us, Shepard? We know you're a pal of theirs, and that you went to Las Vegas a couple days ago."

I stared at him. I hadn't spotted any tail. "You were following me? What for?"

"It wasn't like that. We got a tip that a certain party had flown in from Las Vegas. We checked up on it and saw your name on the passenger list."

"Durance said he thought someone has been shadowing him," I said, thinking aloud.

Watts shook his head. "Not us. We don't get to take many jaunts to Nevada. We're on the taxpayer's dime."

"Why are you so interested in Eddie Durance? He doesn't even live here anymore."

"We're interested in any known gangsters who come to Los Angeles," Watts said. "Word is, some of the boys are trying to start up the rackets here again, and new boys are trying to muscle in from the east. So, yeah, don't mind us if we keep an eye on Durance when he's in town."

A nurse came out of Eddie's room.

"Mr. Durance is awake. You may see him for three minutes only," she said with a firm nod. She looked at me. "Are you Mr. Shepard? He's been asking for you."

Watts and Sangor glanced at each other. Sangor shrugged.

The room was small and windowless. Sangor leaned against the back wall. I sat down in a vacant chair in one corner. Eddie looked limp and wan, lying on a metal cot. He tried to sit up but winced and fell back a little onto the pillow. Watts went to the bedside and helped prop him up.

"You two here again?" Eddie jeered in a faint voice. "Hoping for another look at my bare ass?"

"You in a better frame of mind to talk now, Durance?" Sangor growled.

"It's like I already told you," Eddie said. "It was a stick up. A couple of punk kids tried to hold me up at the signal. I wouldn't give 'em anything so they let me have it. Lucky I managed to steer the car down the hill before I passed out. The crime rate in this backwater is for the birds."

"Yeah, we noticed how it always seems to go up whenever you come to town," Sangor said.

"You ought to be out trying to do something about it, 'stead of bothering me."

Sangor started to reply but Watts caught his eye and shook his head. He turned to Eddie. "We're trying to help you, Durance. Why don't you level with us and tell us who shot you?"

Eddie grinned at him. "Why would anyone shoot me? I haven't got an enemy in the world."

"We'll put a guard on your door 'round the clock."

"I don't need protection from you laws. I can take care of my own affairs. Go on and mooch a free meal somewhere. You look like you need it," Eddie laughed, then started to cough.

The nurse poked her head inside the door, glared collectively at us, and started to shoo us out of the room.

"I wanna talk to Shepard a second," Eddie said. "The rest of you can clear out."

The two deputies hesitated. The nurse ordered them out and they went. She pursed her lips and glanced at her watch then at me.

"One minute," she said.

"If you've got anything to say about what went on last night, Eddie, you ought to tell it to them, not me," I said when the door had closed again.

Eddie's voice was hoarse now, barely above a whisper. "It's about those torpedoes who bothered you. I needed to tell you. They're nothing you gotta worry about any more. The matter's been taken care of."

"What? How…who–?"

I pictured Big and Tall lying in a ditch somewhere next to Short and Fat and smiled at the thought.

"It was Shelly told those guys to put the wind up you," Eddie said. "He was just mixed up. Thought he was doing me a favor. He knows now he fucked up, but good. It won't happen again."

I wanted to ask him if they had been warning me off the Swann case, and if so, how that would be considered helping Eddie, but for the moment I felt nothing but grateful relief and in any case didn't care to argue with a man in his condition.

"Sheldon has a funny way of doing favors for people," I said. "Next time I see him I think I'll tell him how I funny I think he is."

"He's going to hear about it from me in person, as soon as I get out of this shithole."

Eddie winced and leaned back again, his face almost as white as the pillow. He closed his eyes. "Look in on Cathy for me, would you Shepard? She'll be worried."

Cathy Durance was in another ward of the hospital on a different floor than Eddie. Her door was closed. There was no Manny on duty, no police guard on it either.

As I walked up I heard Cathy's panicked voice shout from within, "You– you keep away from me with that thing!" Then she screamed in terror.

CHAPTER 17

I came bursting through the door all at once, just like the tough guys in the movies. A nurse stood next to the bed, her cap askew, with a hypodermic needle in one hand. Cathy lay prone under the covers with the sheet drawn up around her chin, pale beneath her tan. She still had a trace of the shiner, and there were deep bluish shadows under both eyes as well as a fresh bruise on her forehead from where she banged it on the steering wheel. The outline of her body under the thin sheet looked hardly bigger than a child's.

Both women turned to stare at me. "I– uh– just came to see how Mrs. Durance was getting on," I said.

"She's been having hysterics since the news came in about her husband, poor thing," the nurse said as if Cathy wasn't within earshot. "I've given her something to help her sleep." She turned to Cathy and smoothed her pillow. "Now that wasn't so bad after all, was it?"

"I don't wanna sleep," Cathy said in a hoarse whisper. "Not until I know how Eddie is. Why won't anyone tell me?"

"You must rest," the nurse said firmly.

"Could I see her a minute?"

The nurse shook her head. "She isn't supposed to have visitors."

"Oh, don't make him go– please!" Cathy whimpered. "Let him stay an' talk to me. I don't like it here in this place all alone."

"I've got a message for her from her husband," I said.

"You're a friend of his?" The nurse gave me a wary onceover, probably wondering if I was a gangster. "Well, I suppose there's no harm. The doctor will be making his rounds in a few minutes. He'd better not find you here."

She went out, pulling the door closed behind her.

The room was a private one and must've been costing Eddie a mint. Even so it was typically dismal, the only bright note being a vase of yellow roses on the bedside table.

Cathy looked up at me, her baby blue eyes fever-bright. "What did Eddie say? Manny told me how somebody shot him. He's going to be okay, isn't he?"

"Eddie's tough. He'll pull through," I said. "He's more worried about you and who shot you."

"I did it. Eddie knows—"

"You and me and Eddie all know you never shot yourself."

"I did too," she said, scowling now.

"Then what did you do with the gun?"

That stumped her, but not for long. "Why— you mean? Isn't it in the car?"

"Uh-uh. You'll have to do better than that, Cathy."

"Well, I guess I must've thrown it away. I don't remember." She frowned and shook her head. "I just wanna forget it ever happened. It was a dumb thing to do. Eddie's not divorcing me at all. He told me so. He said we're meant to be together. He means it, too. Didn't he come all the way from Las Vegas to see me? Just like I knew he would." For a second the blue eyes flashed with triumph, then drooped and finally closed. Her breath came in short, shallow gasps then became regular. She wasn't going to tell me who shot her, not now. I was gone before the doctor came in.

On the drive home I kicked around a bunch of questions. Like— why was Cathy shot but not killed? These people didn't kid around. If they'd wanted to kill her, she'd be dead. Or had Cathy shot herself, after all, to get Eddie's attention? What happened as a result of her being shot? Eddie came back to Los Angeles. Had that been that the desired outcome all along– getting him here? Or was it that somebody wanted Eddie out of Las Vegas? In either case, the fact is someone made an attempt on his life almost as soon as he arrived. Did it have to do with Eddie's recent troubles in Las Vegas– that business with the casino license for instance? Or did it go back further than that? All the way back, maybe, to the Swann case?

I stopped to tell Paul he didn't have to watch the house anymore and to bring the bill for his hours and expenses into the office in the morning. Then I went up to the house to give Bobbie the good news. We went into the bedroom and held each other close until I fell into an exhausted sleep. I woke to find Bobbie watching over me.

"Let's go get our kid and bring him home, huh?" I said.

At the ranch I brought Buster and Swish up to date on things. Then we didn't think about Eddie or Swann or any of that business anymore, for a while. The kids showed us their collected loot– wagon wheels, bits of rusted harness, agate stones, and Indian arrowheads– I suspected the latter came from a five and dime, hidden by Swish for them to find. We inspected the long-disused pool that was slowly filling with water, Buster having managed to repair the pump. Swish and Bobbie made plans to meet in town to go school clothes shopping for the kids. We had a peek at Diana, who seemed to have grown already. Buster talked some more about his idea of having ex-servicemen come stay at the ranch and showed us a roughly-sketched plan for rebuilding the bunkhouse. We decided that next Friday wasn't too soon to get started on it. Swish suggested we make a weekend of it with a barbeque and a swim to celebrate my birthday, which I'd forgotten all about.

We stopped at the market on the way back to town and did our delayed shopping. Back at the house, Bobbie changed into her bathing suit and took a sunbath on the deck. Donny laid on his tummy in front of the radio and listened to his favorite programs. I read the afternoon papers. The news about Eddie's shooting was splashed across all the headlines. My name was mentioned, but only in passing. Later I cooked hamburgers on the barbeque for supper. It felt good to get back to the normal, family routine.

Around six o'clock, the telephone rang.

"This Shepard?" a male voice rasped at the other end of the line.

"Yeah," I said. "Who's this?"

"I hear you're looking for Jack Burkett."

"Is this Burkett?" I could hear him breathing, but otherwise there was only silence. "Or do you prefer Jake Barnett?"

"Where'd ya get that name?" the voice barked.

"Kay Higgins gave it to me."

He went quiet again. "Whadda ya want with him?" he asked after a while.

"I need to know about Mike Higgins and Axel Swann."

The caller sighed. "Okay. There's a church out Bunker Hill way, on Third."

I knew the one he meant.

"Get there within the hour," he said. "And be alone."

CHAPTER 18

The church was built into the slope of Third Street where it crested at Fremont, looking across the hotel and apartment house rooftops to the backside of Bunker Hill and the endless stream of cars and streetcars flowing through the yawning tunnel portal. A neon sign mounted on the weather-beaten clapboard steeple proclaimed it to be the Unity Gospel Church. I cut through a small flower garden and mounted a flight of wooden steps to the front doors, which stood open. A hand-lettered sign in the tiny vestibule read:

'ALL THE LABOR OF MAN IS FOR HIS MOUTH, YET THE
APPETITE IS NOT FILLED' – SOLOMON
WELCOME, FRIENDS. A PLACE FOR THE SPIRITUALLY HUNGRY
MEALS 8:00, 12:00 & 4:00 DAILY

Dappled early evening sunlight fell in arched patches from upper windows across the well-worn linoleum floor of the main hall, where a stocky, bull-necked middle-aged man in a blue denim work shirt and dungarees was putting rows of folding chairs away. He straightened up stiffly.

"I'm looking for Jack Burkett."

Pale blue eyes, staring out of a ruddy, acne-pitted face,

gave me the long once-over of a man used to reading faces, then nodded. "I'm Burkett. Guess you're Shepard?"

I showed him my detective's license. He frowned, squinting to read the print, then gave it back to me.

"You a friend of Kay's?"

"I just met her. She trusted me enough to tell me where to find you, and your name."

He gave me a wary look. "They said you was asking for me at the Rumpus Room. Kay never told ya I was there. She couldn't 'a. She didn't know herself. So how'd ya track me?"

I told him.

"Yeah, that Smitty struck me as the type who'd turn rat on a guy," Burkett said, shaking his head slowly. "I didn't like the set up, so I blew." He straightened his shoulders and looked at me. "I dunno what ya think I can tell ya about Mike. He's been gone a long time. But come on back."

I followed Burkett down the aisle and past the vestry, into a makeshift kitchen. I sat down at the table while he poured us some coffee from a chromium urn on the wooden counter.

"The Rumpus Room was okay. I liked the folks. But it got to where I couldn't take being in a saloon anymore. Too damn noisy," he said. "But I didn't know what other kind of work I could get after I got outta stir. Then I heard Brother Tom talking on the radio. I kinda liked what he had to say. So I started coming here regular. And Brother Tom, he gimmie a job. I do odd jobs around this place, take care of the lawn, fix whatever needs fixing. And it's quiet."

"You didn't keep in touch with Kay?"

"Naw," he shook his head. "Kay's good people now— respectable, I mean. It don't do for her to get mixed up with an ex-con like me."

"I doubt that Kay would see it that way."

"Naw, and that's a fact. She was never one to high-hat a guy. It just wouldn't be fitting, that's all. Mike never knew how good he had it, with a woman like Kay looking out for him."

"You and Mike were partners?"

"Yeah. See, I knew Mike from a cousin 'a mine. I heard he was out here working for a heist outfit. So when I come out from the north side 'a Chicago, I hooked up with him. That musta been in twenty-five or so. We'd hold up trucks that was hauling alky up from the beaches and sell the stuff in town. Mike and me, we'd clear three, four hundred a night each doing that— sometimes more. I didn't think nothing in those days of dropping a pair of Cs on a suit, and tipping the waiters a sawbuck for any little thing. And Mike, he'd drink up half his pay and blow the rest of it at dice. It was easy come, easy go 'ta us." He looked around the shabby room. "I don't need so much nowadays. I got enough to eat, a place to kip. Brother Tom says the true riches of life are to be found in the soul. I guess he's got something there."

"Who did you work for back then?"

Burkett laughed. "Anybody that would pay us cash money, that's who. We'd have every last bottle sold before we took on a job. But we only ever dealt with the big operators. We didn't bother with small timers. That's 'cos the big boys made the pay-offs to the feds and the coppers so we didn't have to worry about them bothering us, or so Mike said. He was usually right."

"Did you ever work for Gus Taggart? Or Eddie Durance?"

"Oh sure. We did a lot of jobs for both them boys. Mostly stealing the stuff from one and selling it 'ta the other, and stealing it back again the next week." Burkett ran a hand through his thick, sandy hair. "It was pretty easy work. Not like Chicago. Everything was real calm and peaceful-like most of the time. I guess I could handle a Tommy pretty good if I had to, but I never had much use for one out here. There was one time our convoy got ambushed out on the beach road, though. One of the drivers got fogged. Me and Mike were lucky— I took a couple slugs in the leg, he got it in the foot. We were laid up for a few weeks. Mr. Taggart, he come to see us and give us a stack 'a kale. Paid the croaker's bills too. I guess maybe he felt bad on account 'a we got hurt. Once I got well again, I quit the alky racket and he gimmie a job as a doorman at his gambling club."

"What about Mike? Did he work at Taggart's club?"

"That, and more. Taggart made him a kinda personal bodyguard. Mike drove him around and that sorta thing." Burkett made a wry face. "Mike started getting a swelled head about it, thinking he was a big shot or something. He was drinking more than usual, and running around with other women, too. Kay got fed up and called it quits. I didn't blame her. I told Mike he was acting ten kinds of a fool. We got into a brawl about it."

I leaned forward. "Think back to the summer of 1930, Jack. Is it true Taggart was trying to organize the bootleggers? There was supposed to have been a big meeting about it around that time."

"There was some chatter about it, yeah," Burkett nodded. "Mike couldn't resist shooting off his mouth about it 'ta show off what a big shot he'd got to be. I knew something was up, anyway. The boys would meet late at night. All the big 'leggers, even the ones who hated Taggart, like Eddie. I had to pat 'em down and take their rods away from 'em 'fore they came in. It's a good thing I did, I guess. Eddie and Taggart got into a brawl one night. Eddie looked like he coulda killed him. I had 'ta chuck him out."

"Do you know what the fight was about?"

Burkett shrugged. "Eddie called him a double-crosser."

"Did you hear any talk about hiring someone to kill Swann?"

Burkett stared past me at a picture calendar of a waterfall tacked to the wall. "Something was up. I dunno what they talked about, though. I couldn't hear 'em and Mike never said."

I took a photograph of Harry out of my coat pocket and set it down on the scarred wooden table. "Did you ever see this man meet with Taggart or any of the 'leggers?'" I asked, watching his face closely.

Burkett picked up the snapshot and squinted at it. His eyes gave away no sign of recognition. He shook his head. "I never seen him before."

I thanked him, nodding, still thinking about the idea of a gunman being hired for the "job."

"Do you remember anyone in particular hanging around Taggart's at the time, Jack? A stranger, maybe?"

Burkett scratched his head. "There was this one guy.... I didn't know him. He used to come in the joint a lot, though."

"A 'legger?"

"Naw, I don't think so. Just one 'a the suckers. I never knew his name. He liked the dice tables. But he must've been a big shot I guess. Taggart always treated him good, gave him all the credit he wanted. Anyway, he was meeting with Taggart then, up in Taggart's office. Just the two of them. And Mike."

"Do you remember what he looked like? Tall? Short? Old? Young?"

"He was around my age. And short. Real short. A swell type 'a dresser. I looked like a bum next to him. Black hair and mustache. His face reminded me of something. A bird– an eagle, sorta, or maybe an owl. I dunno. He was there all the time, right up until we hadda close up."

"Why was that?"

"On account of after that fed went missing– Swann– the town got too hot even for top men like Taggart. He closed up and breezed it outta town for a while. Mike went with him. I didn't see him again until he called me up about being his trigger man for that warehouse job." Burkett shook his head.

"What happened that night?"

"I dunno. Something went wrong, I know that much for sure. It was supposed 'ta be a cakewalk." Burkett looked down. "That's what Mike said. I didn't want any part of it, at first. But he offered me a pair 'a Cs just to drive him to this warehouse and watch 'ta make sure nothing happened to him. It sounded bugs to me. But I was down to cases since I ain't worked in a while, and four hundred bucks is a lotta kale.

So I drove us down there and we parked around the corner from the warehouse, down the alley, where we could see the loading dock out back, then just waited. It was like in the old days, when we was waiting for the alky trucks. We sorta patched things up between us. He told me how he'd got back with Kay and that he'd taken the pledge. He was sober enough then, alright. Anyway, he musta got the signal 'cos he got out and started down the alley. I seen him get to the door an' open it."

"He didn't break in?"

"It was unlocked. That's when I started to feel real windy. The hair went up on the back 'a my neck, like the time right before we got shot up out on the beach road. I was about 'ta go after Mike and tell him we oughta lam it when I heard shots from a Tommy. Mike dropped. All of a sudden the place was crawling with coppers. I wasn't gonna hang around and get myself fogged too. I knew there weren't nothing I could do for Mike. So I scrammed. Sure, some pal I am," he added, lowering his massive head.

"Did anyone else know you were going to be there that night?"

"I never told nobody," Burkett said. He looked up at me with stricken eyes. "But somebody knew and put Mike on the spot."

"Mike told Kay he was going to meet a policeman that night."

"If he was, he didn't say anything about it 'ta me, but I wouldn't be surprised. He was always working an angle."

"Had he ever met Nick Lundy before?"

"Not that I know of. There were a lotta cops around Taggart's all the time, though."

"What do you know about Mike and a cop named Cyrus Law?"

"Nothing much. Law was a wrong gee," Burkett said. "Always shaking us down, threatening 'ta run us in if we didn't pay up. Got rough with us sometimes, too."

The room was silent except for the ticking of an old fashioned regulator wall clock out in the hall and the usual creaks and groans of an aged building.

"Do you think Mike could have been a police informant?" I asked.

Burkett stared at me. "Mike– turn rat?"

"Did he ever say anything about Swann– that he knew something about his disappearance?"

"N-no– not 'ta me," Burkett said slowly. "Is that why he was killed– 'ta keep him from talking?"

"I don't know yet," I said.

"You know, there was something different about Mike that night. I didn't know what it was then, but now I think I do. See, when you're on the make, you're always looking back over your shoulder, waiting for some smart gee 'ta put the finger on you. Mike that night seemed 'ta me like a guy who didn't owe nothing 'ta nobody. Or maybe it's just I never seen him sober before." He sighed. "It weren't right him getting fogged by that copper like that when he weren't even armed. Me, I scarpered back to Chicago after that. At least there we didn't get the coppers to settle our scores for us."

I thought of Nick Lundy's claim that he'd shot in self-defense, Higgins having threatened him with a gun. I mentioned this to Burkett, who shook his head.

"Mike didn't have no rod on him that night," he said firmly.

It had grown dark outside. Barnett's face was half in shadow, cast by a single bare lightbulb over the sink. I said I had better be getting home.

"You gonna sort it out, about Mike I mean?"

"If I can," I said. "I'm trying to help a pal of mine who's gone, too. You've been a lot of help, Jack. Thank you."

Burkett shrugged. "I used 'ta think a lot about what happened, hating Nick Lundy and whoever put Mike on the spot that night, planning how I'd make sure they got theirs someday. But Brother Tom, he made me see I wasn't doing nothing but disturbing the peace 'a my own heart by carrying a grudge around. He says when ya learn 'ta forgive is when ya truly walk free. I try 'ta remember that. Those guys— they'll get theirs, alright, but it won't be no thanks 'ta me. 'Vengeance is mine; I will repay, so sayeth the Lord.' "

CHAPTER 19

Paul was in the office the next the morning bright and early as I'd asked but refused to take any money from me for his time spent guarding the house. I gave him a new assignment on a job that had just come in– tracking down witnesses in a restaurant negligence lawsuit.

Grace came in with the photograph copies of the Hayward Hotel register. Zankich had sent them over last week as promised and I'd given Grace, who had ambitions of becoming an operative someday, the thankless task of checking the names against any records she could locate to see if by chance any one of them had been party to a divorce in 1930. I didn't hold out any high hopes, but it could explain what Harry might have been doing there. Cases where adultery was suspected often involved taking a nearby hotel room and waiting. One of the least savory parts of the business was having to serve as a witness when the client insisted on bursting in on an unfaithful spouse. Harry usually foisted this duty off on Edith or me– but as Edith had noted, he would handle it himself if the client was an important one or had asked for him specifically.

Grace, however, shook her head.

"It's no soap, boss. I've been through these names and none of them were involved in any divorce actions around that time."

"You mean you were able to track them all down?"

"All of them but one gentleman," she said, pointing to a name on the register with her pencil. "This one here– Mr. A. L. Kyknos. Sounds like a Greek, do you think? Room four-one-seven. Says he lived here in town but I couldn't find any trace of him. He's not listed in any city directories, tax assessor rolls– nothing. I even checked the *Blue Book*. If you want me to keep looking…"

"No, never mind. The name's probably a phony. Thanks for trying, Grace. Good work."

"It's going to drive me crazy," she said and went out, beaming.

I went over my notes on the Swann case, adding what I'd gotten from Burkett last night. His description of the man who'd frequented Taggart's place and looked like a bird– he could have been anyone, but he sounded a lot like Roger de Pietro. Was de Pietro a gambler? And if it was him, what had he and Taggart been meeting about? I dialed the de Pietro's number and got the houseboy.

"Mr. de Pietro out of town," he said.

"When do you expect him back?"

"He not say. Maybe long time. You leave message?"

"No message," I said and hung up.

I wasn't sure I believed him. On the other hand, if de Pietro really was out, I might be able to sugar the nurse into letting me see Margaret Swann again. A few ideas were starting to take shape that I wanted to run by her.

The Buick was parked across the street in front of a talent agent's. I put the top up to keep the sun off my neck and was about to step on the starter when I looked up and saw an older model Rolls Royce lumbering by, headed east in the far right lane. Roger de Pietro was its lone passenger.

He hadn't seen me; he was sitting in the center of the back seat, staring straight ahead. *So 'Mr. de Pietro out of town,' is he?* I thought and fell in behind the Rolls. It was going at a snail's pace as if looking for a particular address. Impatient drivers, used to doing fifty or sixty along this stretch, swerved around me angrily. After about a mile, the Rolls stopped in front of one of the long, low white buildings that were the Strip's answer to colonial Virginia. I pulled over to the curb a few car lengths behind them and watched.

The driver went around and held the passenger door open. De Pietro got out, smoothing imaginary creases from the front of his Palm Beach suit. He stood mopping his face with his handkerchief while the driver rummaged around in the trunk and came up with a bulky item covered by a cloth. The cloth slipped as he lugged the thing over to the sidewalk, revealing a small lacquered wooden box with a handle, like something Napoleon would have carried his spare crown around in. He covered it up again and followed de Pietro inside one of the small shops, ANTIQUES BOUGHT & SOLD according to the hand-lettered sign. I waited. The driver came right back out, empty-handed, and slouched against the Rolls' front fender smoking a cigarette. De Pietro was in there for ten minutes or so. He climbed back into the Rolls and it continued on its way east on Sunset.

If either of them noticed they'd picked up a tail, there was no sign of it. The big car cut up onto Hollywood Boulevard and turned up Nichols Canyon on the south side of the Hollywood Hills. I gave them a long lead and kept out of their sight as we crept up the narrow, winding road. There wasn't any chance of my missing them; with the steep, rocky slopes of the canyon on either side, there were few places to turn off and if they did, I'd spot them. The road was little used. Here and there I glimpsed a house nestled amidst the scrub. No other cars passed us going up or down. I could hear the Rolls chugging along, always one curve ahead of me. The only other sounds were birds, the dry rustling of the leaves in the trees and the faint rush of water from some unseen stream. As the crow flies it was only a few minutes from central Hollywood, but we might have been in some remote backwoods.

We'd traveled for maybe twenty minutes when I

noticed the Rolls' motor had gone quiet. I backed the Buick a few feet to a dirt lane I'd just passed and parked it in the shade of a tree. Then I got my binoculars out of the glovebox and made my way up the hill to a point where I could get a good look, wondering what in the hell de Pietro was up to. He wasn't exactly dressed for hiking.

The Rolls had pulled over at a wide spot in the road overlooking a deep ravine and the next canyon over. Somebody else had had the same idea. A black coupe was parked alongside the Rolls. There was no way to tell if it had been there waiting or had come down from the other direction. In any case, de Pietro had gotten out and stood near the hood of the Rolls, his driver a few feet behind him, and appeared to be deep in conversation with two other men. I knew them. They were my old friends, Short and Fat and Big and Tall.

Short had on a blue and red sports shirt today; Big wore his same green jacket and snap-brim panama. I held the glasses steady. I was too far away to hear the words but it didn't look like they were asking each other for directions. Short yelled something, jabbing his trigger finger at de Pietro's chest. De Pietro reached into his coat pocket and handed something to Big; Big tucked whatever it was under his arm and turned away. Short gave de Pietro a shove. De Pietro staggered. As his driver made a lunging motion in Short's direction, de Pietro steadied himself and shook his head, then climbed into the back of the Rolls. The driver looked as if he still wanted to take a poke at Short but only glowered and slammed the passenger door closed.

It looked like the party was breaking up. I hustled back down to where I'd left the Buick. Presently the Rolls came sailing along, back the way it had come. I let it go. I heard the coupe's motor start and waited for it to pass me. It didn't. I pulled out onto the road and continued uphill. The coupe was nowhere in sight but that didn't worry me. I could guess which way they'd be headed, and sure enough caught a glimpse of the coupe where the canyon road came out at

Mulholland. I followed, winding around above the Hollywood Bowl and down to the Cahuenga Pass, where the coupe merged into the freeway traffic, headed south. In Hollywood they turned on Sunset and went east toward downtown. I kept them in sight but didn't get too close. They didn't seem to notice they were being tailed. We cruised along Sunset at a good clip until the coupe made the hairpin turn onto North Hill, crossed Temple, and shot through the auto-interurban tunnel under Bunker Hill onto South Hill Street. At Third it swung a left and slowed to a crawl past the Fay Building. They seemed to be looking for a place to park. I swore and looked around wondering where I could stash the Buick. The driver behind me honked angrily. I waved him around just as a truck pulled away from the curb a few feet ahead and the coupe slid into the vacated spot. Short and Fat and Big and Tall sprang out and strolled into the Fay Building. I drove on but had no luck. I went around the block and back onto Hill and ended up having to leave the car at an auto-park.

I fought my way on foot through the lunchtime crowds on the sidewalk and rounded the corner at Third when up ahead I saw Big and Tall, with Short and Fat at his heels, come out of the Fay Building again in a big hurry, making for their car. I swore again. There was no time to get back to the Buick and barely enough to flag down a taxi, even if there had been one to flag. The oddly-matched pair jumped into the coupe. I shrugged, watching as it sped away. Your luck runs hot and cold in this business and such was the peril of a solo tail job in downtown Los Angeles near the noon hour.

I decided to try my new pal Pop, sage of the Fay Building newsstand, hoping he could at least give me an idea of where Short and Fat and Big and Tall had gone during their brief visit. I was almost to the doors when a police radio car pulled up and idled, double-parked, in front of the entrance. A patrolman got out of the passenger side and went in. I followed in his wake and saw him disappearing down a hallway at the rear of the building, accompanied by an older, heavyset man who fumbled with a set of keys, the sides of his blue sports jacket flapping as he walked.

I found Pop on duty at his newsstand as before.

"You look like a sportin' fella–" he started. "Oh, I know you. You was in here the other day."

"A lot of excitement around here today," I said, jerking a thumb in the direction of the patrolman and the heavyset man. "What's that all about?"

"Don't know," Pop said. "Didn't ask. If the super wants to get all het up and call the police, it's none of my affair. Someday he'll call to have 'um carry me out of here feet first but that won't be none of my affair, neither, 'cos I'll be dead."

"Not anytime soon, Pop," I said. "How about a racing form today."

I gave him a quarter and took one off the stack.

He bowed in thanks. "Best of luck to you."

"You didn't happen to notice those two guys who came in here a little bit ago? A fat one and a tall one?"

"I ain't kept this stand thirty-odd years by poking my nose in things where it don't belong," Pop said. "I sure didn't notice any little round fella in a blue and red shirt and a tall fella in a green jacket come in and go up to the fifth floor and come right back down again."

"I didn't think you would," I said. "So I guess you wouldn't know if these fellows had ever been around here before?"

"What fellas? I tell you, I never seen any fellas like that, so you'd never hear it from me that they come in here two, three times a week."

A patrolman, a different one, came swinging through the lobby from the Third Street entrance and positioned himself near the elevators. He looked like a boy playing dress up in his father's uniform. I was thinking of having another chat with Cyrus Law, but the patrolman eyed me challengingly.

"You work here, Mac?"

"Just visiting."

"Sorry. I've got orders not to let anyone up except tenants."

"What's going on?"

He shrugged. "Got a leaper, I guess. Somebody went out of a window up on the fifth floor."

CHAPTER 20

A crowd of curious bystanders had gathered out on the sidewalk in front of the Fay Building– boys on bicycles, office workers returning from lunch, pensioners down from the hill to do their shopping. The first radio car had been joined by a second, and three more patrolmen on foot were milling around not doing much of anything that I could see. A faded green Ford sedan pulled up and Jeff Zankich got out of it. He was still hatless, with his dark glasses and a tweed sports jacket this time. He was alone; there was no sign of the sullen Dawson.

Zankich gave a slight nod as he passed me and followed one of the patrolman around the east side of the building. He came back a few minutes later wearing a grim expression and pushed his way inside without glancing in my direction. I smoked a cigarette and waited. Motorists swerved around the patrol cars that were blocking the traffic lane, some slowing to rubber-neck. About a quarter of an hour went by before Zankich strolled out onto the sidewalk again, squinting in the sun. He slipped his dark glasses on and came over to where I stood.

"Hullo, Shepard," he said. "You been to see Law today?"

"Cyrus Law? No," I said.

He looked at me. "But you did see him? He had your card out on his desk."

"Oh, sure. Last week."

"What are you doing here today?"

"I thought of some more questions I wanted to ask him."

"Well, you won't get much out of him now," Zankich said grimly. "Better come see for yourself."

I trailed along behind him down a narrow service passage on the east side and around to the back where the light wells yawned between the building's narrow wings. Zankich stopped at the mouth of one of them and stared into its shadows. It smelled of rotting garbage and was obviously used regularly as a public toilet. There was something else, too— worse even than that. It made me think of the trenches.

A man lay sprawled on his back in the sparse weeds about three feet away, his legs twisted at an unnatural angle. He wore tattered flannel trousers with tan leather suspenders, a red bow tie and a dress shirt that had once been white but was now scorched black.

That was the other smell— burned flesh.

Cyrus Law.

His eyes stared sightlessly at the stingy patch of blue showing overhead; his mouth, the jaw having been knocked out of alignment, hung open as if he was screaming in terror.

I looked up to the fifth floor. A man peered down at me from an open window then ducked back inside again. People were crowded at the other office windows above and behind us, watching.

"Has he been moved?" I asked, noting the dirt and gravel pockmarking Law's face.

Zankich groaned. "Yeah. He hit the ground face down. The idiot who found him turned him over on his back. A janitor in the building. I guess he thought Law was a drunk or something."

"Anybody see what happened?"

"We're just starting to take statements. The coroner will have a better idea, but I'm thinking he must've been asleep and accidentally set himself on fire. See those burn marks near his fly?" Zankich said, pointing. "Maybe dropped a cigarette in his lap. Then went to the window and fell out in a panic."

"Maybe he had help. There's no scorch marks on his hands," I said slowly. "If you woke up and found yourself on fire, what's the first thing you would do?"

Zankich blanched under his tan. "Oh, hell. I should have caught that."

"You'd have got there."

"But what if—" He cut off as two men came around the corner. One was wide-shouldered with an expansive gut and thick black eyebrows in a round moon face; the other was a gray-haired, bespectacled man with a toothbrush mustache lugging a large, oblong bag. "Damn. It's the skipper. That's the deputy coroner with him."

Zankich went over and spoke to the wide man. The older man crouched down next to Law's body and got to work. I turned away and walked back to the street, as a police photographer nearly ran me down. With the coroner's hearse parked at the curb, the crowd out on the sidewalk had doubled, joined now by reporters— a young woman among them— and news photographers wielding Speed Graphics. Two beefy young patrolmen were trying to keep them at bay. Zankich appeared behind me a minute later. He nodded to the officers.

"The cap says you can let them go back now," he said. The press corps took off at a run.

Zankich still looked pale to me. I suggested a cup of coffee in the drugstore. He nodded and told one of the patrolmen where to find him.

We sat at counter stools overlooking the busy intersection. Cars whooshed through the tunnel. Barkers on the sidewalk hawked theater tickets and sight-seeing bus tours. The little funicular railway cars clanked their way up and down Bunker Hill. The other day I'd been looking at the opposite side of the same hillside from outside Burkett's church.

I had to decide what to tell Zankich about Short and Fat and Big and Tall. They hadn't been up there very long; was it long enough to set Law on fire and pitch him out of a window? If they'd been up there before, as Pop said, the police would find their prints. They probably had a file on these guys already. Still, I'd have to tell him about Lou Sheldon. Eddie wouldn't like that, but that was too bad. Zankich would want to bring them in for questioning.

Gradually his color came back. I gave him all of it, starting with them threatening me at the Thriftimart to the meeting with de Pietro that morning. He jotted it down in a little notebook.

"You don't have any idea who these two guys are?"

I shook my head. "You might ask Pop– the old guy who runs the newsstand. You'll want to talk to Pop anyway. I get the feeling there's not much that goes on around here he doesn't know about. And Law had a girl who kept his appointments. She should know. Maybe they were operatives for Law."

"Well, one thing's for sure– you've been busier than I have on the Swann case," Zankich said. "I haven't got much of anywhere with it."

"There were a couple of vice boys at the hospital when I went to see Eddie Durance. Sangor and Watts," I said. "They were pretty interested in him."

Zankich stared out the window absently then nodded. "I think I know who you mean. They're always hanging around, poking their noses in our cases. We're supposed to be cooperating with them and vice versa. Someone seems to have the idea we've got a bunch of eastern hoods moving in here. Durance was a bootlegger in the old days, wasn't he?"

"So was a guy named Gus Taggart. Ever heard of him?"

"I may have come across the name," Zankich said

172

doubtfully. "Why? You got some dope on him I should know about?"

"I'm still working on it. He seems to have had a pal on the force named Nick Lundy. Works for him now at his casino."

"Doesn't ring a bell. Must've been before my time," Zankich said, his face a blank. He took a swallow of his coffee. "Speaking of ex-cops, my skipper back there would probably think I ought to be in a home cutting out paper dolls for saying so, but it's damn funny– two people I wanted to talk to about the Swann case dead within two days of each other."

"Oh," I said. "Margaret de Pietro pass away, then?"

Zankich glanced at his watch. "Oh hell– I better get back. They'll be loading him into the meat wagon by now," he said, fishing some coins out of his pocket for the check. "No, poor Margaret's still kicking as far as I know. It was another retired copper I was talking about. Used to work in missing persons– Frank Ricketts."

I stared at him. "What do you mean about Frank Ricketts? I just saw him not too long ago."

It was Zankich's turn to stare at me. "You hadn't heard? Aw, shit– I didn't know."

"I don't understand. You're saying Frank– he died?"

"He shot himself with his service revolver two days ago. His wife found him. Been worried about his health, she said. Helluva thing. I'm sorry to go blurting it out like that. I always manage to put my foot in it. Was he a pal of yours?"

173

CHAPTER 21

The funeral– Frank's funeral– was the next afternoon at Edwards Brothers on Venice Boulevard, a New England variety of imitation colonial. The chapel was nearly full. It cheered me some that he rated a fair sized crowd. Stubby Vargas was there, in a rusty black suit. Looking out across the high ceiling nave, I recognized a lot of the balding, gray or portly figures as retired police from years past. Some hadn't changed at all. Frank was there, too, for all who wished to view him. I didn't. There wouldn't be any burial afterward; according to the brief notice in the paper, he was to be cremated. That must have been Ruth's idea. Frank, I was sure, would have wanted to be buried with Vera at Evergreen cemetery. Now he'd be kept in a jar on the mantle of that tidy living room, to be dusted twice a day along with the porcelain ducks.

After the service, I waited with Bobbie in the receiving line to offer our condolences to Ruth, who stood in the foyer of the main entrance, shaking hand after hand. The hum of voices filled the chapel as the crowd filed out.

When our turn came, Ruth reached for my outstretched hand mechanically as I murmured the usual empty words of comfort. She looked up, noticing me for the first time and jerked her hand back. I could feel her glare through the heavy mourning veil of her hat.

"You!" she spat. "How dare you show your face here? It was all your doing, this. You brought him to it! Coming around, stirring up old memories best forgotten."

Another day I might have had something to say to her about that. As it was, this was Frank's funeral and she was, after all, his legal widow, so I just walked out into the sunshine without a word. Bobbie looked as if she'd like to have scratched Ruth's eyes out, but restrained herself with effort and fumed silently at my side.

People were milled around the grounds in small clusters, chatting and catching up. I nodded to those I knew. Vargas stood in the shade of a mulberry tree talking to a large man whose back, which was turned toward us, looked wide enough to be rented out as a billboard. Vargas waved at Bobbie and called me over.

"Take your time, Ave. I'll meet you back at the car," Bobbie said.

"Cap, this is my detective pal Shepard. Shep, this is Patrick O'Leary. I was telling you about him the last time you came to see me, remember?"

"Sure, sure. The arrest of Taggart," I said, nodding. "Glad to meet you, O'Leary."

I offered my hand and he gripped it with a big, ruddy paw. His salt and pepper hair was cropped in a crew cut, and he had bright blue eyes capped by unruly black eyebrows and the reddish-brown wind-whipped complexion you could only get by spending a lot of time out on the water.

"Call me Cap. Everyone does. Nice to meet you, too, Shepard," O'Leary said. "If only it was under better circumstances. He was a fine man, Ricketts was, and a credit to the force. I can't say that about all my brother officers. Cyrus Law, for one."

I looked up at the candid, open face, thinking of Law's sneering words about O'Leary and his fondness for drink, and suspected O'Leary's contempt would be mutual. In my business you had to be a quick judge of character. I liked O'Leary right away; I hadn't liked Law.

O'Leary was watching me with one eyebrow raised and a sad half-grin on his face, as if he guessed what I was thinking.

He glanced around. "I guess there'll be another one of these for old Cyrus coming up. I'll be busy in my garden that day, to be sure."

I told them about being there with the police when they found Law's body. I hadn't heard anything more about it, other than what it said in the papers. The coroner thought Law had been dead less than an hour when he was found. He'd been burned over his chest but they hadn't found any smoke in his lungs and concluded, as I'd pointed out to Zankich, that he was unconscious at the time he went out of the window. It was still possible that his fall had been an accident. A coroner's jury would decide at the inquest.

"You've got all the luck, Shep," Vargas groused. "What I wouldn't give to have been on the scene. I'd have written the hell out of that story. Accident, my ass."

O'Leary turned to me. "Our mutual friend here tells me you're interested in the Axel Swann case," he said. "I'm interested that you're interested. Today is not the day for it, but why don't you come see me tomorrow and we can have a long chat about it."

I avoided his eyes. "I don't know. I can take it or leave it. Maybe I ought to leave it."

"I'm sorry to hear it," O'Leary said. He handed me a card, the old-fashioned visiting variety, with his name and address on it. "You'll find me at home most any morning, should you be changing your mind."

I was grateful once again for the normal, family routine. For supper, Bobbie made my favorite summer meal of fried chicken and warm potato salad with a banana cream pie. Later we sat out on the deck and looked at the lights. I talked a little, about Frank and Vera and the old days.

"That awful woman today. How dare she say what she did?" Bobbie said, bristling at the memory. "I broke that stupid lamp of hers on purpose and I'm glad. Poor Frank!"

She burst into tears and I put my arm around her.

"In a way, though, she had a point. Maybe I shouldn't stir up any more old memories."

"Oh, Ave– you can't think it had anything to do with that case you're working on, do you?"

"No. I don't know. Not really," I said.

We looked in on Donny, who'd fallen asleep with the radio on and a yellow crayon pressed into his chubby cheek, before turning in ourselves. I woke up in the wee hours and couldn't get back to sleep. I got up and sat on the deck in my shorts eating cold chicken and watching the lights until they went off.

"The truth is," I said aloud to myself, "the Frank I used to know died a long time ago. He just didn't lie down until now."

I went back to bed and dozed a little longer. When I woke up again I took a hot shower and shaved. After breakfast, I threw a ball around with Donny for a while. Then I went to see Cap O'Leary.

CHAPTER 22

O'Leary lived out in Venice, where the sea breezes came with the odor of creosote and raw sewage. A long time ago, someone had had the bright idea of putting in a bunch of canals there, like they have in Italy. But Los Angeles had more cars than boats so the canals got tuned into roads. There were still a few of them around, though, and O'Leary lived alongside one in a little rose covered bungalow with a white picket fence around a pocket handkerchief-sized yard.

O'Leary was reclining on a porch swing in dungarees and a denim work shirt, reading a paper-backed detective novel and smoking a pipe. A tan and white terrier, lying at his feet, stirred and started to bark as I opened the gate. O'Leary patted the dog's head and grinned at me.

"There, there now, Reg– that's a good boy. It's just a friend of Papa's, come to call. Beautiful day isn't it, Shepard? Come on in. I'll introduce you to my bride."

He led the way into a living room, cheerful with white painted wood beams and brass lamps. Seascapes dotted the walls on either side of a brick fireplace, the mantle crowded with framed photographs. A kitten was napping next to a knitting basket on the cushion of a chintz slip-covered sofa. A low table in front of it was scattered with newspapers and magazines. In the dining room just beyond, a small, dark-haired woman had her head bent over a pile of papers on the table, a bowl of apples at her elbow. She was Edna, O'Leary's wife.

"And himself didn't say a word about us expecting company," she said with a look of mock reproof at O'Leary. "Forgive my mess, Mr. Shepard. I haven't a crumb in the house, either, but will you take an apple? A cup of coffee?"

I thanked her and said I'd eaten and had my fill of coffee already.

"Well, you'll stay for lunch anyway won't you? I insist. I'd better get back to it until then, if you'll excuse me," she said, gesturing at the table. "I'm up to my ears in curriculum."

"I married a schoolmarm, Shepard," O'Leary said. "Don't worry, darlin' girl, we'll just take ourselves for a bit of a constitutional and get out of your hair."

O'Leary selected a soft cap and a well-worn cardigan-type sports jacket with big patch pockets from an oaken hat rack just inside the front door and I followed him out into the late morning sunshine along a narrow footpath and up to the street. The canals looked murky, with a layer of greenish foam skimming their surface, and gave off a faint sulfuric smell. In the distance, the oil derricks loomed like blackened trees after a forest fire. We wound our way out to the beach and strolled along the concrete promenade, settling on one of the benches where we could look out over the water. O'Leary breathed deeply, not seeming to mind the sewer smell; he was used to it, I supposed.

The shore was not yet crowded; only a few sun worshippers were stretched out on the sand in front of us. A sailor dozed in the shade of a quarantine sign. Some high school boys paddled in the surf between the piers. A lifeguard passing by paused to give O'Leary a friendly salute.

"One of my boys," O'Leary said, and told me how he'd volunteered for shore patrol during the war, and taught Coast Guard recruits the ropes. "A lot of excitement around here we had then. Now it's all changing. For the better, so they tell us. I'm not so sure."

He glanced over at the amusement pier, where the arcs of the coaster swooped and fell like waves. The place was largely silent, with an unkempt, deserted look about it. The auto park, next to a replicated Spanish galleon, stood empty but for a handful of cars, and no more than a dozen people were wandering among the ramshackle collection of popcorn stands, palm readers, lunch counters and gag photo booths.

"Now, about the Swann case," O'Leary said after a while. "Found him, then, have they?" I nodded and he eyed me shrewdly. "What's your interest in the case? Or are the police so short-handed these days they're relying on private help again?"

I told him about the visit from Zankich and Dawson, and their suspicions regarding Harry.

O'Leary stared out at the horizon. "I knew Harry Price when I was still wet behind the ears as a detective," he said slowly. "He worked with us for a time back then. The force did have to rely on outside help in those days. Anyone could call himself a detective and get a tin star. There were some who abused it. That's how we eventually came to need a licensing law, if you don't know it. But Harry, he was one of the good ones. I won't pretend I always agreed with him, but I never had any doubt about his trustworthiness, or his honesty. Not that he wasn't above taking the law into his own hands if he thought it was really justified. I couldn't blame him, myself. Some of my brother officers didn't care what happened after we made an arrest. If a guilty man got himself a clever lawyer and didn't pay for a crime we knew him to be guilty of, it was no skin off their nose. There were times I must say when I envied them."

"You're telling me you think Harry was capable of killing a man?"

He raised a disheveled eyebrow. "Don't you, if you're honest?"

"Hell no," I said, then sighed. "Okay, maybe he was capable of it, but not over a gambling debt, for money. That I would never believe of him."

"We're both of us in agreement there, now," O'Leary said. "Any man who asked Harry Price to put a man in his grave like that was more likely to wind up in the hospital himself, and that would be that. No, this Zankich fellow will have to do better than that."

I nodded. "But he did point out that hotel register. Frank had to have known Harry was there. But he never said anything then, and he sure wasn't interested in talking about it when I went to see him."

O'Leary looked at me. "Frank was a good man and a loyal friend, but he was a good copper first. He wouldn't have kept quiet if he'd thought there was anything wrong about Harry being there. You can bank on that."

"I know it. But why not just say?"

"Might be he was protecting somebody else and it had nothing to do with the case," O'Leary said after a pause. He shrugged. "What else have you got?"

"Not a whole hell of a lot," I admitted. "There was a man named Mike Higgins who worked for Angus Taggart. He was supposed to know something about Swann, but was shot by a cop named Nick Lundy. I think Cyrus Law put Higgins on the spot that night and Lundy shot him to keep him from talking. I can't prove any of it, of course."

"No," O'Leary said, "Lundy and Law would take care to cover their tracks. I worked with both of them, of course. Lundy was as nasty a piece of work as they come. There's some that say men like him are needed on the force today—pah!" He spat in the sand. "It was good riddance to bad trash when that lot got the boot. As for Law, my missus would have my hide for speaking ill o' the dead, but if he had help going out of that window, it was only what he had coming to him. Maybe he didn't start out as a crook, but a crook is what he became. He was a good detective when he wanted to be. If he'd been straight, I dare say he'd be remembered today as a great man. Clever, he was. Knew how to curry favor where and when it counted. But let's just say his methods reeked like

181

this stench around here if you were a decent copper."

"Was Higgins a police informant, do you know?"

"Could be he *thought* he was. But if he trusted Law, he made a mistake."

"You think Law was on Taggart's payroll?"

"Oh, I think they had some sort of arrangement— maybe not one as cut and dried as that. Law, I believe, liked using his position to do favors for those he thought it might prove useful to have beholden to him. A dangerous game to play with men like Taggart."

He paused to light his pipe, watching a group of pretty girls in bathing suits who had spread their blankets out on the sand near us.

"Where was I? Oh, Taggart. Yes. I knew of him, you see, from when I walked a beat on Central Avenue. He was a flashy dresser in those days, he was— the windowpane check suit and diamond stickpin type. He was just a small time gambler then, ran a little hand book operation out of a cigar store. I must've brought him in a dozen times. Ambitious little weasel, though, Taggart. He wanted to move on to bigger and better things, so he got himself in with the right people— Charlie Crawford and all of the crooked bunch who pulled the strings at City Hall. They let him run some of their big casinos. It went to his head. That's when he started dressing like a banker and calling himself a real estate man. He might have changed his style, but he was the same small-time bunko artist underneath."

"He branched out into liquor, too?"

"Like I say, he was ambitious. I suppose it could be 'twas just Taggart's good fortunate that his star started to rise right as old Charlie's was falling, but Mrs. O'Leary didn't raise any fools. No, I've always had a suspicion that he was at the back of Crawford's man in liquor getting arrested. Right over there, as a matter of fact." He pointed to the Spanish galleon, which for years had housed a notorious café. "And the man who helped put him away, the one who worked out of the Venice division here? He became chief of police. Taggart had that kind of influence."

"Was Taggart behind your getting kicked off the force, too?"

He sucked on his pipe, nodding. "A car came out of nowhere and I hit it. They tried to say I'd been drinking. Now, I'll be the first to admit I was fond of a nip now and then in those days. That was before I took the pledge. But I hadn't had a drop that night, and that's a fact. I had myself tested by the force doctor, and my personal doctor. But no matter. They wanted me out and they needed cause, so that was that."

"But they took you back, didn't they?"

"For a few months, sure. I had a good friend, an ex-police commissioner. And Taggart thought he'd taught me a lesson, I suppose. Anyway, they made sure I wasn't in any position to interfere with his plans anymore."

"You worked for the D.A. after that?"

"I did. I was there when Axel Swann called 'round and asked to see me."

I stared at him. "Swann– wanted to see you?"

O'Leary grinned, enjoying my reaction. "I've really got your attention now, I see. Yes, indeed he did. It was all very hush-hush. He didn't trust anyone, not even his fellow agents, with what he wanted to say. So he took a room at the Hayward Hotel and we met there."

"The Hayward," I repeated slowly.

"That's right. He told me he wanted to go after the big fish– the ones who always got away. Arrests of the small-time bootleggers weren't curbing the liquor problem. They were a dime a dozen. If one of them got caught, the big fish soon replaced them."

"What exactly did he want from you?"

"Information on Taggart, mostly. He'd heard about our little adventure at the beach." O'Leary glanced over his left shoulder and nodded. "Just a wee bit south of this spot where we're sitting now is where it happened. I had the bastard dead to rights, and he walked clean away." He shook his head. "Anyway, Swann wanted to know about Taggart's whole organization– who his Canadian agents were, those who arranged the sales of the stuff before they shipped it down here; his local sales agents; the names of his lieutenants– everything. I didn't have the kind of details he needed, but I could give him some pointers on ways he might go about getting it."

"Such as?"

"Well, I suggested he ought to go after the next tier down– the big bootleggers outside of Taggart's circle. There were rumors that he was trying to bring them into the fold and meant to squeeze them out if they didn't go along. Seemed to me one or more of them wouldn't have much interest in seeing Taggart rise any higher."

"Did he take your advice?"

O'Leary shrugged. "I wouldn't know. I never saw him again, so I can't say whether he found anything out or what he'd been up to. He disappeared a couple months after we had our little chat."

"After Swann went missing, the D.A. never questioned Taggart? I mean, you told him about your meeting with him?"

"Certainly I did," O'Leary said, his ruddy face darkening. "I suspected the worst, right away. I told him he ought to bring Taggart in, but I didn't have anything to go on. Just my suspicions. The D.A. was cautious. He was running for governor at the time. I think he wanted to appear tough on crime without actually doing anything. It was easier for him to blame it on eastern gangsters and send them packing, which I'm sure didn't do Taggart's business any disservice. The other investigators assigned to the case had a theory Swann had gone down to Mexico to get evidence on a rum case, and ran into trouble down there. Malarkey of course."

"So nothing happened?"

"Nothing a-tall. Oh, our mutual friend, Vargas, wrote some things that might have made Taggart squirm a bit, but on the whole...." O'Leary threw up his hands. "I didn't like what I saw as far as the way the case was handled in the D.A.'s office. A lot of things I didn't like, but that was the corker. I resigned over it after a while. I had my pension, and I got a good job working security at the aircraft plant just down the way here. Retired from that about two years ago. Now I fish and putter around my garden and read books, and sit out here and look at the girls. And I've got a part interest in an old fishing boat that some of the boys and I are fixing up. It's a nice life. Edna and I are happy. I've got no regrets. But I always did hope they'd find out what really happened to Swann, and that Taggart would get his, too. It's reaching for the moon, I know. In books they always wrap it up neat with a bow in the last chapter, but myself, I never saw much of that."

We sat looking out at the sea for a while longer then went back to the cottage, where Edna had a picnic lunch ready on the porch. Afterward O'Leary walked me to my car and I drove back to Hollywood, wishing Edith was still around to talk it all over with. We'd gotten a cable from her, letting us know she made it to Honolulu safely.

When I got to the office, Grace had been and gone, this being her half-day. She'd left some phone messages on my desk along with the mail. There was a note from her on top of the pile.

> *Went downtown to the Greek church this a.m. hoping to find something on our mysterious Mr. Kyknos. It was a bust. They've never heard of any such person. All the rev. could tell me is that Kyknos is Greek for swan, which is interesting but not very helpful, I'm afraid.*
>
> *—Grace*

CHAPTER 23

They'd transferred Eddie out of the surgery wing to a room in the recovery ward since the last time I was there. I was half expecting to have another run-in with Sangor and Watts, but the waiting area was empty save for a stocky, pasty-looking man reading a newspaper.

Even Manny had deserted his post outside Eddie's door. It was open a crack and laughter came from within. I tapped on the door before pushing it open. Eddie was sitting up stiffly in the bed, one hand beneath the blanket, the muscles of his face and neck looking taut and strained. Cathy sat next to him in a wheelchair beside the bed. Eddie relaxed and sank back against the pillow.

He was still pale but not nearly as bad as the other day. I could see the bulky outline of his bandages under the thin folds of his hospital gown.

"Hey, Shepard," he said, grinning at me. "How you doing? The doc just upped my chances to fifty-fifty. I told him I'd take those odds. Some pair we are, huh? I was just saying to Cathy, it's gonna be a long time before we do any more rhumbaing together, or anything else. Right, baby?"

Cathy convulsed with laughter. She looked almost well again, dressed in a pair of ice-blue pajamas with a lace bed jacket tossed over her shoulders and fuzzy pink slippers on her feet. Her hair had been combed and stood out in soft curls around her head.

"I don't care, Eddie– just so long as we're together," she said.

A nurse poked her head in the door then entered. "Knock, knock," she said in a bright voice. "It's high time I took you back to your room, Mrs. Durance. We can't have you getting over tired, now can we?"

"That's a good idea," Eddie said. "You run along, baby and get some rest."

"Well...I guess so," Cathy said. Eddie gave her hand a squeeze before the nurse maneuvered the chair around and wheeled her out. Eddie craned his head, watching them go. When the nurse's white skirt was out of sight, he sat up in the bed.

"Close that door, will you, Shepard."

I did as he asked. "Now look, Eddie–"

"Was there anyone out there when you came in?"

I shrugged. "Just some man..."

"Fat guy? White faced? Brown hat?"

"I guess."

"I thought so. He's been out there half the morning. Who the hell is he?"

"Probably just waiting on a patient," I said. "Where's Manny? I'm surprised he's not here."

"I had him take the Caddy to a garage to get it all fixed up," Eddie said, his eye still on the door.

"If you're worried, you could always call the police. They offered."

"Who says I'm worried?" Eddie said. "Besides, anybody tries anything, I can take care of myself." He reached under the blanket and brought out a small revolver. "Manny slipped it to me."

"And you without an enemy in the world."

He gave me a sharp look and tucked the gun back under the blanket. "I read about Ricketts. It sure the hell is

187

rough, losing a pal like that. You go to the funeral?"

"Yeah," I said.

"I oughta have sent a wreath or something. Maybe it's not too late. Have you got a cigarette?"

I lit one and handed it off to him. "About the Swann case—"

"Not that bullshit again."

"—what do you know about Swann trying to get the goods on Taggart?"

"Who says he was?"

"An ex-cop I ran into."

"How should I know anything about it?" Eddie shrugged, wincing.

"Did you ever meet Swann at the Hayward Hotel?"

He sat up and glared at me through narrowed eyes. "For a smart guy, Shepard, sometimes you're awfully dumb."

"You saw Harry there that night, is that it?"

Eddie stared at the wall, smoking his cigarette in silence.

"Swann used the Hayward as a meeting place. Maybe you knew him better as Kyknos."

"You son of a bitch—" Eddie flung the blanket back and started to get up, groaned, and sagged against the pillow again. "You got it all figured out. Whadda you need me for?"

I crossed my arms and looked at him, not saying anything. It was an old trick of Harry's.

"What, you think I owe you?" Eddie said after a long while. "After what you did for Cathy and saving my life, I guess I do at that. What do you want me to say?"

"The hell with it," I said and put my hat on. I started to yank the door open but Eddie called me back.

"I don't get you, Shepard. You been riding my ass about this, then I say I'll talk and you go and walk outta here? What gives?"

"All I wanted to do was clear Harry in this thing."

"Sit down," Eddie growled. I sat. "So Taggart calls a meeting of all of us bootleggers and says he's taking over the liquor rackets. He says he's got it all fixed with the higher-ups and no one will bother us. All we gotta do is come in with him, and it's only gonna cost us twenty percent. That's his cut. I told him where he could go. None of the other boys liked it too well, either. It's not long after that, I start getting double-crossed. All the same, when Swann asked me to help him, I told him to go to hell. I'm nobody's stool pigeon. But I got to thinking, if he breaks up Taggart's operation, well, that'd be okay by me. Things could go back to the way they were– maybe better, even. Taggart always muscled me out when I tried to open up a gambling joint. It might be my big chance."

"So you agreed to help him?"

"Yeah," Eddie stared up at me, granite-faced. "In my business, that makes me a stoolie. For all the good it did me."

"You got the information he wanted on Taggart's operation?"

"What I could. I told Taggart I'd changed my mind about coming in with him, but I needed his guarantee that he could deliver the protection he promised. I found out plenty. Some of the rest of it I got from Higgins. He drank and he talked too much. That was his trouble."

"Do you think that's why he was shot?"

"I dunno. Probably." Eddie shrugged, wincing. "Somebody put Higgins on the spot– that much is for sure. I shoulda known better than to bring a rummy into it. The last time I met with Swann, he had the wind up. He told me he thought Taggart might be getting wise."

"When was that?"

"The day he disappeared."

"You and he would meet at the Hayward?"

"Yeah." Eddie fell silent and stared at the wall with a slack expression. "We couldn't risk anyone seeing us together. He'd take a room and I'd slip in through the back way once the coast was clear. Anyway, I kept my ear to the ground, and sure enough, later that day, I heard something was up. I didn't get the details. Just that someone was gonna put Swann on the spot, and he was gonna go for a one-way ride. Swann didn't like us talking on the phone in case his wire might be tapped, but I hadda take a chance, and I called him up. He wasn't home so I left a message with the help for him to meet me over at the Hayward at seven o'clock. I went down there and waited for him, but he never showed. I tried calling him a couple more times."

"Is that when you saw Harry?"

"He was there, alright. But it's like I been saying, it wasn't anything to do with Swann. He had a dame with him."

I stared at him, remembering Edith's surmises about a woman in Harry's life that summer.

"Do you remember anything about her?"

"I dunno." Eddie frowned. "A looker. Real class type."

"Did Harry see you?"

"I doubt it," he said, shaking his head. "I wasn't exactly advertising the fact that I was there. Anyway, the dame left by herself after about half an hour, and Harry not long after that. So, there isn't any way he coulda had anything to do with Swann going missing– see?"

He was breathing heavily and his voice had gone raspy from the effort of talking. I poured a glass of water from the bedside table and gave it to him.

"That's all there is to it," he said after a while.

"You didn't tell anyone?"

"Are you kidding me? Don't be a sap, Shepard," Eddie sneered. "Tell who? Think any laws would take my word for it? I couldn't prove anything. I didn't know for a fact what happened to Swann. For all I knew he decided to leave me hanging out to dry and blew town. That's what the papers kept saying. His going missing when he did left me in a bad spot. Word got around I'd turned stoolie, I'd have gone for a ride myself."

"You think Taggart was behind it?"

"What's it to you? I told you what you wanted to know, didn't I? Harry's in the clear." He asked for a cigarette and I gave him one. "Goddamn Taggart. He's still trying to muscle in on me, can you beat it? You know, he wanted us to let him run the casino operation at the Oasis. Offered to cut us in for twenty percent. Twenty percent of my own goddamn casino! I told Shelly, tell him to go fuck himself. Next thing I know, the city's pulling my fucking gambling license. Now I know Taggart was at the back of that. I oughta be in Vegas, handling it. Get the nurse in here, will you? I need her to bring me a goddamn phone so I can call Shelly and find out how things went today. He was supposed to be meeting with the licensing board."

I hesitated with my hand on the doorknob. "Are you sure you can trust Sheldon?"

Eddie gave me a sharp glance. "Sure I'm sure. You know any reason why I shouldn't?"

I told him about seeing Sheldon and Lundy together that night in the casino of my hotel. "I can't say for sure they were talking to each other. But that's what it looked like to me."

"Why the hell didn't you tell me about this before now?" he barked, throwing the covers off himself again.

"It didn't seem important," I said. "But seeing how Lundy is Taggart's man—"

Eddie swung his feet over the side of the bed and groaned.

"What are you doing? Wait while I call the nurse."

"Never mind the damn nurse. I'm getting out of this place," he said.

"Are you crazy or something? You're not in any condition to be up and around yet."

"Watch me."

"Where are you going to go?"

"Home," Eddie said flatly.

"The doc will never allow it," I said.

"Oh yeah? I'd like to see him try and stop me," he glared. "I can get well just as good at home as this place. Or I should just lie around and let the two of them finish me off?"

191

Our eyes met. Eddie's had the hard, flinty look. "Did he do this?" I asked, nodding at his bandages. "Because of the casino deal?"

"What're you talking about? I told you it was just some punk kids," he rasped. "I just meant Shelly might be trying to screw me over. He thought all along I oughta make a deal with Taggart."

"You're not in any shape to do anything about it, much less travel."

"I don't mean I'm going to Vegas. I'll rest up at the house here. Let them come to me. They'll come, alright. All I need is to find out what the hell they've done with my pants."

"It's your funeral," I shrugged. Glancing around the room, I spotted an alligator club bag under the bed and hoisted it up onto the mattress next to him. Eddie shrugged off the loose hospital gown, fished some shorts, a shirt and his trousers out of the bag and started to dress, slowly. Beads of sweat broke out across his forehead from the effort. I shook my head and started again to go.

"Hold on a second, Shepard." I turned around. Eddie paused in the act of buttoning his shirt and looked up at me. "I need you to do something for me."

"No," I said, my hand still clutching the doorknob.

"You haven't even heard what it is yet. I just want you to help me get Cathy out of town."

I shook my head. "Why me? Can't Manny drive her to Vegas?"

"I don't mean there. I was thinking of someplace farther away– away from all this bullshit that's been going on." The blue eyes were pleading now. "I want her stashed someplace safe for a little while, while I sort this thing out. Someplace sunny. She hates the cold."

"There's Palm Springs," I said after a while.

"Nah– it's too close," Eddie said. "We know a lot of people there."

"Miami?"

"Too far. She wouldn't like it."

I sighed. "What about Mexico? It's only a few hours by plane."

Eddie grinned. "Now that's an idea. That's perfect. She could stay at a hotel in the city for a couple days. I'll send Manny down with the car and he can drive her to this little spot I know of on the beach."

"It's at least a five day drive from here."

"Manny can make it in three," Eddie shrugged, gritting his teeth in pain. "Fix it up with her for me, will you, Shepard? You know— put the idea in her head and convince her she's got to go."

"Shouldn't it come from you?"

"She'd just think I'm trying to get rid of her or something."

"Well, aren't you?"

"It's for her own good. She'll trust it's legit if you tell her. She likes you. She told me so." He nodded as if it was all settled and finished buttoning his shirt. "You break it to her and get it all fixed up with the flight and everything, then take her to the airport— make sure she gets off okay, huh? Manny can get a jump on her, start down there tonight."

"I'd have thought you'd want Manny here."

"I can take care of myself." he said, struggling to knot his tie.

"Look at you. You can barely dress yourself," I said. Eddie ignored me. "Those cops the other day— they said you could have protection if you wanted it. Why not take them up on it?"

Eddie stopped what he was doing and looked up at me. The corner of his lips turned down in a half-grin. "Yeah?" he said softly. "So who's gonna protect me from them?"

The waiting room was empty when I left. As I trotted down the steps into the hot afternoon sunshine, someone darted out from the shrubbery and grabbed my arm. It was Sandy, in a white sundress with a floral print scarf tied over her dark hair and a pair of oversized dark glasses, which, if intended as a disguise only made her look more conspicuous.

"Avery– thank God! I've been going crazy. No one will tell me anything." She burst into tears. I took her elbow and steered her down the rest of the steps and into the shade. "Please– I have to know. How is he? He *is* going to live, isn't he?"

"I gather the docs seem to think he'll pull through." I said, passing her my handkerchief. She removed the sunglasses and dabbed at her eyes.

"Really? You're not just saying that?"

"You can see him for yourself if you wait around a while. He says he's going home."

"He is?" She blinked up at me, then wrinkled her nose. "Oh, but *she'll* be with him. His wife. She has a very suspicious mind. She might get the wrong idea about Eddie and me."

"What's the right idea? Seems clear enough Eddie's more than just a boss to you."

"If you mean am I in love with him– I guess I am, a little. I know it's hopeless." Sandy put her sunglasses back on and looked away. "He might like to play around with me, but I don't mean anything to him at all. Besides, he'll never leave her– that lush of a wife of his. He wants to, he told me so once. But he can't. I pity him, if you want to know the truth."

I tried to see her eyes behind the dark glasses. "You didn't mention to anyone where he was going to be the night he was shot, did you? Sheldon– or you father?"

Sandy frowned. "Why would I? I told you, I hardly even know my father. I don't have much to say to him about anything." She blew her nose and squared her drooping shoulders. "Anyway, I'm catching the next plane home," she said flatly. "I just didn't want to go without knowing about Eddie."

CHAPTER 24

I did what Eddie wanted, of course. Like Sandy, I kind of felt sorry for him, too, in a way– him and Cathy both. So I called up the American Express office and through them arranged a plane ticket for Cathy to Mexico City, a hotel reservation, and some traveler's checks. That was the easy part. Convincing her to go was the real job. I didn't get anywhere. She wouldn't leave Eddie, she said; he just wanted her out of the way so he could carry on with the new nurse the hospital was sending home with him. In the end it was Bobbie who put it over. She just kept telling Cathy about our honeymoon in Mexico, what a romantic place it was, and how nice it would be to relax and work on her tan before Eddie came down to join her, until Cathy finally warmed to the idea.

Late the next afternoon we dropped Donny off with a friend of Bobbie's before heading over to the Durance's to collect Cathy and take her out to Burbank. A young, blonde nurse in a crisp white uniform let us in, a pair of scissors in one hand. She brought us into Eddie's little office next to the front door.

Eddie was there leaning up against the desk with his shirt off. The nurse, it seemed, was in the middle of changing his bandages. The sofa had been made up into a bed for him, probably because he wasn't up to climbing the stairs.

He straightened up slowly, and came over to shake hands with us, holding on to Bobbie's longer than was strictly necessary it seemed to me.

"This is really nice, you coming along, Mrs. Shepard," he said, fixing Bobbie with drowsy blue eyes. "Cathy really took to you, you know. She's upstairs packing."

"I'll run up and see if I can give her a hand, Mr. Durance," Bobbie said.

"Call me Eddie."

Bobbie headed upstairs while the nurse finished up with Eddie's bandages.

"There. That ought to hold you for a few hours. You really shouldn't be up and about," she said in a stern tone that was undercut by a smile that played around the corners of her red lips. "I'll just fix up your supper tray for you, then I've got to scoot along. I have other patients to see tonight."

Eddie grinned at her. "The hell with them, and to hell with a lousy tray. Why don't you come back later? We'll go out to Ciro's and get some real food. I'm so well, I feel like dancing."

"You're supposed to be in bed early, remember? Doctor's orders."

"I was counting on it."

"Now, now, Mr. Durance," the nurse said, wagging a finger at him.

"I really I appreciate what you're doing, Shepard," Eddie said when she had disappeared, blushing, down the hall to the kitchen. "I owe you."

He put on his shirt back on and walked over to a mirror on the wall to fix his tie, humming a little tune.

"You can make it up to me by telling Zankich what you told me yesterday– about Harry I mean."

"Hell, Shepard, you never give up, do you?" he said, turning to grin at me. "I can't think about that business right now. Come around and see me tomorrow. I'll talk to my lawyer. He'll work something out. You want a drink?"

The telephone bell jangled.

"I gotta take that," Eddie said.

"Go ahead," I glanced at my watch. "I'll see if the girls are ready for me to bring the suitcases down."

Cathy's room was at the top of the stairs. It looked like a bomb had gone off in the dress department of Saks Fifth Avenue. Garments littered the floor, with still more draped over the backs of chairs and heaped on the silvery-blue satin bedspread. A large pigskin wardrobe case and an overnight bag lay open on a padded bench at the foot of the bed, spilling over with nightgowns and negligees, brightly printed playsuits, bathing suits, and shoes. Against the window, a mirrored dressing table had been emptied of bottles and jars, leaving only traces of leftover powder and a silver-framed photograph of Eddie.

Cathy, in a slip and her fuzzy mule slippers, reclined on a tufted peach satin chaise lounge, buffing her nails and thumbing listlessly through a movie magazine. Bobbie emerged from the depths of the dressing room holding up a black cocktail dress with a lace-trimmed wraparound skirt.

"This will be perfect for informal little dinners out of doors," she said. "You certainly have some lovely things, Cathy."

"You can have anything of mine you want, except this bracelet and my husband," Cathy said. She went on buffing her nails while Bobbie folded the dress in tissue paper and placed it in the suitcase. She added a few more things, keeping up a steady stream of friendly chatter all the while.

"Gosh, I wish I could wear this color... I think one hat ought to be enough, wouldn't you say? What about this darling turban for daytime? It doesn't take up much room. You'll want to buy a few little things when you get there anyway... Oh, I use this brand of sun cream, too. Don't you just love the scent?... Packing for a trip is such fun, isn't it? It's the unpacking I don't like... There...finally. That is going to have to do it." She turned to me. "Ave, do you think you can manage to close this bag? I'm afraid it might explode if I add one more thing."

With effort, I shut and locked the case and lugged it downstairs along with the overnight bag while Bobbie stayed behind to help Cathy dress.

Eddie was just hanging up the phone. He stood at the desk, staring out the window, his hand still on the receiver.

"Everything okay?" I asked.

"Yeah, sure," he said with a grimace. "How about that drink?"

"No thanks," I said.

We went into the living room. He mixed himself a highball and we chatted about nothing in particular. The doorbell rang.

Eddie tensed and flattened his back against the wall while I went to answer it.

It was the American Express agent. He shoved a blue folder at me containing Cathy's ticket and all the rest of it. I gave him a tip and he departed.

"Do you see a guy out there, sitting in a gray-top convertible?" Eddie hissed as I started to shut the door.

I poked my head out but the only parked car on the street I could see besides the Buick was a little green Plymouth coupe.

"That's the nurse's heap," Eddie said.

Bobbie came down a couple of minutes later with Cathy, who had changed into a suit of white wool, with a little peplum at the waist, and a bright red blouse that matched her platform pumps. She had a white handbag slung over one deeply-padded shoulder and wore a tall, brimless straw hat that had probably cost half a month's rent and looked like nothing so much as a horse's nose bag.

Eddie sidled up to her and put his good arm around her waist. "You look beautiful, baby,"

Cathy looked up at him and crossed her arms. "I don't wanna go," she said.

"Let's not have another big scene, honey." Eddie said, cupping her chin in his palm. "You're all set. You just relax and enjoy yourself down there."

"You just want to get rid of me so you can move another woman in here with you," Cathy said, glaring at him. "That blond dragon, I bet. I saw how you were looking at her."

"Keep your voice down, will you?" Eddie said with a glance toward the kitchen, where from the sound of things, the nurse was busy cooking his dinner. "It isn't true, baby. There's nobody for me but you. You ought to know that," he added in silkier tones, patting her cheek gently. "I'll be down to join you as soon as I can."

"When's that gonna be?"

"Not until I'm well enough," Eddie said.

"Well, why can't I just stay here until then, so we can both go down together?"

"Because…there's things I gotta take care of first. It doesn't make any sense for you to hang around here," Eddie said impatiently. "Look, honey, we've been over this a million times already–"

He glanced over at me and made a nodding motion with his head. I looked back at him and shrugged. What did he want me to do– carry her kicking and screaming onto the plane?

Once again, it was Bobbie who saved the day.

"But I've brought you a wonderful guidebook Cathy, and underlined all the cafes and shops I was telling you about," she interjected. "How lucky you are, to be able to do all of your shopping before your husband joins you. Men haven't got the patience for that sort of thing. Then when he arrives, you two can just relax and have fun."

"That's right," Eddie said. "I'll be there before you know it."

"Well…" Cathy hesitated, looking from Eddie to Bobbie, to me, and back to Eddie again. "I still don't see why I can't stay, but okay."

Eddie shot Bobbie a grateful smile

I picked up the bags and edged toward the front door. "We'd better hustle if we're going to make the flight."

"I guess this is it," Eddie said, taking Cathy's hand. "*Hasta manana*, baby."

"What's that? You mean like the song?"

"It's just something people say down there. It means I'll be seeing you soon."

We left the two of them to say their private good-byes. I put the bags in the trunk and helped Bobbie into the Buick. Cathy came weaving down the concrete stairs, wearing her dark sunglasses, a handkerchief balled up in one gloved hand. Bobbie made room for her in the front seat. Eddie stood against the railing of the porch, his eyes darting up and down the block. He raised his arm in farewell as I pulled away from the curb.

The Pan American terminal at Lockheed Airport was a crossroads of humanity that evening. Partings and greetings played out across the black and white checkered floor in Chinese, French, Spanish and still other languages I couldn't place. Babies cried. Couples held hands and whispered to each other in the corners. A loud speaker blared unintelligibly. I left Cathy's bags at the ticket counter to be weighed while Bobbie went with her to pick out some magazines to read on the plane. When her flight was called, Cathy burst into tears and threw her arms around me. Still sniffling, she went off across the tarmac with the stewardess. We stood in the open air waiting area, waving, until she'd climbed aboard, then went over to the Sky Room cocktail lounge in the main terminal. From its big windows we could watch the constant ballet of planes landing and taking off. I ordered myself a scotch highball and a black velvet for Bobbie.

"I'm glad that's over with," I said.

"Frankly, so am I. I feel drained," Bobbie said. "Oh, Ave– that poor girl. I thought my life was a hard luck story but she– well, she never really had a chance. She told me all about herself while I was packing her things. Her mother left and her father was a mean drunk. He entered her in a beauty contest when she was only thirteen. She won, but the judges made her give the prize money back when they found out she was underage. Her father had already drank it up, so he made an arrangement with one of the judges. There was more, but you get the idea. It sounds as if every man she ever met just used her up and threw her away like an old tissue, until Eddie," she sighed. "He seems so nice. Not how I imagined a gangster, I mean. And so handsome. She's crazy about him."

"I think Eddie really cares for her too, in some strange sort of way," I said.

Bobbie put her hand on mine. "It isn't like our way, is it?"

Our drinks came and we clinked glasses. "To you, sweetheart," I said.

"I'll have to switch to milk before too much longer," Bobbie said.

"Honey, you mean you're—"

She laughed. "Don't get excited yet, Ave— it's too soon to tell. Call it a hunch. I get them sometimes too, you know."

"We better keep trying, in the meantime, just to be sure." I glanced out the window then looked at my watch. "There she goes, right on time."

We watched as the big Clipper taxied along and lifted off, climbing elegantly into the purplish-blue sky. I made another toast, to Cathy this time.

CHAPTER 25

We picked up Donny on the way back to Hollywood. He fell asleep in midsentence, telling us about the exploits of his current hero, "Royrogers," in the movie they'd been to see. Bobbie held him across her lap and snuggled up against my shoulder.

"I forgot to tell you— Joe and Peggy invited us to their house rewarming party next Saturday. I said we'd go. We've hardly seen them all summer."

My lawyer, Joe Gill, and his family had been staying down at Del Mar for the racing season while their place here was being decorated.

"I'll be sure to ask Joe about all this money we're supposed to have," Bobbie added in a teasing tone.

"I don't know how he can swing it with what things cost these days— that big house in Pasadena, and their kid starting college soon, too. Sometimes I think I'm in the wrong business."

"It's just as well I didn't have to go to him," Bobbie said with mock seriousness. "I mean, maybe he's been playing the horses with his clients' money. I might've caught him up short."

I braked hard at the red light and stared at her.

"That's it," I said. "Of course..."

"Oh, Ave, I was only kidding. You know I don't think Joe would really–"

I leaned over and kissed her. "I love you, honey. It wasn't Joe I was thinking of."

The Filipino houseboy bowed and ushered me in without a word. De Pietro was outside on the loggia, seated at the glass-topped table in his dressing gown. He didn't bother to look up as I approached, but went on staring out into the dark void beyond the balcony.

"I wanted to see you the other day," I said. "You were a regular at Angus Taggart's gambling club, weren't you?"

"Yes," he said, still staring.

"Did Swann know you'd lost all the money he had invested with you?"

"I only needed a couple lucky turns and I'd have made it all back," de Pietro said in a flat tone. "If the damn markets hadn't wiped me out...."

"And you owed Taggart, but he offered to forget the debt if you helped him out. What did he want you to do?"

De Pietro didn't answer.

"He wanted you to get Swann to be at a particular spot that night, is that how it was?"

"I didn't have any choice. So I called Swannie and asked him to go to dinner with me. He said there was something he wanted to discuss with me, too. I knew what that meant. He'd found out. And he had. But he wasn't going to turn me in, he said. He'd give me the time to pay the money back. *I'm not going to prosecute an old friend, Rog,'* he said. He forgave me, you understand? But it was too late to call it off, even if–"

"There was still your gambling debt to Taggart. He wouldn't forgive you like Swann. So, Swann was to be snatched off the street after he left the restaurant?"

"I begged him not to leave alone, to let me give him a lift. But he was stubborn. He insisted on walking. He always was bull-headed."

"Is that why you called his house later?"

"Yes," he said. "I thought perhaps– that if Margaret raised the alarm, he could– that is, they might not..."

"It wasn't just about the gambling debt, was it? Were you in love with Margaret?"

"Oh, what does it matter now?" de Pietro sighed. "Yes, I was. She was so lovely. And to think, she was going to divorce him. She thought he was having an affair, meeting another woman at a hotel downtown. She even went so far as to hire a detective. She saw a message written on a pad that he was to meet this person at the hotel that night, so she went down there, with this detective along as a witness, thinking she'd catch him in the act."

"Only Swann never showed," I said.

De Pietro's face looked haggard. "The fact is, she changed her mind. She didn't care what he'd done, she didn't want a divorce. She went home to wait for him. After he went missing, she never spoke of it. I only found out myself recently. She'd say things, under the morphine, you see. She was never happy with me, in our marriage. He was always between us. She convinced herself he was still alive. I could have told her...crushed her hopes. But I never did."

"Maybe you wanted to pretend to believe it too. So you wouldn't have to face the fact that you sold out your friend for money."

He winced.

"Why did you sent the wire to Swann's secretary, pretending it was from him? That was you, wasn't it?"

"I had to do it. I'd cooked up a second set of books, but the police were going to check Swannie's own records."

"What about Cyrus Law?"

De Pietro shrugged limply. "I owed some money, betting on the horses. Law was trying to collect it, that's all."

"Did he know about Swann?"

"Yes, I suppose he did," de Pietro said. He sighed. "What will you do?"

"The police will have to know. About your part in all of it, I mean."

"I won't leave Margaret." De Pietro's voice quivered.

A gleam of metal winked in the lamp light. I looked down and saw he had a gun in his left hand and was leveling it at me.

"Why couldn't you stay away and leave us in peace as I asked?" he said, rising.

I took a step back. Another time I might have made a play for the gun; de Pietro hadn't struck me as a tough guy but in his state, who knew what he was capable of. Then all at once he seemed to crumble. The gun made an awful crashing sound as he dropped it onto the glass table. His hands shook. I shoved the gun out of reach and helped him to sit back down.

"I'm having one of my attacks," he gasped.

"Should I call your man? Or a doc?"

"No, no– I'll recover in a moment." he said. "It was just the shock of it all, you see." He looked up at me. His face had gone pale and there a look of defeat in the hooded eyes. "You'll turn me in to the authorities if I don't surrender myself, I suppose?"

I stared down at him, not saying anything.

"Very well," de Pietro said wearily. His face was white and still. "Only give me a few hours, I beg you. Just until the morning. They'll be coming to take Margaret away then. My dear wife has passed on, you see. As of ten minutes past six o'clock this evening."

CHAPTER 26

Sunset Boulevard slept, still partly shrouded in the misty blue fog that rolled in from the coast and would be gone within the hour. The nightclubs and restaurants were shuttered and dark, their parking lots bare, having sent the last of the merrymakers rolling home only a couple of hours earlier. Banners with famous names on them fluttered in the light breeze. OPENING TONITE. CLOSING TOMORROW. I rolled past vacant lots and billboards for Eastside, Acme, Calvert and Old Crow, Jantzen bathing suits and Quaker Oats. The shades were still drawn on the auction houses and art galleries, antique dealers and interior decorators, photo studios and beauty salons, and gift shops full of overpriced brick-a-brac no one in their right mind would want to give or get. Someone's idea of a dream castle, turreted and crenelated within an inch of its life, was perched on the hillside. Sleek modernistic service stations rubbed shoulders with the imitation New England colonials and ye olde English Tudors, together with a sprinkling of Normandy villages and Spanish villas, pink stucco bungalows and tar-paper shacks. The used car lot was empty, both of customers and cars. A lone attendant at the drive-in café hosed down a bare parking lot that later in the afternoon would be ringed by expensive-make cars. A woman in pink slacks and a brassiere top waited

206

for a bus on a bench that advertised FINE FUNERALS at $68 (AND UP). I passed my own office and eased around the curve where the Strip officially petered out. The barkers had not yet settled under their bright yellow and orange umbrellas and gaudy signs, hustling maps to the film stars' homes. The maple trees lining the bridle path were a shimmering silver canopy; there were no riders this morning. Red geraniums in window boxes stood out sharply against the light stucco of the boulevard's famous hotel, where I turned off and wound my way down below Wilshire to Eddie's.

I could have used the extra sleep myself. I'd spent half the night combining my notes and going over what I was going to tell Zankich.

That Harry hadn't had any hand in Swann's murder was clear to me now. He had been working a divorce case, after all. Frank had befriended Margaret Swann; she must have taken him into her confidence. Frank had protected Margaret's privacy, as Harry had. Like Margaret, he and Harry may have figured Swann for an unfaithful husband, nothing more. They had no reason to connect his covert visits to the Hayward Hotel with anything sinister, had no way of knowing what he had really been doing there or who he had been meeting. Eddie could tell that bit, if he was willing. I hoped to find him in a receptive mood.

Eddie's block was silent and still; not so much as a leaf stirred as I climbed the steps to his front porch.

The blue door was standing partway open.

If I was smart, I'd have turned around right then, got back in the Buick, and driven clean away as fast as I could.

I wasn't smart. I pushed the door open. The reek of gunpowder, faint but unmistakable, lingered in the gloom of the hall. I took a step inside.

"Eddie?" I called out, knowing I didn't expect to get any answer.

I took another step and glanced to the right, into Eddie's study. It was empty. The couch-bed looked unslept in.

"Eddie?" I called, louder this time, and stepping forward, looked down into the living room.

The venetian blinds were closed as they had been the afternoon before, keeping the strong morning sunshine at bay. In the light of a floor lamp beside the armchair I could see that one of the smooth black glass tiles surrounding the fireplace had been shattered. Eddie wouldn't like that. But he was beyond caring. His head, what was left of it, was pressed into the cushion of the armchair as if he'd fallen into a deep sleep. Blood was splattered across the stark white wall behind him and had soaked into his once-white his tie, suggesting otherwise.

It wasn't until I'd started toward him that I saw the woman. Or rather, I caught a glimpse of a white skirt, half hidden behind the sofa where she'd fallen.

Sandy? I thought. But a second look revealed that this woman was a blonde. *So the nurse had come back, after all?* Or was she someone else altogether? *So much for true love.* Maybe Cathy had been right all along– that Eddie just wanted her out of the way.

I went around to the other side of the couch but even in the dim light it was clear there was nothing I could do for her, whoever she was. She lay slumped on her side in a pool of dried or drying blood, her legs twisted grotesquely as if she'd gone sprawling before she fell. One foot was bare, the other still clad in a red platform pump. I froze. I'd seen that shoe before. Last night. Cathy Durance had been wearing it.

Kneeling, I made myself look at the distorted face. It was her. It was Cathy, one blue eye staring sightlessly in Eddie's direction.

I rose and beat a hasty retreat outside, leaning against the metal porch rail to steady myself. Birds chirped away in the tall trees next to the house, unaware that it was now a crime scene. I kicked the railing and swore viciously.

"I don't understand," I said. "I put her on that plane myself."

The birds didn't pay me any mind.

After a while I turned and went back into the house. I wasn't in any danger; whoever had done this would be long gone. It still wasn't too late to be smart. All I had to do was walk down those thirty-two steps, let the nurse find them when she came around to change Eddie's bandages.

I didn't glance into the living room again but went into the little study off the entry hall where the telephone was. Cradling the receiver under my chin, I dialed the number for Stubby Vargas.

CHAPTER 27

"How in the hell some goddamn reporter got hold of it before we did, that's what I'd like to know," Zankich fumed, using a rolled up copy of Vargas' front page exclusive to swat a fly crawling across a corner of his desk.

I sat across from him in a hard-backed wooden chair. It was just the two of us; Dawson was apparently off being surly someplace else. Other detectives and a few uniformed officers passed by, answering the endlessly ringing telephones and chatting about what they'd done over the holiday weekend.

Zankich had bluish-purple circles under his eyes. His tie was more subdued today– if red, green and yellow swirls could be considered subdued; that was on account of the inquest, I supposed. As the person who'd found the bodies, I'd had to give testimony, too. In the end, the jury concluded, to no one's surprise, that the victims died of cerebral hemorrhaging caused by two gunshot wounds each: one to the head and one to the chest, execution style, inflicted by person or persons unknown. Further investigation was recommended.

"Just a lucky break, I guess," I said.

Zankich brushed the fly to the floor with the paper. "Well, it stinks. Things are bad enough without the press floating their cockamamie theories." He looked at the headlines of the other papers, which had since picked up the story. "Murder-suicide. Love triangle. Gang revenge. They probably tampered with the crime scene, too. There was a lamp on inside that living room."

"No, it was on when I found them. Otherwise, I wouldn't have seen– her." I shook my head. "Why couldn't she have just stayed on the damn plane?"

One of the stewardesses on the Mexico flight had told of Cathy throwing a fit soon after she boarded, demanding to be let off. Since she was free, white and twenty-one, they let her. A Burbank taxi driver came forward to report that he had driven her from Lockheed on the evening in question and dropped her off in front of the house. It had been dark, he said; he'd seen no one, and nothing. Nobody had. One of the neighbors reportedly heard muffled gunshots, but had assumed at the time it was kids setting off late firecrackers. Another said he had been half asleep listening to a crime program and thought the shots were part of the show.

"Durance was expecting company, that much is for sure," Zankich said. "Had himself quite an arsenal. There were two guns found on the rug next to him: a thirty-two snub-nose and a thirty-eight long barrel. Both had been fired recently."

"That doesn't mean he fired them."

"No, sure, of course not. But they found a bullet lodged in the living room wall next to the door, a thirty-eight. Like our lab guy said at the inquest, looks like it was fired from Durance's revolver. Then the paraffin test found traces of nitrate on his hands. Seems to confirm he'd fired a gun lately."

"Was there any powder residue on her hands?"

Zankich fussed with the band of his watch. "The results weren't conclusive. She was wearing gloves."

"What about the other gun?"

"Well, that's kind of funny." He picked up a file folder from his desk, opened it and glanced over the top

211

page. "That guy Sangor from vice sent this over. That is to say, my skipper called his skipper and forced him to hand it over. So much for the spirit of cooperation. It's his report on the earlier shootings of Durance and his wife. They recovered some bullets out of the Cadillac. One was a thirty-two, the other two were thirty-eights. That little thirty-two? It matches the gun she was killed with at the house. One of the ones we found next to Eddie."

I stared at him. "What? I don't believe it. Whoever killed them must have left it behind."

"Maybe. But after all, we know he had fired a gun..."

"Yeah, but it doesn't have to be that gun. Did you find his prints on it?"

"Nothing we could use. It's got a rubber grip. But there's another thing," Zankich looked up from the pages he was sifting through. "The thirty-eights in the Caddy don't match the two slugs that killed him. And the revolver we found with him was the one that made the hole in the wall by the front door. There'd have to have been a third rod." He gave me a sidelong glance. "You're sure you didn't see it?"

"I didn't notice any guns. But then, I didn't think to look for them. Most likely the killer left one gun and took the other one away with him."

He looked at me. "Don't suppose you know who it was Durance was planning to meet?"

I shrugged. "He didn't take me into his confidence. I've got one or two ideas. 'Course, they're only cockamamie theories, but I could tell you about them."

Zankich studied the giant map of the Los Angeles metropolitan area on the wall behind me as if he'd never seen it before. "Okay, how do you like this?" he said finally. "There was no sign of a break-in. Stands to reason Durance or his wife let the killer, or killers, in, but like I said, he was expecting trouble. If you didn't turn that lamp on, and you're sure the damn reporters didn't do it, Durance must've had it on himself. So maybe, they're having a nice little chat, then things get heated. This other party gets up to leave in a hurry,

Durance takes a crack at him and misses– his bum shoulder's bothering him– and the other guy fires back, kills 'em both. From what you say, no one was expecting the wife to be there. She just got in the way."

I didn't answer. My own theory was that Eddie had been sitting in the dark, waiting, when Cathy came back. Whoever he had expected to come walking through that door, it wasn't her. He'd have heard a fumbling at the latch, and when it opened, he'd fired. Maybe Cathy had called out at the last minute and startled him. The shot went wild. I imagined Eddie switching the lamp on in disbelief and Cathy running toward him, scared. Distracted, neither of them would notice the killers step out of the shadows to stand in the open doorway, one armed with a thirty-two, the other with a thirty-eight. They hadn't been expecting Cathy, either. The thirty-two may have been left there by mistake, in the confusion.

"Could be it was her gun," Zankich went on. "Says here she claimed to have shot herself."

"Then where has it been all this time?" I said. "Doesn't the report mention that it wasn't found in the car?"

"Yeah." He closed the folder and tossed it onto the heap of papers on his desk. "Okay, so maybe it was Durance who shot at her the other night, too."

"He was in Las Vegas at the time."

"Might've flown in earlier than he said," Zankich shrugged. "It was a charter flight. He say why he wanted her out of town?"

"That's part of my cockamamie theory."

Zankich leaned back in his chair with his hands laced behind his head. "Let's have it."

I'd already told him most of it– what I'd found on Taggart and Higgins, and how Eddie had secretly been helping Swann. I added the bit about Eddie's recent beef with Taggart, owing to Taggart's effort to take over the running of the Oasis casino.

He stared at me. "You think this was about the

213

Swann case? Or all this gambling business?"

"Both, maybe," I said. "I think Eddie tried to use what he knew about Swann and Taggart as leverage against Taggart trying to muscle in on his casino operation. The trouble for Eddie was there was only so much he could say without letting on that he'd been the one giving Swann the goods on Taggart. But Taggart might've figured it out anyway. He was safe so long no one talked and Swann stayed a missing person case. Once it became a murder, things started happening. Like Cyrus Law."

"You think that was Taggart, too?"

I shrugged. "Law fixed things for Taggard back in those days. He helped get rid of Higgins, who they thought might've turned stoolie. And Law was the ex-cop, wasn't he, who told the insurance investigator that Harry did favors for bootleggers?

Zankich nodded. "I asked him about it, but he said he couldn't remember saying it. I wanted to question him about it again but I never got the chance. To tell you the truth, I didn't think much of his story. Especially after talking to you folks. And from what I've heard about Price, it didn't fit. But I don't know that there's necessarily any connection between Swann and Law going out the window. From what I hear, Law had his fingers in a lot of shady pies."

"Like what, for instance?"

"Well, seems he was more or less running the collection end of a bookmaking outfit, one that until a couple days ago was operating out of a joint on the Strip. Those two characters you saw there that day worked for them."

Short and Fat's real name it seemed, was Patsy Truro; Big and Tall was named Joe Egan. They'd skipped town, but the coroner's report had Law dead about an hour before he was found, so that let the two of them out. They'd been meeting with de Pietro at the time.

"Yeah," Zankich went on, "I gather there's something doing with the racing wire service lately. The guy that used to run it back in Chicago got bumped off not too long ago.

Before he died he said Al Capone was behind it all."

I raised a questioning eyebrow. "Al Capone?"

"What? It's possible. I've seen the reports myself that Capone and his outfit are trying to muscle in on the race wire out here. If Law crossed any of them…"

I didn't argue with him, but it seemed like a stretch to me.

"I'd still ask Taggart about it," I said. "You'll be questioning him in the Swann case, anyway."

"Mm-hm."

"You are planning to bring him in, aren't you?"

"My skipper's talking it over with the D.A."

"Did you get anything more out of de Pietro? Or hasn't he woken up yet?"

"From what I hear, chances are he won't wake up at all," Zankich said.

De Pietro's servant had called the Receiving Hospital later that night that I was there. His employer had collapsed– an overdose of morphine, most likely snatched from Margaret's nurse when she wasn't looking.

"Even if he doesn't croak, they'd still need another witness to corroborate his story," Zankich went on. "Someone who heard Taggart and de Pietro planning to bump off Swann but wasn't involved in it himself. It stinks, but that's the law. You can't convict anybody on the testimony of a co-conspirator. The case would never stand up. And with the D.A running for attorney general, he won't want any bad publicity."

And the police department won't want a lawsuit from Taggart, I thought.

Zankich rubbed his eyes. "God, I'm tired. I feel like I could go to sleep for a week."

A policewoman in street clothes came in and handed a stack of wires to Zankich. He read through them with a puzzled frown, then looked up at me.

"What do you know about this Herman Stanley guy?"

"Who?"

"Supposed to have been Durance's bodyguard or something."

"Oh– Manny. I don't know. Not much. Why?"

"They just picked him up in Mexico driving Durance's Caddy. He had a suitcase with a hundred grand in cash. Says Durance gave it to him but Stanley claims he didn't know what was in it– that Durance just told him to bring it and the car down there."

"That much is true," I said. "He was supposed to pick up Cathy."

"With all that dough? What was it for?"

I shrugged. "I can't tell you anything about that."

"Can't– or won't?"

"I don't know anything about it. That guy Sheldon in Vegas seemed to have the impression Eddie was more or less one step away from the poorhouse. My best guess is he had some cash stashed away for a rainy day that nobody but him knew about."

Zankich put the telegrams down. He dumped the newspapers into the wastepaper basket and lit a cigarette. "Your best guess, my best guess. All we've got is guesses. It's all we'll ever have."

EPILOGUE

He was right. Zankich put in his twenty years and retired to a fishing lodge in the mountains but the Durance case went down in his books as the one that got away.

The sensational double slaying made national headlines, pushing aside Molotov and even the Cary Grant-Barbara Hutton divorce. They came out with a new motive every day– a disgruntled casino patron, a dispute over the race wire service, a revival of old gang feuds among the local gambling contingent, revenge for some unknown infraction. The worst was the one they called the "Love Triangle" angle. Building on the fact that Eddie's wife was supposed to have left to go out of town, and a neighbor who told of seeing a woman who was decidedly not Mrs. Durance arriving at the house with Eddie earlier in the week "at a very late hour," the tabloids speculated that Cathy, "having returned home unexpectedly," may have walked in on Eddie with another woman and a scuffle ensued, during which both Durance and his wife were shot. According to this theory, the same "mystery woman" had made the earlier attempt on Cathy's life and possibly Eddie's too, though they were a little fuzzy on the last part.

A smaller story, easy to miss, was the death of Roger de Pietro. "Despondent over the recent death of his wife," it said. The same could have been said of Frank, minus the recent part.

I gave my statement twice, once for the official police record and again for the D.A. I told them everything I knew or thought I knew. They thanked me very politely then forgot about it.

Gus Taggart was questioned at length about Eddie and the Swann murder– not by the police but Stubby Vargas. Taggart laughed off the suggestion that there was any lingering bad blood between him and Eddie.

"I'm a businessman," he said. "I run a legitimate business. I didn't have many dealings with the late Mr. Durance because I don't think people of his character do our business any favors. But I never had any trouble with him." Pressed about Axel Swann, he'd only shrugged. "Never heard of him." He died of a heart attack a few years later, fondly remembered as a successful casino owner and respected pillar of the community. His connections to illicit liquor, if they were referred to at all, were swept under the rug by most reporters as part of his "colorful" past. He left an estate worth over a million dollars to his young widow and son; there was no mention of Sandy, who I'd heard had long since forsaken Las Vegas for the City of Lights.

The Los Angeles D.A. did interview Lou Sheldon about the Durance murders, but according to the papers, was "unable to give any clues" as to possible suspects or motives. "I have no idea who could have done this," Sheldon said. Eddie had been popular in the desert city, he insisted. Las Vegas, for its part, seemed to develop a collective amnesia about Eddie. Other club operators said that they'd liked him and had wished him every success. The chief of police called him a swell guy who never gave him any trouble.

Eddie's baby, The Oasis Casino, had a big, splashy gala reopening in April 1947 as Lou Sheldon's Oasis Resort. We saw the advertisement in the local papers. Not that we'd have considered going, but in any case Bobbie and I were busy— Bobbie a lot more so than me— having a baby of our own. Two of them, in fact— our twins, Mark and Matthew.

For whatever reason, the Oasis was not a success. I never heard of a casino not making money, but Sheldon couldn't manage to keep it afloat. Within a year, a local syndicate bought him out, remodeling and renaming it once again. The place changed hands a few more times after that, before it finally burned down and someone built a warehouse on the property.

If Eddie had lived, maybe he might have been able to make a go of it from the sheer force of his personality. But the airport traffic he had been counting on never came. Not long after he died, the city opened up a new one south of town, and the highway resort development followed, starting with the gangster Siegel's Flamingo Club— which did open for business, after all. Not that Siegel got to enjoy it for long. He got his in June of the following year while relaxing in a Beverly Hills mansion. His murder was never solved, either. Nor was the double shooting of Patsy Truro and Joe Egan in Hollywood a few years after that. I was in Hawaii at the time, if anyone wants to know.

I had other cases that took me to Las Vegas over the years, and Bobbie and I visited a few times, usually with the boys on our way back from fishing trips at Lake Mead. We didn't care much for the gambling but had a good time lounging beside the pool and taking in all the shows at the Strip resorts, always amazed that they managed to squeeze in another one. After a couple of days, though, the place began to pall and we were always glad when the time came to pack up again and go home.

AUTHOR'S NOTES

Los Angeles observed the first anniversary of the Japanese surrender, V-J Day, on August 14, 1946 with quiet celebrations of peace and tributes to the fallen, eschewing the raucous revelries that had marked the war's end a year earlier. But even as it stood united in solemn remembrance of a bloody war that had left few Southlanders untouched, there was no mistaking that Los Angeles was a very different city than the one it had been before Pearl Harbor.

There were a lot more people, for one thing. In a survey of returning servicemen conducted in early 1946, thirty-five percent said they planned to make the Los Angeles area their permanent home. Combined with the civilians who had migrated here during the war years to work in defense plants and stayed, the city's population swelled from 1,504,272 in 1940 to 1,805,687 as of July 1946, with even more flooding into the county.

Of all the attendant problems associated with the metropolitan area's rapid growth, the most pressing was an acute shortage of low-cost housing, compounded by a scarcity of essential building materials and soaring labor costs. The problem was not unique to Los Angeles, but, as National Housing Agency administrator Wilson W. Wyatt proclaimed on a visit here in October 1946, the area had the greatest housing problem in the nation. Throughout much of 1946, Los Angeles could tour developer Fritz Burns' "Post-War House" model-demonstration home on Wilshire Boulevard, which *House Beautiful* magazine called "the stuff better dreams are made of." For many of the thousands of visitors, a home of any kind would remain a dream, at least for the immediate future. A special census taken in July 1946 revealed that there were 300,000 World War II veterans living in Los Angeles County, of which 50,000 families were in urgent need of permanent shelter. Some were living in converted busses and streetcars, tents, trailers, garages, even chicken coops. One frustrated vet camped out with his wife and children under Mayor Bowron's window on the lawn of City Hall.

Federal, state and local housing authorities scrambled to provide much-needed temporary emergency housing like Rodger Young Village in Griffith Park. Created from war surplus Quonset huts, it was the largest project of its kind in the country when it was dedicated on April 27, 1946. Designed to house 1,500 families, there were 13,000 applicants.

In the private sector, subdivisions of new homes sprang up in all the outlying areas of the city, particularly in rural San Fernando Valley. Industrialist Henry J. Kaiser applied his shipbuilding experience to housing, teaming up with Fritz Burns to create mass-produced, affordable "Kaiser Community Homes" geared toward the veteran market. Built partly at Kaiser's factory and finished on-site, the company completed over 2,000 homes around Los Angeles between September 1946 and February 1947.

Traffic congestion, while not a new problem, worsened. With gas and tire rationing at an end, car-loving Los Angeles took to the road in epic numbers. The phenomenon was touted as part of California's enviable and unique lifestyle by *Life* magazine, which wrote in its October 22, 1945 issue that, particularly in the southern half of the state, "they spend much of their time in automobiles, think nothing of driving twenty miles on a routine shopping trip."

In December 1946, the State Department of Motor Vehicles reported that the number of out-of-state vehicle registrations had doubled since 1941, to 200,000. Overall, Los Angeles County registrations totaled 1,411,881 for 1946– more than one-third of California's 3,442,051 cars.

Plans for a system of freeways, on hold since before the war, were accelerated. Ironically enough the housing crisis delayed the start of construction on the Hollywood Freeway, as it would have entailed displacing a number of residents. Work did get underway on the Santa Ana Parkway near the civic center, with structures being relocated rather than demolished. In the coming years, entire hillsides would disappear and great, gray swaths of concrete sliced through neighborhoods, transforming the city.

Then there was the smog that cast a gloomy, gray haze over the city center. First noticed in 1942, it was attributed to unavoidable war conditions that would probably go away once victory was achieved. But a year after the war's end, the downtown area still suffered from this atmospheric snafu. In the sweltering temperatures of August and September 1946, smog that reddened eyes and irritated nostrils hung around for days on end.

The crime rate rose. According to the Federal Bureau of Investigation's annual statistics, murders in Los Angeles increased from eighty-six in 1940 to 116 in 1946. Traffic deaths and petty crimes were up also. State lawmakers called the city the "vice and gambling blackspot of California." The understaffed Los Angeles Police Department blamed the upsurge on the burgeoning population, which, according to reports, included a flood of "eastern gangsters."

There were other worries: the adequacy of the water supply; overcrowded schools and colleges; racial tensions, unemployment. For all the shortcomings, though, people continued to come, and most would have to agree, if they were honest, that Los Angeles was still a pretty nice place to live– *if only there weren't so damn many people!*

While real life events, places and people are mentioned, this book is a novel and anyone with a "speaking part" in it is a fictional character. Ex-saloonkeeper Charles Crawford was indeed the unacknowledged leader of the Los Angeles underworld before his murder in May 1931. His loosely organized syndicate included Albert Marco, who ran bootlegging and prostitution, Bob Gans the "slot-machine king," bookmaker Tutor Scherer, gambler Farmer Page, and former vice cop Guy McAfee. In 1925 City Councilman Carl Jacobson began conducting investigations into vice conditions and uncovered the system of "protection" that allowed the syndicate to operate with only token interference from law enforcement. One night in August 1927, LAPD detective Harry Raymond, with three other high-ranking officers and reporters in tow, ostensibly responding to a disturbing the peace call, arrested Jacobson on "morals offences" at the cottage of an attractive woman constituent. Jacobson maintained that he was the victim of a frame-up. It was certainly not the first time such tactics had been used to silence a political foe, nor would it be the last.

A decade later, cafeteria owner Clifford Clinton picked up where Jacobson left off, leading a group of citizen activists known as CIVIC in an investigation into the protected vice that had continued to thrive in the years since Repeal under the administration of Mayor Frank Shaw. The underworld attempted to discredit CIVIC and succeeded in keeping their findings out of the public eye until January 14, 1938, when a crudely-rigged car bomb exploded, blowing the lid off corruption in civic government. The intended victim was Harry Raymond. Now a private investigator, Raymond had been conducting a vice inquiry of his own. The bomb was soon traced to a police officer with ties to the top levels of City Hall. Shaw was duly recalled from office. His replacement, Fletcher Bowron, let it be known that Los Angeles would thereafter be a closed town, putting its "high gambling chiefs" on notice and purging the police department of twenty-three officers suspected of being on the underworld's payroll. McAfee, Page and Scherer left town and established legitimate casinos in Las Vegas. There were indications that this exodus had less to do with Mayor Bowron's reform policies than the presence of a new arrival who had muscled in on the local gambling rackets: Benjamin "Bugsy" Siegel. In any case, Siegel himself soon upped stakes for Las Vegas, where the rivalry continued until his untimely death.

For more about Los Angeles history as it relates to *Midnight Blue* please go to www.jhgraham.com.

RESEARCH

The background for *Midnight Blue* is largely based on original research using historical newspaper articles, magazines and journals, photos, court documents, state and federal government reports, maps, phone books and other miscellaneous ephemera. While some of these sources are from my own collection, others are maintained by libraries, archives and museums.

Recreating the Los Angeles of 1946 was greatly aided by the digital photo archives and collections of the University of Southern California, the University of California Los Angeles, the Los Angeles Central Branch Library History Department, and the California State Library (CSL) in Sacramento. The CSL's California History Reading Room has a large collection of historical Los Angeles newspapers on microfilm while the Government Publications section retains the reports of Governor Warren's Special Crime Study Commission on Organized Crime (formed in 1947 after the murder of Bugsy Siegel); the final report of May 1953 includes an LAPD's retrospective survey of gangland killings in the Los Angeles area from the turn of the century to 1951. Thanks to film preservation efforts, it is also possible to see glimpses of postwar Los Angeles in living celluloid in *The Blue Dahlia, Somewhere in the Night, The Black Angel, The Killers, T-Men, I Love Trouble, Nobody Lives Forever, Out of the Past, The*

Street with No Name, Pitfall, He Walked by Night, Criss Cross, The Crooked Way, The Set Up and White Heat, to name just a few.

Although much has been written about the Prohibition Era and rum-running, very little of it covers how it played out in Southern California. Among hundreds of magazine and newspaper articles used for reference, several by *Los Angeles Times* reporter Albert F. Nathan were particularly useful in filling in the blanks: "The Rum-Runners" (August 1, 1926), "How Whiskey Smugglers Buy and Land Cargos" (August 8, 1926), "Death Sudden and Mysterious is Fate of Hijacker" (August 15, 1926) "Rousting System Earns Curses of Rum-Runners" (August 22, 1926), "Are Gangsters Building Another Chicago Here?" (March 29, 1931), "California's Homegrown Racketeers" (May 24, 1931) and "What's Become of the Rum-Runners?" (September 16, 1934). Curiously, while independent rum-runners like Tony Cornero figure prominently in these pieces, Nathan makes no reference to Crawford's kingpins such as Albert Marco. It is worth noting that Nathan accompanied the LAPD on the Jacobson raid and gave damaging testimony against the city councilman in court. *Liberty* magazine's six part series, "The Lid off Los Angeles" by Dwight F. McKinney and Fred Allhoff (November 11, 18, 25 and December 2, 9, 16, 1939), drawing heavily from Clifford Clinton's investigations, gives a more complete picture of the underworld and its system of "protected" vice. George Creel also covered the subject for *Collier's* in "Unholy City" (September 2, 1939) as did Guy Finney in his 1945 book *Angel City in Turmoil: A Story of the Minute Men of Los Angeles and their War on Civic Corruption, Graft and Privilege.*

Visualizing Las Vegas in 1946 would not have been possible without photographs, newspapers, scrapbooks, and many other materials maintained by the Nevada State Museum, Las Vegas Cahlan Research Library, the University of Nevada, Las Vegas Special Collections Library, and the Las Vegas Library's Jack I. Gardner Special Collections Room for Local History & Gaming. The National Museum of Crime in

Las Vegas (also known as the Mob Museum), housed in the beautifully rehabilitated former U.S. Courthouse where the Kefauver Committee gave Bugsy Siegel's former associate Moe Sedway a few uncomfortable moments in 1950, has special exhibits relating to the impact of organized crime on local history and is well worth a visit. Wesley Stout's feature article on the city, "Nevada's New Reno" for *Saturday Evening Post* (October 31, 1942) was instructive, especially when compared with *Life*'s profile of just five years later, "Las Vegas Strikes it Rich" (May 26, 1947). The details of Siegel's Las Vegas activities during the summer of 1946 are documented in his heavily redacted FBI file, available from vault.fbi.gov. I was also able to draw on my mother's childhood memories of spending summers in Las Vegas and seeing the gangsters with "their boys" lounging around the pool of El Rancho Vegas, the first casino-resort on the Strip (The Flamingo was third).

SELECTED READING:

Anderson, Clinton H. *Beverly Hills Is My Beat.* Popular Library. 1960.

Behr, Edward. *Prohibition: Thirteen Years that Changed America.* Arcade Publishing. 2011.

Buntin, John. *L.A. Noir: The Struggle for the Soul of America's Most Seductive City.* Crown. 2009.

Coffey, Thomas M. *The Long Thirst: Prohibition in America, 1920-1933.* W. W. Norton & Co. 1975.

Cook, Fred J. *A Two-Dollar Bet Means Murder.* Dial Press. 1961.

Friedrich, Otto. *City of Nets: A Portrait of Hollywood in the 1940's.* Harper & Row. 1986.

Garrigues, Charles Harris. *You're Paying For It! A Guide to Graft.* Funk & Wagnalls. 1936.

Gragg, Larry. *Benjamin "Bugsy" Siegel: The Gangster, the Flamingo, and the Making of Modern Las Vegas.* Praeger. 2015.

Helmer, William with Rick Mattix. *Public Enemies: America's Criminal Past, 1919-1940.* Chronicle Books. 1998.

Henstell, Bruce. *Sunshine & Wealth: Los Angeles in the Twenties and Thirties.* Chronicle Books. 1984.

Hess, Alan. *Viva Las Vegas: After Hours Architecture.* Chronicle Books. 1993.

Jennings, Dean. *We Only Kill Each Other: The Life and Bad Times of Bugsy Siegel.* Prentice-Hall. 1967.

Kobler, John. *Ardent Spirits: The Rise and Fall of Prohibition.* Putnam. 1973.

Lewis, Oscar. *Sagebrush Casinos: The Story of Legal Gambling in Nevada.* Doubleday & Co. 1953.

Lieberman, Paul. *Gangster Squad: Covert Cops, the Mob, and the Battle for Los Angeles.* Thomas Dunne Books. 2012.

Mappen, Marc. *Prohibition Gangsters: The Rise and Fall of a Bad Generation.* Rutgers University Press. 2013.

Marquez, Ernest. *Noir Afloat: Tony Cornero and the Notorious Gambling Ships of Southern California.* Angel City Press. 2011.

McWilliams, Carey. *Southern California Country: An Island on the Land.* Duell, Sloan & Pearce. 1946.

Ralli, Paul. *Viva Vegas.* House-Warven. 1953.

Rayner, Richard. *A Bright and Guilty Place: Murder, Corruption, and L.A.'s Scandalous Coming of Age.* Doubleday. 2009.

Reid, Ed and Ovid Demaris. *Green Felt Jungle.* Trident Press. 1963.

Richardson, James H. *For the Life of Me: Memoirs of a City Editor.* Putnam. 1954.

Starr, Kevin. *The Dream Endures: California Enters the 1940s.* University of Oxford Press. 1997.

Turkus, Burton and Sid Feder. *Murder, Inc.* Manor Books. 1951.

Walker, Clifford James. *One Eye Closed the Other Red: The California Bootlegging Years.* Back Door Publishing. 1999.

Weinstock, Matt. *My L.A.* Current Books. 1947.

Acknowledgements:

    To HJK for once again taking on the painstaking and thankless task of editing; and the Fulton-Graham women of Los Angeles and Las Vegas who beat the odds even when the deck was stacked against them.

Brief Prohibition Chronology for Los Angeles

08-01-1917 Eighteenth Amendment language introduced in Congress prohibiting the sale, transportation, manufacture, importation and exportation of alcohol.

11-16-1917 City of L.A. passes the Gandier Ordinance, banning sales of strong liquor and limited where and when intoxicating beverages of minimal alcohol content could be sold.

12-18-1917 Eighteenth Amendment passed by Congress.

04-01-1918 Gandier Ordinance goes into effect. Many of the city's 200-odd saloons close.

11-11-1918 WWI ends.

11-18-1918 Congress passes the Wartime Prohibition Act, forbidding the sale of intoxicants above 2.75 percent alcohol content. L.A. police and café men clash over whether this "war brew" beer constitutes an "intoxicating liquor" and therefore forbidden under the Gandier Ordinance.

01-16-1919 Eighteenth Amendment fully ratified.

06-30-1919 Wartime Prohibition Act goes into effect.

10-28-1919 National Prohibition Act ("The Volstead Act"), the enabling legislation allowing for enforcement of the Eighteenth Amendment, enacted over President Woodrow Wilson's veto.

01-17-1920 National Prohibition Act goes into effect.

01-08-1921 Los Angeles County adopts Ordinance No. 650 (the "Little Volstead"), modeled after the federal law and considered more stringent.

11-10-1922 California passes the Wright Act, a state version of the Volstead Act.

05-16-1927 The U.S. Supreme Court decides in *the United States vs. Sullivan* that gains from illegal liquor traffic are subject to federal income tax.

06-04-1928 The U.S. Supreme Court decides in *the United States vs. Olmstead* that evidence from a telephone conversation obtained by wiretap without judicial approval does not constitute a violation of a defendant's Fourth or Fifth Amendment rights.

03-02-1929 The Increased Penalties Act (the "Jones Act") enacted, imposing greater punishments for bootlegging.

05-31-1930 Canada outlaws exportation of liquor to the United States.

07-01-1930 Prohibition Bureau transferred from the Treasury Department to the Department of Justice.

11-08-1932 Californians vote to repeal the Wright Act.

03-04-1933 Franklin Delano Roosevelt inaugurated as the thirty-second president of the United States.

03-22-1933 The federal Cullen-Harrison Act (the "Beer Bill"), legalizing sale and manufacture of beer with alcohol content of 3.2 percent, signed into law.

03-27-1933 Los Angeles County Ordinance No. 650 repealed.

04-07-1933 Cullen-Harrison Act goes into effect.

05-02-1933 Gandier Ordinance repealed.

08-01-1933 California's Alcoholic Beverage Tax takes effect.

12-05-1933 Twenty-first Amendment repealing the Eighteenth Amendment fully ratified.

ABOUT THE AUTHOR

J.H. Graham is a third generation Los Angeles native and the daughter, granddaughter and great-granddaughter of gamblers. She has an M.A. in History from California State University and worked as a researcher and architectural historian before starting to write fiction. She is a proud member of Sisters In Crime, The International Association of Crime Writers, and The Detective Writers of America. She now lives in Northern California.

www.ingramcontent.com/pod-product-compliance
Lightning Source LLC
Chambersburg PA
CBHW032212190626
46810CB00019B/2671